Saving
Laurel Springs

**Center Point
Large Print**

Also by Lin Stepp and available from Center Point Large Print:

Makin' Miracles

**This Large Print Book carries the
Seal of Approval of N.A.V.H.**

Saving Laurel Springs

a smoky mountain novel

Lin Stepp

CENTER POINT LARGE PRINT
THORNDIKE, MAINE

This Center Point Large Print edition is published in the year 2015 by arrangement with Kensington Publishing Corp.

The text of this Large Print edition is unabridged. In other aspects, this book may vary from the original edition. Printed in the United States of America on permanent paper. Set in 16-point Times New Roman type.

ISBN: 978-1-62899-764-4

Library of Congress Cataloging-in-Publication Data

Stepp, Lin.
  Saving Laurel Springs : a Smoky Mountain novel / Lin Stepp. —
  Center Point Large Print edition.
      pages cm
  Summary: "In a heartwarming novel set amid the lush splendor of the Great Smoky Mountains, Lin Stepp reunites two kindred spirits in a charming story of first love and surprising second chances"
  —Provided by publisher.
  ISBN 978-1-62899-764-4 (hardcover : alk. paper)
  1. Mountain life—Great Smoky Mountains Region (N.C. and Tenn.)—Fiction. 2. Large type books. I. Title.
  PS3619.T47695S28 2015
  813′.6—dc23
                                                          2015032465

This book is dedicated
to my brother David and his wife, Sandy
—who have always loved camping in the
Smoky Mountains. I'm sure they would
enjoy bringing their motor home for a long
stay at Laurel Springs campground
were it a real place!
Happy travels, David and Sandy
. . . and happy reading!

Acknowledgments

There is always something to be thankful for in every day and someone to thank in every day for helping your life to be rich and joyous.

Special thanks to Martin Biro, my editor at Kensington Publishing, for his wonderful support and encouragement. He is my ongoing champion and always helps to make my books the best they can be.

Grateful acknowledgment to book cover art director Kristine Mills and to my talented book cover illustrator Judy York.

Many thanks, also, to my hard-working publicist, Jane Nutter, to production editor Paula Reedy, to Kensington copy editor Brittany Dowdle, and to Guy Chapman, inventory manager, who ships out my needed books so expediently.

Closer to home—loving gratitude to my husband, J. L. Stepp, my business manager, traveling companion, and biggest fan. Thanks also to my daughter Kate Stepp for her graphics expertise with my author's Web site at www.linstepp.com and for her talented design help with social media sites such as Facebook and Twitter.

Last but never least . . . thanks to the Lord for guiding and directing my path and for His ever-present help and blessing in all my work.

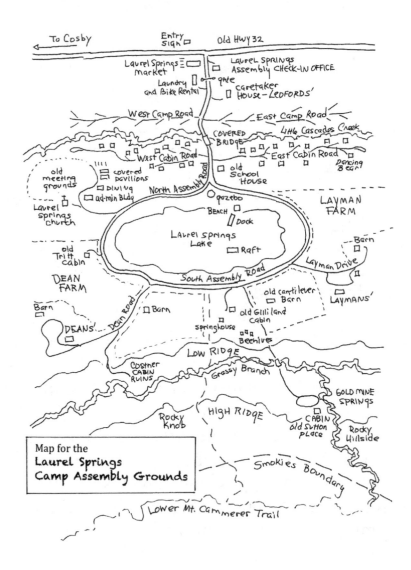

To Cosby

Entry sign

Old HWY 32

Laurel Springs market

Laurel Springs Assembly CHECK-IN OFFICE

gate

Laundry and Bike Rental

caretaker House — LEDFORDS'

West Camp Road

East Camp Road

COVERED BRIDGE

4H6 Cascades Creek

West Cabin Road

East Cabin Road

old meeting grounds

covered pavilions

DINING

ad-min Bldg

old School House

Dancing Bear

North Assembly Road

gazebo

LAYMAN FARM

Laurel springs church

BEACH

Dock

Laurel springs Lake

Raft

old Tritt cabin

Barn

DEAN FARM

South Assembly Road

Layman Drive

Barn

Dean Road

Barn

old cantilever Barn

LAYMANS'

DEANS'

springhouse

old Gilliland Cabin

Beehives

LOW RIDGE

Costner CABIN RUINS

Grassy Branch

HIGH RIDGE

GOLD MINE SPRINGS

Rocky Knob

CABIN old Sutton Place

Rocky Hillside

Map for the
**Laurel Springs
Camp Assembly Grounds**

Smokies Boundary

Lower Mt. Cammerer Trail

Chapter 1

"Ugh. Are we about finished, Rhea?" Jeannie asked, balancing a load of dirty sheets on her hip while she pushed open the screened door of one of the assembly grounds' picturesque cabins.

"Yes. Just about." Rhea looked up from sweeping the front walkway of Azalea House, a cute pink cottage with white gingerbread trim. She watched her best friend angle her way down the porch steps and, with a strength surprising for her petite size, heave her load of sheets into the back of a green pickup truck.

Rhea grinned, but felt her smile fade as she noticed some of the letters of *Laurel Springs Camp Assembly Grounds* flaking off the door of the truck.

Jeannie caught her gaze and waved a hand dismissively. "No sense in wasting worry over a little paint picking off, Rhea. Nearly everything shows a well-worn look around the assembly grounds these days."

Sighing, Rhea sat down on one of the front steps of the house. "Yeah, and I hate to see things getting so run down."

"I know." Jeannie gave her shoulder an affectionate pat before settling down on the step below her. She leaned back against the porch rail and blew out a long breath. "Whew, it sure feels good to sit down. We've been busy today."

"Don't be regretful for that, Jeannie Ledford." Rhea shoved her playfully with a foot. "We need the money, and it's always a blessing to rent more than half our cabins on the weekend." She pushed a stray strand of honey-brown hair off her face.

Jeannie gave her an impish smile. "Wouldn't it be great to win the lottery and get a big pile of money, Rhea? What would you do if you won a half million dollars or something?"

Rhea leaned back against the porch rail to think. "I'd fix up all the rental cottages, repave the roads and the campsite pull-in spaces, and put a strong roof on the covered bridge coming over the creek."

She leaned toward Jeannie, warming to the subject. "I'd buy a dozen rental bikes and nice washers and dryers for the coin laundry, a new cash register for the store, and updated computers for the administrative offices. I'd paint the assembly church and fix that broken stained-glass window near the front door. I'd hire someone to resurface the swimming raft and put fresh rails on the gazebo by the lake, and I'd buy a few new canoes." She paused. "I think I'd reseed the meeting grounds where the grass has worn away to dirt, too, and buy a popcorn machine for the market. I think we could make some extra money if we popped corn and sold it every day."

"Stop! I wish I hadn't asked." Jeannie laughed. "I should have known you'd spend it all on Laurel Springs." She leaned back and sighed. "As for me, my mind veered more toward how nice it would be to take one of those luxury cruises in the Caribbean about now. That would be sweet."

Rhea studied her. "Would you really like to do that?"

"Absolutely." She closed her eyes dreamily. "I'd leave little Beau with my mother, and Billy Wade and I could have a second honeymoon on one of those big ocean liners—sitting on the deck in the tropical sun and sipping little pineapple drinks with umbrellas in them."

"You think Billy Wade would like that?" Rhea smirked at the idea, trying to picture it.

"I'd be sure Billy Wade had a *good* time, if you know what I mean." She giggled. "Besides, he works too hard. I'd like to see him enjoy a real vacation—and if not a cruise, then something else."

Rhea sighed. "Seems like we often talk about wishes and what-ifs."

"Oh, don't be getting all serious and down-in-the-dumps on me 'cause I was doing a little dreaming at the end of a busy day." Jeannie punched Rhea's arm playfully. "It's not like cleaning tourist cottages is a real glamour job, you know. It would be fun to use some of that lottery money to hire cleaning help for this place.

I remember when a lot more staff worked at Laurel Springs."

"So do I." Rhea sighed again and checked her watch. "You'd better take the truck and the laundry on back. You'll have time to throw a couple of loads in the washers before you need to pick up Billy Wade and drive him to Newport to get his truck at the shop. Nana Dean said she'd keep Beau until you got back, but I don't want her to get too worn out."

"Your grandmother is a peach to keep Beau for me so often. I know at six he's a handful."

Rhea stood up and stretched. "Nana enjoys him. She says Beau helps to keep her young."

"I feel just the opposite." Jeannie laughed and headed toward the truck. "By the end of some days, that child makes me feel old!"

She paused at the truck door, turning to give Rhea one of her crinkly grins. "You going to ride up to the front of the camp with me?"

Rhea looked across the road toward a brown cottage, called the Dancing Bear, tucked under a group of pine trees. "No. I still need to sweep off the porch at the Bear. I'll clean and check inside, too. A family from Indiana is coming tomorrow to stay there for a week. I want to be sure everything looks good. I'll walk back when I finish."

"Okay." Jeannie bounded into the truck with her usual enthusiasm and then turned to wave two fingers cheerily in good-bye.

Rhea envied her carefree disposition. "You always bounce around all cute, cheerful, and bubbly like the proverbial cheerleader."

Jeannie wrinkled her nose. "So? You know I coach the cheering squad at the high school. It makes me feel young and carefree—reminds me of my own cheerleader days, too." She sent a sunny smile Rhea's way. "Besides, you cheered, too, when we went to Cosby High."

"I know." Rhea grinned at the memory. "You coached me so I could make the squad even though I was too tall and not very good."

"You did fine." Jeannie shut the truck door and laughed. "We had some great times in high school on all those game weekends, too—you, me, Billy Wade, and Carter."

Rhea smiled thinking of Jeannie's husband, Billy Wade. "Everybody still calls Billy Wade the best wide receiver Cosby ever had."

"And Carter made a good kicker before he injured his knee." Jeannie giggled. "After he got sidelined, I remember Carter took pictures at every game during senior year and wrote up great articles for the newspaper."

"Well, that was a long time ago. Nine years." Rhea frowned and picked up her broom and started toward the cottage across the street.

Jeannie's voice, in a softer tone, followed her. "I wasn't going to tell you, Rhea, but Carter is coming in for a vacation soon."

Rhea kept her eyes toward the Dancing Bear cottage and didn't look back at Jeannie. "So? Why should you not want to tell me that? Carter's family lives on part of the grounds; they co-own the Laurel Springs Camp Assembly Grounds. It figures he'd wander in sometime. He is Wes and Mary Jane's only son, after all."

"Yes, but, like you said, he hasn't been home in nine years, Rhea, not since he went away to college and then got married. It's been a long time." She paused. "Mary Jane said he's bringing his little boy to visit. His wife's been gone a whole year now."

"What's your point, Jeannie?" Rhea turned to glare at her friend. She knew her voice snapped more sharply than she intended it to.

Jeannie twiddled with her watchband. "Well, you and Carter were special to each other before he went away."

Rhea gripped the broom handle with clenched hands. She didn't like the direction this conversation was heading. "Yes, and then Carter went away, got married, started a family, and made a new life. I went to college here and made my own life, too. Time has marched forward a long time since high school, Jeannie Ledford. There's no sentimental, yearning spot left in my heart for Carter Layman. So don't start playing around with that idea in your mind."

"All right." Jeannie shrugged. "But I hope

maybe you and Carter can be friends again when he comes back. It would be fun for the four of us to get together while he's here. Like old times."

"I wouldn't count on it." Rhea turned and started toward the Dancing Bear. "And it wouldn't be like old times. Ever. Those times are gone."

In the background she heard Jeannie blow out a breath, start the truck, and drive away. Only when the sound of the truck's engine faded into the distance did Rhea turn to look after it. When she did, there were tears dripping down her cheeks she hadn't wanted Jeannie to see.

She kicked at a pinecone on the cottage's walkway as she headed toward the porch steps. *If it wasn't summer and the height of tourist season, I'd take off on a trip somewhere to avoid even laying eyes on that traitor again.* Rhea started sweeping the Dancing Bear's porch with a vengeance, furious she'd spared even a tear for the memory of Carter Layman. She shouldn't feel even a twinge of pain anymore after all this time.

"I hate him for what he did to me and how he hurt me. I really do." She spat the words out, needing to give vent to her thoughts as she whacked the broom against a porch rail, her anger kicking up. "Jeannie must be crazy to think I'd want to buddy up to Carter Layman and be chummy friends again. No, sir. I'm going to stay as far away from him as possible while he's here for his little visit."

Checking inside the cottage later, Rhea's thoughts drifted to Carter again, despite her intention not to think about him. They'd grown up together, she and Carter, been best friends through childhood and sweethearts later on.

It was hard to sweep away a lifetime of memories, even if you tried. She heaved a sigh. And she certainly had tried.

Walking into the boys' bunkroom in the Dancing Bear, Rhea encountered still more unwanted reminders of Carter Layman. Old prints of classic cars from the sixties and seventies marched in a somewhat crooked row across the wall. Rhea straightened them with reluctance—hating to even touch them in her present mood. Carter had chosen and framed these car prints one summer when they painted and fixed up the cabin's bunkroom.

Rhea ran a finger across the faded photo of a red convertible. She didn't know the make of the car, but Carter would know right away. He loved vintage cars. Especially that old red Pontiac Firebird convertible he'd fixed up and driven through junior and senior year of high school.

She pressed down the sweet memories trying to creep into her thoughts as she looked at the photo. *Oh, no you don't. Don't you dare go soft thinking about Carter Layman even for one minute. He's a snake. He didn't prove true to you—or even to his own professed dreams.*

Turning away and encountering her own troubled face in the dresser mirror, she shook a finger at herself. "You keep in mind that Carter Layman drove off to California to college in his Pontiac convertible. Drove off to study computer gaming so he could make a lot of money to help save Laurel Springs. Or so he *said*." She snorted. "Remember all that big talk? All those big plans? And then he became a hotshot computer game developer, married some rich man's daughter—and never came back. You keep that firmly in mind, Rhea Dean, and you remember just how much you can trust Carter Layman. Not one inch."

She stomped out of the room and pushed open the door to the back porch, where she began to sweep the leaves and debris away with a fury.

An hour later, Rhea's long strides took her back along the East Cabin Road, following the dusty tracks left by the assembly truck, and then up the paved North Assembly Road toward the main entrance of the camp on Highway 32. She'd vented out her frustrations and anger in work and felt calmer now. As she approached the historic covered bridge over Little Cascades Creek, she could see a car parked inside in the deep shadows.

Rhea frowned as she started toward the bridge. It could be dangerous to stop on the bridge. What were those people thinking? The road through the bridge was a narrow two-lane one, long and dark inside; traffic could hardly see a stopped vehicle from either direction.

With annoyance, she moved closer to the entrance of the bridge and called out a warning to the driver. "You need to pull your car out of the covered bridge. It's dangerous to stop in there."

Hearing the vehicle start up now, Rhea stepped back off the road, leaning against the fence rail out of the way.

As the car nosed out of the shadows of the bridge, a familiar voice floated out before it. "I see you're still as bossy as ever, Rhea Dean."

Rhea gripped the rail behind her to steady herself as her heartbeat escalated. She'd know that voice anywhere—even after a hundred years.

Into the summer sunshine drove Carter Layman, his familiar black hair a little too long, his dark eyes still mischievous and sleepy, his mouth tweaked in that old sardonic, know-it-all smile. He pulled the white convertible to a stop beside her, draping an arm over the door to study her slowly from head to toe.

She could have died right then. She wore a soiled white T-shirt, a shabby jeans romper with a faded overall top, and battered canvas shoes. Terrific. Her hair straggled down her back and stuck out from under the barrette she'd tried to pin it back with. Any semblance of makeup had faded over the day, and dirt streaks undoubtedly decorated her face from sweeping and cleaning.

She still carried her dilapidated work broom, too.

It was definitely not how she'd wanted to look when she saw Carter Layman again for the first time, but, of course, she'd never let him know that. Lifting her chin, she studied him back, giving him the same once-over he'd given her, steeling her face not to give away a shred of discomfort.

She let her eyes sweep over him casually. Dastardly man. He looked heartbreakingly the same—and yet different somehow. She'd seen occasional pictures of him through the years, so she shouldn't be shocked at how he'd matured, filled out, and become more sophisticated. He seemed tan and fit, easy with himself, his dark coffee eyes watching her with amusement, his even white teeth flashing in a typical Carter grin. Despite the casual clothes he wore, he reeked of money, too. A big diamond ring winked on a middle finger of his hand, and she stood close enough to see the word *Cartier* on the watch on his arm.

And the car. Good heavens. Her eyes swept slowly over that now. A classic white Mercedes convertible—certainly a cut above the old junker he'd left Laurel Springs in years ago.

He caught her glance assessing the car. "Nice convertible, huh? It's a 1970 280SE Benz classic, fully restored."

Rhea tossed her head. "You always did like old cars," she said in an unimpressed voice.

He chuckled and let his eyes drift leisurely over her again, more intimately than she'd have liked. She crossed her arms defensively and glared at him. "I heard through the grapevine that you finally planned to visit your parents. You sure they'll still allow you home after all the years of neglect?"

A slow grin spread over his face. "My mom said she made me a blackberry cobbler and my dad's cooking ribs. That sounds like a promising welcome."

"Maybe." Rhea leaned back against the fence, making an effort to assume a relaxed pose. "Wes and Mary Jane always have been hospitable. Even to strangers." She stressed the last word.

Carter laughed. "Guess that witch's broom you're carrying sort of fits your mood today, Rhea Dean."

A small voice piped in. "Are you *really* Rhea Dean?" A dark-haired boy leaned around Carter to study Rhea with wide brown eyes. "Dad said you were his best friend *ever* when you were kids."

Rhea gripped the fence rail behind her for added support as she realized this was Carter's child. A pain ripped through her heart at the sight of him. He was the spitting image of Carter at the same age. Well, almost. She looked more closely. The child possessed a sweetness and vulnerability she didn't ever remember seeing in Carter. Carter had always been a rogue.

She struggled to find her voice. "Your father and I were friends once in the past," Rhea said to the child.

Her eyes shifted to Carter's. "But that was a long time ago." She emphasized the word *long*. "We don't know each other anymore."

"That could change." Carter's voice softened as his eyes met hers.

"No. Actually, it couldn't." She said each word slowly and emphatically, not dropping her eyes from his.

Rhea thought she saw a wince of pain pass over Carter's face before his old smile returned. "Rhea, this is my son, Taylor Layman. Taylor turned six in January and I thought it was about time he got a chance to see Laurel Springs."

"Well, summer is a good time for it." Rhea picked up the broom she'd leaned against the fence rail and started around the car, wanting to put an end to this conversation.

A large brindled mutt of a dog—maybe an Airedale terrier mix—lifted a sleepy head to eye Rhea curiously from a backseat carrier. He didn't bark; he just watched her walk by.

Nearing the covered bridge, Rhea paused and looked back. "Why did you stop on the bridge?" she asked impulsively.

Taylor answered before Carter could. "To listen to the water," he told her with solemn eyes. "It sounds like magic to hear the creek rushing under the covered bridge, and Dad said it was good luck to drop a penny through the bridge cracks into the water below."

The child leaned over the backseat to pet the big dog's head through the crate. "I dropped in *two* pennies for double luck." His bright eyes met Rhea's, and then he gave her a concerned look. "Do you think that's all right, to put in two instead of one?"

"Sure. I'd say so. However many you want." Rhea tried to keep her voice nonchalant. She and Carter used to drop pennies through the bridge rails—making wishes, planning dreams, whispering and talking in the dark shadows of the covered bridge. Touching, kissing when they grew older. Rhea stopped her thoughts from moving on.

She saw Carter's eyes probing hers, watching.

Offering a practiced smile, Rhea turned to start up the road again. "I need to get back to work."

Carter's voice followed her on a soft note. "See ya later—and love you forever, Rhea Dean."

She bit her lip not to react to the old greeting they'd always called out to each other through their lifetime, willing away the memories the words tried to conjure up. Increasing her pace, Rhea marched into the covered bridge, leaving Carter Layman and the pain he'd brought her quickly behind.

Chapter 2

Carter wished, at that moment, he could do something to change the pained look he'd seen in Rhea's eyes. He knew Taylor's words had ushered in an unwelcome rush of intimate memories of the two of them stopping underneath that dark old bridge to listen to the water, to make wishes and share dreams, to kiss and discover the sweetness of first love. Carter felt the fingers of the memories stir him as pictures flooded his mind—of the spreading maple and oak trees around the old bridge a blaze of red and orange, aflame like their young passion. He never saw autumn colors or a scene of a covered bridge anymore without remembering.

Taylor turned and gave him a sweet, young smile. "I like Rhea, Dad. She's nice."

"Yeah, Rhea's something else." He grinned. *Nice* was hardly a word to ever describe Rhea Dean. Strong, passionate, intense, competitive, loyal, aware, zealous, determined—those were all words he might use. And he knew yet another side of her few others saw, too. Tender, shy, sometimes sentimental, full of wonder, hard-working, curious, intelligent, eager to be understood but never acting as if she cared what people thought.

How he'd missed her.

Taylor's words interrupted his thoughts. "Dad, can I walk Jinx for a minute? He needs to get out to—you know." He rolled his eyes. "I'll walk him around near that tree." He pointed toward a big maple off the side of the road.

Carter nodded, leaning over the seat to open the crate, snap a leash on Jinx, and help the big dog out the door with Taylor. It wouldn't hurt the boy to walk around, too, before they headed on to his parents' house.

He'd watched Taylor squirm restlessly in his seat for the last hour. Carter felt grateful he hadn't tried to drive all the way from California to Tennessee. Originally, he'd thought it might be fun for him and his son to see the USA together, to travel across country, enjoying an adventure—especially after the hard year since Judith died. Instead, he'd arranged a deal to get his car on an auto transport load going to Nashville, flew in to meet the car, and then drove from Nashville over to Cosby. It had been a long enough day for the boy, and for Jinx, confined first in the airplane and later in the car.

Taylor walked the dog nearer the car now, zooming his arms out like an airplane. "How many miles did we fly today, Dad?"

"We flew about two thousand miles from Sunnyvale to Nashville."

"That's *far.*" Taylor blew out a breath. "And it took forever."

"It took about four hours, buddy—not forever. And the drive from Nashville took another four." Carter grinned at his son. "You slept through most of it, anyway. I don't know why you're grumbling so."

"Because I wanted to *get* here." He glanced back toward the long rustic bridge over Little Cascades Creek. "Can I drop another penny through the bridge into the creek for luck? Rhea didn't think it would be bad luck to do more than one." He dug into his shorts pocket and fished around. "I have *one* more penny, too," he announced, holding it up with a big smile.

"Sure, sport, but stay toward this end of the bridge and watch for cars."

It didn't take a lot to make a kid happy, Carter thought. He remembered those innocent days when life held so few problems and every day seemed filled with possibilities. He wanted to taste that kind of joy again—and he wanted his son to have more innocent pleasures.

He closed his eyes, remembering the scene that had just occurred with Rhea. She certainly hadn't expected to see him today—that was obvious. But like a hungry man before a feast, he'd let his eyes examine every inch of her. She'd matured, filled out richly in several delicious places—but still had those full, pouty lips and that pert nose. She looked more beautiful than ever, if that was possible, her skin tanned from the summer sun, her honey-brown hair falling down over her shoulders. It was longer than he remembered, and a messy tumble today. Carter had longed to put his hands in it, to straighten it and comb it through his fingers. When his gaze touched her eyes—still smoky blue with flecks of gold—she'd glared at him in suppressed anger and resentment. He shouldn't have felt so surprised to see the anger there. He'd expected it, hadn't he?

She'd assessed him, too, the minx. He chuckled to remember it. She did it in defiance to let him see he hadn't gotten one up on her. Typical of Rhea. She'd always been like that. Never giving an inch. Never letting him know she cared a whit. Always a challenge. Other girls would flirt with him. Simper and flatter. But never Rhea.

She'd been upset he'd seen her in old work clothes, too, after so many years apart. Angry that he'd caught her off guard—not ready for him, not giving her time to bury her emotions carefully below the surface where he couldn't see them. As if she could do that.

They'd played together since their toddler years, known each other the way only longtime friends could. Yet, once they'd matured and discovered each other in a new way, their relationship took on a new dimension, strong and intense, with passion and sexual tension always sizzling just below the surface. Powerful feelings always welled between them—sometimes exploding and stunning them both.

Lord, there was no one like Rhea.

Just as saucy and as much a smart-ass as the day he left.

Taylor came running back to the car, pulling Jinx along. "I made an extra special wish, Dad."

"Good," he said, opening the door for boy and dog to climb in. "Let's get on over to your Mamaw and Papaw's place now, Taylor. They'll be eager to see you."

Carter drove from the bridge down to the beginning of the loop road that circled Laurel Springs Lake and then swung left. He could see the rutted bike and walking trail along the side of the road.

"This will be a good place for you to practice riding your bicycle, sport."

Their bikes were strapped securely on the bike rack on the back of the car. "The trail goes all the way around the lake."

"I *know,* Dad." Taylor heaved a sigh. "I've heard a million-zillion stories about Laurel Springs. You've drawn me maps, showed me pictures, and told me about *everything.* Remember?"

Carter bristled defensively. "Well, it's my home, Son."

"I know that, too, Dad. It wasn't boring or anything. Don't worry." Taylor patted his arm in an overly adult fashion for a six-year-old. "I like hearing about it. And it was neat seeing the big sign over the road you always told me about when we drove up. It said 'Laurel Springs Camp Assembly Grounds—Retreat Center, Campgrounds, and Rental Cabins'—just like you said it would—and I knew most all the words myself."

"So you did." Carter grinned.

"The Laurel Springs Market was right across from the sign and the other buildings, too."

"The bike rentals shop and the coin laundry."

Taylor nodded. "And the road after the entrance was all shaded over with trees like a tunnel, just like you told me." He pulled a metal airplane from his pocket, a gift from the airport, and launched it into the air from the dashboard. "All the roads were exactly like on the maps you drew me, Dad, the East Camp Road and the West Camp Road where people come with their tents and campers and stuff and the other roads after the bridge with the cabins and houses on them for people to rent. It's neat."

"You have a good memory, Son."

Taylor rolled his eyes. "You've been telling me about Laurel Springs since forever, Dad."

"Yeah, I guess I have."

"Look, there's a tractor!" Taylor pointed toward the farm field with excitement. He loved vehicles of all kinds at six—and as a city boy was eager to point out tractors, mowers, and farm machines.

As the road circled around the side of the lake, Carter watched for the familiar turn leading to the Layman farm and house. A two-storied white farmhouse soon welcomed them at the end of the lane, with a rambling front porch, a high front gable, black shutters, a red front door, tall brick chimneys, and soft gray roofing. Big red barns and weathered gray farm sheds dotted the landscape around the farmhouse—and as they drew close to the house, the car slid under a row of overarching shade trees along the drive.

Carter's father, Wes Layman, and his Grampa Preston, or Preacher Layman, as everyone called him, sat on the porch—obviously watching for them. They must have called out to his mother, because she flew out the door with her face wreathed in smiles as they drove up. The homecoming had started. And it felt good to be back.

An hour later, after Taylor set off to explore the farm and ride the tractor with his Papaw and Great Grampa, Carter sat in the kitchen, finishing off a glass of milk and an uneaten half of one of Taylor's cookies. His mother caught him up on family news while working on preparations for dinner.

"Have you been over to the Deans'?" she asked. "Nana Dean is looking forward to seeing you."

Carter picked at the chocolate chips in his cookie without answering.

His mother turned to study him. "Are you worrying about seeing Rhea?"

"I've seen her." He told his mother briefly about their encounter at the bridge. "She isn't happy with me. I wish we'd had more time to talk. But with Rhea, things don't always work out like you plan."

His mother chuckled. "That's a fact. But I think it's never a good thing to avoid what might be unpleasant or uncomfortable. Take the courageous route, Son. Go right on over to the Deans' and pay your respects, despite what things happened in the past to create some misunderstandings. I know for a fact that Nana will be glad to see you. And perhaps you'll get another chance to talk to Rhea."

She looked toward the kitchen clock. "It will be at least two hours before we have dinner. And Taylor is well occupied. We'll look after him and keep him entertained until you get back."

Carter blew out a breath. "I think I've dreaded seeing Lillian as much as Rhea. She can be a hard woman."

His mother shook her head. "Lillian is all business and has always been as tough as nails. Not the type to be warm and emotional. But she's intelligent and fair. She won't roll out the red carpet to you, Carter—not as Rhea's mother. You shouldn't expect it, but she won't fail to offer you welcome. The Deans and the Laymans share a long history. And she's known you since you were a baby. She may never let you know she's glad to see you, but she will be."

Carter stood up. "I guess you're right. The visit there will hang over my head until I get it past."

His mother came to give him another hug. "It's good to see you here again, Son. I keep wanting to pinch myself every time I look at you. I can't tell you how happy I am that you've come."

"Well, at least someone is glad to see me." He gave her a kiss on the cheek.

"I know someone else who will be pleased to see you again." She smiled at him. "See if you can slip out the back way so Taylor doesn't see you and head down to the barn. Traveler could use a run today, and he'd be pleased to take you over to the Deans', don't you think?"

Carter grinned in answer.

"His saddle and bridle are in the usual place. You'll get there and back quicker if you ride." She looked out the kitchen window toward the barn. "But be sure to ride out the back way up along Low Ridge, Carter. If the boy sees you, he'll want to go, too, and I think this visit is something you need to do by yourself right now."

Carter soon learned that horses have a long and warm memory. Traveler, one of the Laymans' matched pair of red chestnuts, remembered Carter easily, nuzzled him with affection, and readily welcomed him as a rider. He acted as though it had been only yesterday since the two of them galloped across the back field to the ridge, the horse little more than a yearling then.

They climbed Low Ridge behind the farm to follow the well-worn path along the banks of a shallow stream called Grassy Branch. The trail led through the woods to a break in the old rock wall between the Laymans' and the Deans' properties, crossed a back road, and wound appealingly through more woods to finally emerge behind the back fields of the Deans' home on the other side of the assembly grounds.

Carter made his way down to the house and tied Traveler to a fence post under a shady maple tree where he could munch a little green grass. Where the Laymans' farmhouse was white and trimmed in black, the Deans' place was a soft gray trimmed in barn red. It had picturesque front and side porches and several small gables around the upper story. The barns and outbuildings, like those at the Layman farm, were rusty red or weathered gray. In a side field, one old barn still had the words *See Rock City* painted on the side of the building. No one could ever bear to think of taking that barn down.

Under Nana's nurturing hand, an abundance of flowers bloomed in the front yard, and Carter knew a profusion of herbs flourished in a garden around the back porch.

Rhea's grandmother, Nana Dean, opened the

door to him with a warm smile and stretched out both arms to hug him before he could even walk inside. She'd grown older, her hair fully white now, her face and hands more wrinkled—but her smile was still the same.

"You're a sight for sore eyes." She patted his arm with fondness. "And I'm mighty glad to see you, boy."

She stepped back to study him once he stood inside the entry. "I think you've grown even more handsome. And you always were a pretty thing."

She gestured toward the hallway. "Go on back to the sitting room beside the kitchen. You know the way. I was in the midst of a phone call." She caught his expression. "No, nothing of importance. Just prattling with one of the ladies in my church group. I'll go hang up and be right on back. Lillian's there, and she'll be wanting to see you."

With slow feet, Carter made his way down the familiar hallway to the cozy den off the Deans' kitchen. Lillian sat in an armchair by a sunny window reading the newspaper. A small blond boy sprawled on the floor working a puzzle. He was about the same age as Taylor, and Carter's words of greeting caught in his mouth as he gazed at the honey-haired boy.

Lillian looked up at him with a catlike smile and lifted an eyebrow. "Looks a bit like Rhea, doesn't he?"

Carter could feel his heart beating too rapidly,

and he couldn't seem to get his mouth to speak.

"She could have had a boy since you've been gone. Reckon he'd be about this age. Did you ever give that any thought, Carter Layman? You found someone else, had a child. Maybe Rhea did, too." She studied his face. "How does that thought feel?"

Nana walked into the room. "Quit nettling the boy, Lillian." She took a seat in a cushioned rocker and motioned Carter to a chair. "This here's Jeannie and Billy Wade Ledford's boy, Beau. Beau, say hello to Carter Layman, one of your pa's best friends all the way through high school."

The boy looked up with a shy grin.

Carter sent a scowl Lillian's way but received no remorseful look from her in return.

"So. You decided to grace us with your presence again after all these years," she said. "To what do we owe the honor?"

Nana shook a finger at her. "Lillian, mind your manners. The boy has a right to come home whenever he will. And he's come to see us as soon as he's gotten here." Nana smiled at Carter. "Never mind Lillian. You know she's pleased to see you."

Carter wasn't so sure.

However, the visit moved on, awkward but not unbearable. Nana chatted with amiable pleasure, and Lillian managed more cordiality after a while. Even Beau warmed up and joined in the conversation when he learned Carter had a son his age.

After a requisite twenty minutes, Carter stood to tell them he needed to head back home. Nana saw him out the door and followed him to where he'd tied Traveler.

She saw Carter look around, scanning the property. "She's not here, boy. She came in upset and left in a huff about something." She raised her eyebrows thoughtfully. "Did you see her earlier?"

Carter nodded.

Her gray eyes studied him. "I guess something happened then that got her riled up."

Carter ran a hand through his hair. "Nothing in particular. Just seeing me after so long, Nana."

The old woman considered this. "You were hoping to see her here again when you came, weren't you?"

"Yes." There was no point in denying it. Carter or Rhea had neither one ever been able to lie to Nana. It was of no use. She always saw right through it, even if you lied artfully.

"Why did you want to see her?" Nana asked, moving closer, watching him.

"Maybe to smooth things over. To talk a little more." He dropped his eyes. "I'd like to at least be friends."

Nana weighed this idea and then looked up toward the ridgelines above them. "Well, I reckon

I could mention this. She got Jewel out of the stable and took off up toward the mountain. You can probably figure out about where she might go if you think on it. If you happened to ride up that way and ran into her, then I guess you would."

Carter leaned over and gave the white-haired woman a kiss and a hug. "If I happen to ride up that way, I'll keep it to myself how I happened to be there." He grinned.

"That might be wise. The girl is a little wrought up right now." She patted his cheek fondly.

Carter mounted Traveler and started back down the pathway that brought him to the Deans'. Only this time as he got to Low Ridge, he encouraged Traveler across Grassy Branch at a well-worn crossing and started up a hill through the woods to the upper ridgeline, called High Ridge, on the mountain behind it.

As he crested the ridge, Carter and Traveler followed the narrow trail along the edge of the ridgeline leading out to Rocky Knob, a rocky shelf of high rocks protruding from the mountainside. If you knew the way, you could find a rough pathway behind several higher rocks and walk right out onto a wide, flat rock angling out from the mountain. On a clear day, you could see all the way down the valley from this point—and could see almost the entire property of Laurel Springs Assembly.

Carter knew the spot well. He and Rhea Dean

had come here ever since they discovered this rocky point at seven years old.

He tied Traveler with Rhea's dappled gray horse, Jewel, in the woods behind the rocks, and then he made his way through the rocky maze and out to the point. Rhea sat on the rock with her knees pulled up, looking out on the valley below.

"Go away," she said, without turning around. "I don't want to talk with you anymore today."

"We don't always get what we want in life," he answered, coming out on the rock to sit down beside her.

Chapter 3

To Rhea's annoyance, her dog Dutchie ran with eagerness to wrap herself around Carter's legs before he started out on the rock. He squatted down with pleasure to greet the black-and-white mutt, mostly Border collie, with her tail wagging like an eager flag.

"Traitor," Rhea muttered to the dog.

Carter chuckled. "She hasn't forgotten I rescued her the day that man drove by the lake and threw her out his car window—straight into the water all tied up in a gunnysack."

Rhea set her jaw, her anger stirring at the remembrance. "That horrible man stopped his car and threw her off the bridge into Douglas Lake!"

"Good thing she barked or we might not have known a pup was in the sack at all." He scratched Dutchie with fondness behind her ears.

A flash of remembered fear hit Rhea as she recalled how scared she'd been that day when Carter dove off the bridge to rescue the dog. It had been a long dive, even from the shallow end of the bridge. "You dove in and swam out to save her. You could have drowned yourself."

"But I didn't." Carter edged his way carefully out on the rock to sit down beside her. Dutchie, more cautious of the rocky ledge, stayed back in the shade of a deep overhang.

He sighed. "Best view in the world."

Rhea edged herself away from him on the rock, hugging her knees in her arms. The silence stretched out between them as they looked down over the valley and the property of Laurel Springs.

At one time, Rhea would have been happy and content to have Carter here beside her, looking out over their world together. But not today.

"What are you doing here?" she said at last.

He turned to look at her, pulling his sunglasses down so she could see his eyes. "This is my home, Rhea. And this is my spot as much as yours."

She frowned at him. "No. Not anymore. You're only a visitor now and not a very welcome one. At least not to me."

"I'd like to work past those bad feelings," he said quietly.

She crossed her arms, appalled at his words. "Bad feelings? That's an understatement. Is that how you express the fact that you left Laurel Springs, abandoned all your dreams and promises, and haven't come back for nine years?" Her mouth tightened. "Honestly, Carter, I feel it's extremely charitable of me to even be talking with you at all."

"There might be reasons for why I haven't come back. There might be more to what happened than you know." He reached out a hand to brush a stray hair back from her face.

Rhea slapped his hand away. "Don't start trying to work your way back into my good graces, Carter Layman. We may have known a deep friendship once, but you ended that when you abandoned Laurel Springs and when you abandoned . . ." She caught herself before she finished her sentence, biting off the word.

"When I abandoned you?" Carter asked softly. "I know it seems that way."

"No, Carter, it *was* that way." She pulled her arms tighter around her knees, moving farther away from him. "We may not have been formally engaged, but we were committed. You, of all people, know that's true. We were pledged and you broke all your promises to me."

Carter picked up a small rock and flicked it with anger over the rim of the rock. "You broke some promises to me, too, Rhea Dean. I'm not the only one at fault in what happened. We'd both planned to go away to college in California. Only I had to go alone."

Rhea looked toward him in annoyance. "My father had a heart attack the month before college started. Remember? I couldn't have left then— left Mother and Nana with all the worry and care—and with all of Daddy's responsibilities at Laurel Springs to shoulder alone. It was tourist season. I couldn't go."

"Maybe." His jaw took on a familiar stubborn line. "Or maybe you didn't want to enough. That was our dream, Rhea—to go to California, to get our degrees and find a way to make big money so we could come back here and fix up Laurel Springs."

He ricocheted another stone off the ledge and down into the valley. "I had to go alone and I missed you. You promised you'd come at mid-term, but you found another excuse not to come."

"Daddy wasn't much better," she interrupted. "You know that. I was needed here."

He turned angry eyes toward her. "I needed you, too, Rhea. And I couldn't come home that summer. Then, as summer ended, you didn't come again. You promised you would and you broke that promise, too."

Rhea blew out a breath. "You were working on your first big game that summer, while I was here trying to keep Laurel Springs going, trying to keep up Daddy's jobs and responsibilities. I meant to come in the fall, but as you well know, Daddy died."

"And still you didn't come." His voice was quiet.

Rhea shook her head in exasperation. "Things changed, Carter. My father died. I could hardly pack up my bags and head out West. I was my parents' only child. Who would handle Daddy's responsibilities?"

He slanted her a sharp glance. "Your mother would have managed. She's a strong woman. And she and Nana would have understood if you left them. They knew I had to go on to California alone and be without you for a year." He pitched another stone over the cliff in irritation. "Dash it all, Rhea, how do you think I felt? I felt abandoned when you didn't come. I felt you didn't care."

She began to lose patience. "Well, poor little you. So you just had to go out and find yourself a rich California girl and get married to console yourself."

Carter clenched his fists. "You're ticking me off."

"Good. So go away and leave me alone. I don't want to kiss and make up now that your little wife has died." She spit the words out angrily.

He grabbed her arm, provoked. "Do you ever think how you sound when you lose your temper and spout off like this—how you make people feel?"

"I hope I make you feel horrible." She jerked her arm away and inched her way back off the rock to stand up on more solid ground. "I hope I hurt you like you hurt me."

Carter followed her off the rock and stood up to grasp both her arms. "You don't really mean that."

"Yes, I do." She tried to pull away from him. "What are you doing back here anyway, Carter Layman? What's brought you back now after all this time? I hoped you'd *never* come back."

Carter studied her face, and his voice grew soft. "You don't really mean that either."

Tears threatened at her eyes, but she fought them back. "Yes, I do. I *hate* you, Carter Layman —for how you hurt me, for how little your promises meant. Do you hear me, I hate you." She struggled now to get away from his grasp, hitting at him, trying to kick him.

He fought her, wrestling her into a steely grip in his arms. And then his lips came down to lock on hers with anger.

Rage simmered between them as Rhea struggled to free herself—and then reason and logic vanished and passion crashed over them. Carter pressed her against the rocky ledge, his hands moving over her. She whimpered, drawing him closer, letting her hands touch his face, his arms, all the angles and curves of him—so familiar to her heart even after all these years. Rhea felt Carter's fingers in her hair, his lips explore her neck and shoulder. She felt the fire that always exploded between them sizzling in the air.

He brought his lips back to hers, and the world seemed to fade away in the blaze of feelings that always erupted between them. Carter moaned and drew her even closer, pressing her tighter against the rock, and Rhea wrapped her arms around him, wanting to feel every inch of him touching her.

It wasn't until he drew back and smiled at her with that irritating, satisfied smile of his that she came to herself. What the devil had she done? She'd let him slip past her defenses! Let him hold her and touch her again when she'd sworn that would never happen.

"You don't hate me, Rhea." He reached up to trace a finger down her face, his voice husky. "It's still there between the two of us."

He leaned in to kiss her again, but she pushed him away. "There's always been a little passion between us. Who knows why? But the fact that it ignites—like a sudden brush fire—doesn't mean I feel differently."

She pulled away. "And it doesn't mean I like you—or could ever trust you or respect you again." She rubbed her hand across her lips, as if trying to brush away the traces of the kiss. "Nothing's different because of this little moment, Carter. So don't think it is."

She struggled away from him and around the rock path to her horse. He followed her, trying to reach out to touch her again as she reached Jewel and started to mount.

"Don't touch me again." She slapped at him and swung herself up into the saddle. "You keep your hands off me."

Rhea paused then, looking down at Carter, who watched her carefully, that smug look still lingering in his eyes.

Her temper rose again. She wanted to slap his face.

He'd always been so devastatingly handsome —with such a sexual charisma. Even other girls in school noticed it, from elementary years on. In high school, she fought jealousy often, watching other girls flirt with him . . . sometimes wondering if he was true to her.

He always teased her about it, telling her there would never be anyone for him but her. Promising no one else held any appeal but her. Obviously, that hadn't been true.

She tried to angle Jewel around Carter, wanting to get away.

Seeming to sense her thoughts, Carter put a hand on her leg and smiled up at her. "See ya later—and love you forever, Rhea Dean."

She kicked out at him. "Don't start telling me your lies again about loving forever, Carter Layman. You married someone else—remember?

You have a son. Would you be here flirting with me if she hadn't died? And next month or next year, if someone else comes along who takes your fancy, will you offer them your sweet talk, too? Touch them and make their blood sing?"

He raised a knowing eyebrow at her. "Did I make your blood sing, Rhea? You did mine."

"You're impossible!" She reined Jewel around him to start down the trail. "I hope you're planning to go back home to California soon."

"And what if I'm not?" His voice was soft, and she saw his eyes watching her carefully with a question in them.

Rhea felt a shiver and paused. "What do you mean?"

"Maybe I'm not planning to go back soon." He walked toward her, reaching out to take Jewel's reins in one hand, looking up at her with those dark eyes that always seemed to see far into her soul. "Maybe I'm not planning to go back at all."

Her voice came out in a choked whisper. "Why would you stay?"

"There are some old dreams here unfinished."

Irritated, she lifted her chin. "Like what?"

"Laurel Springs. There's a lot I'd like to do here."

She felt her anger rising again. "Laurel Springs has been here for a long time and hasn't drawn you back through all these years."

His eyes flashed. "You don't know about my life through these years. You don't know what I've been feeling." He gave her a hard look then. "You wouldn't even write to me."

Rhea rolled her eyes. "You were *married.* Or don't you remember that?"

"Don't get hateful again, Rhea." He glared at her.

She jerked Jewel's reins out of his hand. "This conversation is getting us nowhere. I'm tired of it. And you haven't given me even *one* good reason why you've come back at this particular time in history—or why you're talking like you might stay. Laurel Springs must seem tame compared to the fancy California life you've been living. I can't think of anything here that would hold your interest long enough to keep you happy."

Carter swung up onto his horse and brought Traveler up beside her where he could look into her face.

"Give this some thought." His gaze burned into hers. "I've come back for Laurel Springs—for our old dreams and to make her grand again—no matter how you taunt me for it. It's time and past time."

He reached out to touch her face, tracing a finger down her jaw before she jerked away. "And I've come back for you, Rhea Dean—so get used to both of those ideas, like them or not."

He spurred Traveler down the path then, leaving Rhea with her mouth hanging open. *Blast him for getting the last word in!*

Chapter 4

It didn't surprise Carter that Rhea avoided him for the next week. He expected it after what happened between them at Rocky Knob. She'd let her guard down, let him know she still found him desirable. It was heady knowledge—and warmed Carter's thoughts daily. Even if Rhea said she hated him, he knew now she didn't. It was a beginning.

He sat on the porch this fine Monday morning talking with Billy Wade Ledford, their six-year-old boys playing in the yard. Beau and Taylor, now fast friends, had discovered cowboy hats and gun-and-holster sets in an old trunk in Carter's childhood room yesterday. They chased across the yard now, shooting each other in pretend games from behind bushes and trees.

Carter smiled to see Taylor fall to the ground, groaning and feigning a hit. "It's good to see Taylor running and playing like this, Billy. The last year or two took an unhealthy toll on him."

Billy picked up a chipped mug and took a swig of hot coffee. "You mean because of his mother dying? I guess that was a hard time for him. And for you. She had Lou Gehrig's disease, didn't she? Seems like I read women don't get that much. Mostly men."

"Yeah." Carter propped a foot up on a wooden stool. "Lou Gehrig's, or ALS, usually strikes men. But women aren't exempt. That's why it took the doctors a little longer than usual to know what Judith had."

"What exactly is that—ALS?"

"It's a fatal neuromuscular disease. Starts with being tired, losing energy—tripping, dropping things, having muscle cramps—and gradually moves to more advanced muscle atrophy." He shook his head, remembering the last years. "Taylor and I watched Judith lose her ability to walk or use her hands for the simplest acts of daily living, buttoning her shirt or tying her shoes."

Billy gave him a sympathetic look. "That must have been hell."

"Yeah, at least that." He blew out a breath. "The disease worsened to where Judith could hardly talk, swallow, or even breathe—though her mind stayed strong. It's a place no one should have to go."

They sat quietly, two old friends glad to be together again. Billy Wade wasn't a guy who probed too deeply, and Carter felt grateful for that.

"I'm sorry about your wife's death," Billy said at last, clearing his throat. "Jeannie showed me a picture of her once in one of those celebrity magazines. A beautiful woman, almost regal-like, wearing a long, sparkly dress and going in to some gala event. Can't remember what now."

Billy frowned trying to remember and then turned to Carter with a grin. "Awful fancy city girl for an old country boy like you."

Carter grinned back. "Yeah, you got that right."

He watched Beau run around the house when Taylor wasn't looking and then wriggle under a bush to line up a good shot on him. Taylor looked around innocently, not seeing where Beau had gone.

"Taylor's about to get taken down." Carter shook his head. "He's stayed in too much, Billy. Not had a chance to get out, to socialize and learn to play smart. He's too serious for a little kid. Worries too much. I'm hoping being here at Laurel Springs will change that."

They watched the boys run whooping through the yard—Beau, towheaded like Billy's wife, Jeannie, and Taylor, his hair as black as Carter's.

"How long are you staying here, Carter?" Billy asked after they'd watched the boys fake a few more shoot-out deaths.

Carter shifted in his seat. "I'm thinking of not going back at all."

"No kidding?" Billy sat forward with surprise. "But what about your work? Your position with Quest and all your new games coming out? I read those *Time Traveler* games are being made into animated movies or something. That will be big, Carter." He scratched his head. "You've made a real name for yourself in the video gaming industry. That doesn't sound like something you ought to just walk away from."

Carter grinned. Billy always had a way of cutting right to the chase.

"I don't have to give it up to live here." He considered what to tell Billy. "I'll continue to work as a developer and consultant with Quest. And I've hand-trained a successor to continue a large portion of my work in California."

Carter drank the last of his coffee before finishing his thoughts. "I can still create the ideas—the story line, characters, and sketches for a game. Gather data. Do research. And then send it to my programmer and his team. I can fly back and forth as they produce and develop the game. It takes about a year to get a game out. I can test any ongoing game from here and fly over to help get it finalized and put into production. Quest has a small company jet; I can connect with that for the trips back and forth."

"Your boss is okay with this?" Billy seemed surprised.

"Yeah. He's okay with it." Carter's boss, wealthy magnate Morgan Adelman Benton, creator of Quest One Corporation and heir to billions through Benton Electronics, was also Carter's father-in-law. There was a lot more to this story than Carter wanted to share with Billy right now.

"My boss is Judith's dad," Carter added, hoping that would be enough to satisfy Billy's curiosity.

"Well, heck, that's sweet!" Billy Wade reached over to punch Carter on the arm companionably. "Since you're going to hang around, you can help me with the little kids' football team I've gotten myself roped into."

"Whoa, boy." Carter grinned at him. "I've got a lot to do already without helping to coach football. That's the reason I set this time today to come over to talk to you."

Billy feigned a pout. "And here I assumed it was all about spending time with an old friend."

"That, too, Billy. You know it."

"So what's on your mind?" Billy leaned back in his chair and crossed one ankle over his leg. He was still a big man and well-muscled, his hair cut close to his head, his jaw square. Today he wore faded jeans and an old T-shirt that showed his broad shoulders and strong arms. He'd taken his strength and natural dexterity of hand into the contracting and electrical business his family owned. Carter had checked him out. He rated the best in the area. And Carter trusted him.

"I want to fix up Laurel Springs, Billy, and I was hoping you and your crew would take the job on."

Billy's eyes lit up. "Dang, Carter. It's good news to think I can have a part in bringing this old place back to life. I do my best as the part-time caretaker here, living on the assembly grounds like I do, but there's never much money. It's mostly a series of patch jobs that Hiram Denton and I are able to do." He paused. "You remember Hiram, don't you? He'll want to be a part of any renovations we do, if it's okay."

"Yeah, I remember Hiram." Carter smiled. "We used to make bets to see who could get the most words out of him. The man never had much to say."

Billy laughed. "Still doesn't. But he's good with his hands, Carter. And steady. He grew up right across the street from Laurel Springs—where he still lives today. His family worked at Laurel for two generations and now he and his wife, Estelle, both work here. Hiram mows the property, does odd jobs, helps with the farm work, fixes all the bicycles that break down. Estelle works at the store, bakes, makes lunches to sell. Does great baked goods."

Carter hardly needed the reminders. He could see Hiram in his mind, a quiet, slow-moving, and somewhat homely man, always such a contrast to his fast-moving, talkative, and outgoing wife.

"Does Estelle still make those thick bologna sandwiches and fried apple pies?"

"Still does." Billy grinned. "Keeps the store hopping with local business at lunch time."

He turned to Carter with a more serious expression now. "How much renovation are you thinking about doing here, Carter? Do you have an idea of exactly what you want to do—or do you want me to work up an estimate based on the amount you want to spend and the needs I see?"

"I've got some ideas." Carter pulled out the leather folder he'd brought with him and took out a set of papers to hand to Billy.

Carter watched the boys play while Billy looked over the plans. Like most six-year-olds with short attention spans, they'd lost interest in gunfights and lay sprawled under an oak tree now, driving Matchbox cars over dirt roads scratched out where the grass had thinned.

After reading through the papers, Billy looked up, his eyes wide. He whistled. "Contracting may not be your field, but surely you realize you're looking at a bucket load of money to do all this."

"I've *made* a bucket load of money, Billy. And I can't think of a better way to spend it." He caught Billy's eyes. "You know I always wanted to bring Laurel Springs back to life. It's what I went off to California for."

Billy scratched his chin. "Yeah, well, I guess I remember that talk when you were a kid. But a lot of time has gone by. You married and made a new life." He shifted and looked uncomfortable now.

"Spit it out, Billy. Don't stand on ceremony with me."

He scratched his neck. "Well, I guess I was wondering what Rhea thinks about all of this."

Carter scowled. "I've talked to my parents and to Grampa, and I expect to talk to Lillian and to

Nana. They own the land and so the decisions about what renovations can be done *really* lie in their hands—not in Rhea's or mine."

Billy squirmed in his seat. "Yeah, I know that, but Rhea has been working here all these years. Finding ways on a shoestring to make improvements, to draw in new tourists, to keep the place going." He searched for the right words. "I've sort of found myself a lot of times working more for Rhea than for Lillian or your folks."

"You're saying Rhea has sort of been running things?"

"Well, yeah, in a lot of ways. Although Lillian does most of the administrative work and keeps the books over at the ad-min building—and your dad keeps up with the property and farm aspects." He hesitated. "But it's Rhea who keeps things going daily. Jeannie works with her a lot, too."

He frowned. "While the economy has been down and times have been bad, they've scrubbed, cleaned cabins, painted, and mended. Bargain shopped for anything and everything. Run garage sales and rummage sales for extra money. Given historic tours and old-time demonstrations."

Billy gave Carter a determined look then. "It matters what Rhea thinks. And what Jeannie thinks, too."

"And you think that might be a problem?" Carter watched him.

Billy crossed his arms. "Well, sure. I heard

through Jeannie you'd already had one disagreement with Rhea."

"Is that right?" Carter was interested. "What disagreement was that?"

"Well, I heard how Rhea ran into you at the covered bridge—and how things didn't go so well." He dropped his eyes. "Jeannie told me Rhea said she isn't much interested in reinitiating a friendship with you."

Carter bit down on the smile that yearned to slip out. Evidently Rhea had kept quiet, even to her best friend, about their meeting on Rocky Knob. He guessed she didn't want anyone knowing about that.

"I'll deal with Rhea," he told Billy Wade. "I know you feel proud of all that Rhea's been doing. I do, too, Billy." He paused. "I've been keeping up with all that through my parents."

Carter saw Billy's surprise.

"It's the truth and there's more." Again, Carter considered what to tell Billy. "Did you know I've been funneling money into Laurel Springs through my parents over the last seven years?"

"No." Billy shook his head, obviously surprised.

"Rhea doesn't know that, either. So I'd appreciate it if you wouldn't tell her—or Jeannie—just yet." He sent Billy a firm look. "I just wanted you to know I've been doing my part, Billy. I may have been away but I've still kept caring about Laurel Springs."

"Well, dang." Billy gave a low whistle. "This sure has been a day of surprises."

Carter returned to business. "So, Billy, do you think you'd like to take on the contracting renovations for Laurel Springs?"

Billy reached over to clap him on the back. "I'd be downright mad if you asked anyone *but* me. And Ledford Electrical and Contracting will be glad for such a big job. I'll start working on the estimates right away if you'd like. The next time we meet, you can tell me the priorities you have in mind. Where you'd like to start. What you'd like to see to first."

"I'll do that. I have some blueprints for a house for Taylor and me that need priority." Carter pulled them out of the leather folder to pass to Billy. "Dad and Grampa said I can build on Low Ridge on the old Costner ruins. You'll know the spot; we used to play there. I don't want to impose on my folks too long."

"I sure will enjoy working on that project." Billy grinned, beginning to unroll the blueprints to look at them.

Carter stood up. "I've got a lot to do today, and I know you do, too. Thanks for the time you've given me."

"Heck." Billy stood up and gave Carter a clumsy hug. "You're my best friend from back since we were kids. I hope we'll be spending a lot more time together." He grinned. "I'll have to see if you can still catch a football one day."

"We'll do that." Carter smiled as he reached over to gather up his folder and extra papers. Out of the corner of his eye, he saw Billy's grin fade to a thoughtful frown.

"What's worrying you now, Billy?"

Billy shifted uncomfortably. "I guess I was just wishin' you and Rhea could make some sort of peace. So maybe the four of us could have some good times again like before."

Carter gave him a sly glance. "I have a better convertible for us to ride around in now."

Billy laughed. "Well, that's a fact!"

"And I'm working on Rhea." Carter realized regretfully that his voice dropped and softened as he admitted it.

He saw Billy watching his face. "You still got feelings there, Carter?" His voice dropped to a softer tone. "You don't have to say nothin' if you don't want to."

Carter looked at the face of his old friend. "I never stopped having feelings there," he replied honestly.

Billy's eyebrows lifted in question. "Is that so?"

"Yes, but that's a complicated subject and a story for another day." He sent Billy a telling look. "And nothing to talk about, you hear?"

"Don't worry. I can keep a confidence." He grinned again. "Even from Jeannie when I have to."

Carter clapped him on the arm. "I remembered that fact or I wouldn't have said anything at all."

He started down the steps and then turned back to reach his hand out to grasp Billy's in a firm handshake. "It's good to be back, Billy—good to see you, and great to be doing business with you."

"Back at you," Billy said, his grip firm in return.

Billy held his hand a moment longer as a thought came to him. "I hate to put a damper on things, but there's one worry I ought to share with you if your folks haven't."

Carter propped a foot on one step. "What's the worry?"

Billy ran a hand over his head. "Well, there's been some trouble around the place for a couple of months."

"What kind of trouble?" Carter's interest pricked.

"Little break-ins around the property. Vandalism —but with strange happenings with it. Spots dug up around old buildings, like someone's looking for something. Doors and windows broken out in some of the old cabins." He paused, thinking. "A few times folks have said they saw someone but we didn't get much of a description."

"That seems odd for Laurel Springs. Has anyone been hurt or threatened?"

"It is odd. And it's hard to imagine anyone could be looking to find anything around here. Most folks know Laurel has fallen on hard times. There's nothing of much value around the property except in the rental cabins—and they haven't been targeted. Just the old buildings." He frowned as he considered this. "No one's been hurt or threatened, but there's been a sighting or two of someone dressed in dark clothes with something like a ski mask on skulking around. That ain't normal."

Carter didn't like the sound of this. "Has the sheriff been called?"

"Yeah, Lillian called Ursell Wheeler over after the old Tritt cabin was broken into. There's all that spinning stuff there and the quilting frame and it worried Nana when some of that was pushed around in the break-in." He paused. "You remember Ursell?"

Carter grinned, remembering the sturdy, reliable, no-nonsense sheriff. "Yeah, he policed a few of our events around the high school, if I remember right."

Billy laughed. "Let us off for a few minor mishaps we could have gotten ourselves in some trouble for at home."

Moving his thoughts back to the problem at Laurel, Carter asked, "Did Ursell find anything? Figure out what was going on—or what motive might be involved?"

"Nah, it's a mystery, I guess." Billy shrugged. "Ursell figured it was just some kids goofing around. I hope that's all, but it strikes me as peculiar, and that's a fact. I haven't had a good feeling about it. This has always been a safe place. We've never had problems here."

"It's something to keep an eye on—especially if there are more incidents. Thanks for telling me about this." He scanned the yard to locate Taylor. "You let me know if you hear of any more problems, okay? We might decide to do some stakeouts or something."

"Yeah, sure." Billy followed Carter out to his car. "It's probably nothing. But I thought you ought to know, with our boys running free around the property. I've told Beau to keep a watch out."

"I'll talk to Taylor, too."

Chapter 5

Rhea sat on one of the picnic tables at the old Laurel Springs meeting grounds, waiting for the last of the tourists to arrive for the Saturday morning tour. It had been a tradition at Laurel Springs since the earliest of times to tour the grounds. In earlier years, a matched set of horses pulled visitors around the property in a long wagon with slat seats down either side. Now they used an old tram for the tours—bought used from an area amusement park and repainted.

Sam Dean, an outgoing, gregarious man and Rhea's father, always gave the tours with verve and pleasure until his heart attack. Now Rhea gave them. She lacked her father's hearty humor but found she possessed a good gift for storytelling. Rhea smiled to herself, remembering how scared she'd been the first time she led the tours at seventeen. Now she could do them in her sleep.

Checking her watch, Rhea stood up to greet the people who'd arrived. There were three couples from the cabins—the Brileys, the Reeveses, and the McMahans—and a group of six college-age kids from the East Camp Road. An even dozen today.

"Good morning," she said, putting on her tour-guide smile. "I'm glad you came to take our tour of Laurel Springs Camp Assembly Grounds today. I hope you'll enjoy learning a little about the colorful history of the campground and about the surrounding area."

She made introductions, had everyone put on name tags, and then gestured toward a wide field in front of them, starting the tour. "This is the old meeting ground where revivals and camp meetings were held in the 1800s. The Great Revival, with its outdoor brush arbor meetings, swept many parts of the United States in that era, and this mountainous region enjoyed its share of itinerant preachers passing through for fervent meetings and long days of preaching. The earliest ministers to travel this Appalachian section were Methodist circuit riders. Two famous ones who rode this section of the Great Smoky Mountains were Francis Asbury and William McKendree."

"I've seen Asbury's grave in Baltimore," Jim Briley said.

Rhea walked over to a rough covered stage near the field's edge. "The platforms where clergy preached looked much like this hand-built stage. Rough benches were also constructed to seat the outdoor congregation along with a mourner's or sinner's bench up front. A Methodist preacher often rode a five hundred–mile radius holding camp meetings that usually lasted three to four days. Meetings were held on the lands of area farmers, where there was ample land for camping and a good supply of water. It is easy to see why this site became popular for camp meetings— with its broad, flat field near both a mountain stream and a spring-fed lake."

"It certainly is beautiful here," Mrs. Reeves put in. "And I love the little white church."

Turning to point toward the church across the field, Rhea continued. "Churches, like the Laurel Springs Church here, often grew up on the grounds where the revivals and camp meetings were held. The original log church at Laurel Springs burned, and this framed white structure was later built to replace it in the 1900s."

Rhea started walking her group toward the church. "There is still a nondenominational service held here in the Laurel Springs Church every Sunday. Reverend Preston Layman conducts the service and the Gabes Mountain Band, a local gospel and bluegrass band, leads the church music and performs special numbers."

One of the college boys, named Pete, waved a hand. "We came to service Sunday and that group was great. They've won some awards in bluegrass and gospel, too."

"Yes. They're well-known and we're lucky to have them." Rhea smiled. "Several members of the Gabes Mountain Band are related to the Layman family, who co-own the assembly here, and many in the group were raised in the Laurel Springs Church. The band also uses the church to practice in."

The tourists toured the square white church with its broad double doors and handmade, stained-glass windows and then craned their necks to read the faded Scripture paraphrased from Hebrews above the church door: *Don't forsake assembling together.*

Rhea frowned. The letters needed repainting badly—as did the entire church. And one of the stained-glass windows was still broken.

She focused her mind back on the tour.

"There is a small cemetery behind the church." Rhea walked them toward the small fenced area. "In the past, community members made the caskets when a death occurred and dug the graves. You'll notice all the graves face east toward the rising sun and the Second Coming."

Rhea pointed toward a trail weaving into the woods behind the cemetery. "Within walking distance from either side of the Laurel Springs property are two other cemetery grounds, the Tritt and the Gilliland cemeteries. Both are about a three-mile hike in either direction. Maps to both places are available in the store or the administration building. Rough dirt roads drive in to both, too, if you're not a hiker." She grinned. "But expect a slow, bumpy ride on either, and be aware that you have to drive through the creek on the Gilliland Road."

She led them away from the church toward the large two-storied administrative building nearby. "The Laurel Springs Administrative Assembly Building was created in 1918—the year when Samuel Kolton Dean and John Carter Layman bought this property from several landowners eager to sell and move to the western frontier. The land the assembly grounds stand on was originally owned by Tritts, Costners, Suttons, and Gillilands —all familiar family names in Cosby and Newport heritage. You will see old cabins and evidence of their earlier way of life as we tour the grounds today."

Rhea piloted the tour group into the administrative building to see the hand-hewn, rock fireplace in the main entry room and the many framed photographs of the original Dean and

Layman families in the library behind the entry room. The two-storied white building also contained six workshop and conference rooms of various sizes and held the campground's administrative offices.

Visitors always seemed to enjoy the display of historical photos in the library, and Rhea loved talking about the history of Laurel Springs. She walked over to a black-and-white photo of loggers in front of a stand of giant trees. "In the early 1900s, rich tourists and industrialists came into this Appalachian area. Many came with the logging industry that began to develop here; others came driving the new motorcars becoming popular in America. Tourists were drawn to the mountains for the sweet, clean air and healing springs. Many resorts and assembly grounds developed in this region, such as Carson Springs near Newport and Kinzel Springs near Townsend, Tennessee. A Methodist assembly grounds developed on seventy-five acres behind Gatlinburg where Mynatt Park is today—but later moved to Junaluska, North Carolina, in the 1930s when more property was needed."

She pointed to a large photo of two couples on the wall. "Here is an early photo of the Deans and the Laymans. In the background is the Grove Park Inn in Asheville. Samuel Dean, his wife, Rhea Ansley Dean, John Layman, and his wife, Marguerite Dodd Layman, were mutual friends and wealthy New Yorkers. They came to vacation in this mountain region in the early 1900s and fell in love with the Smokies."

Rhea smiled. "Women's roles were limited then, and their dress restrictive, as you can see, but wealth gave much privilege." She pointed to another photo. "Here are Rhea Ansley Dean and Marguerite Layman in riding and hiking clothes. Both couples loved exploring the mountains and that is how they discovered this old assembly grounds near Cosby. A tour guide brought the four of them here to camp and hike. They were captivated by the spring-fed lake and the mountains rising up majestically behind it, and they decided to buy the land, if possible, to develop a resort for wealthy family and friends from the northern industrial states."

She led her tour group to another group of pictures. "After buying the needed land, the Deans and Laymans divided the property equitably and built personal homes. Then they hired an architect to draw the resort and campground plans." Rhea pointed to a frayed, yellowed map framed on one wall. "After plans were approved, a building crew erected the assembly store and entry buildings on the highway and constructed paved roads into the grounds. They created the administrative building here beside the original assembly grounds field —which also once served as a dining hall. They built the covered bridge over the creek, improved the old campsite roads, and built bathhouses. Their architect also designed two dozen charming summer homes, which were built on roads excavated along Little Cascades Creek."

Mrs. Reeves spoke up again. "All those little cottages along the creek roads are so colorful and cute. They look like the summer homes on the Chautauqua grounds near my home in New York."

Rhea smiled. "Do you mean the Chautauqua near Jamestown in Western New York?"

"Yes, that's the one." Mrs. Reeves nodded. "It's on the National Register of Historic Places and is still in operation. I read that over ten thousand people still come to it in the summers."

Rhea was pleased that Mrs. Reeves had introduced the topic of chautauquas. Few people even knew what they were—or knew how popular they once were as summer resorts in America. "Actually, the concept of Laurel Springs was patterned after the chautauquas that developed in the eastern United States in the late 1800s and early 1900s. Like the New York Chautauqua, built on an old Methodist assembly grounds on Chautauqua Lake in New York, Laurel Springs was built on a Methodist assembly grounds, too."

Rhea warmed to her subject. "Laurel Springs once hosted lectures, devotional services, concerts, and offered many outdoor activities. The early chautauquas, almost like educational summer camps, were widely copied. Their widespread growth actually spawned the Chautauqua Movement to encourage learning through educational events and entertainment in outdoor settings."

She pointed to several pictures of ladies and gentlemen playing outdoor games. "The early owners of Laurel Springs erected croquet and badminton courts for leisure, created a sand beach by the lake for bathing, and built a charming gazebo. Because the spring-fed lake is so large, they offered canoe rentals and provided bicycles for leisurely rides on the circular road around Laurel Springs Lake."

"It certainly looked beautiful then." Mrs. Reeves sighed as she studied the gracious women in long dresses and the men in their elegant suits and hats.

"Yes, it was." Rhea felt a clutch around her heart as she looked at the old photos. "Laurel Springs quickly developed a reputation as a charming summer resort and many famous people stayed here." Rhea pointed to pictures of several well-known Americans who had visited.

"It seemed likely in the 1920s and early 1930s that this area of the Smokies would grow and flourish like Asheville and Gatlinburg. Logging had brought a mix of prosperity and devastation to the area, but plans were underway to create a national park. The Deans and Laymans thought tourism would inevitably spread into the Cosby area because of its proximity to both Asheville and Gatlinburg. Although there had been extensive logging in areas near Cosby, this area had largely escaped being raped of its forestland and still maintained its natural beauty."

She escorted her group out of the administrative building. "The Weeks Act of 1911 led to the establishment of national forests in the eastern United States, and then in the 1920s the Great Smoky Mountains Park Commission began buying land for a national park. The families were optimistic that the Cosby area would soon be bustling with opportunity."

"What happened?" a young man named Kent asked.

Jim Briley, the banker from Ohio, answered quickly. "The stock market crashed in 1929 and the Great Depression began. That hit this part of the world hard—where many people already experienced subsistence living back in the hills."

"That's exactly what happened, Mr. Briley." Rhea turned to smile at him. "It proved a struggle for many to simply survive in those times. Sadly, many mountain families had just sold their lands to the government for the national park and put their land money in the banks before they crashed. They lost everything they had. Other families, who still owned land, had to find innovative ways to make do and survive through the hard Depression years."

"Some made moonshine around here." One of the college boys made a swigging motion with his hand and then laughed.

"Yes," Rhea agreed. "Or hunted ginseng or raised bees to sell honey or made crafts to sell to tourists in Gatlinburg. They did what they had to. Hunted, fished, raised their own food. Their natural self-sufficiency helped them in a difficult time. So did new jobs that opened up—work with the CCC after 1933—building park roads when the national park was created—and later, in the 1940s, new jobs helping to build nearby Douglas Dam."

One of the college-aged girls, named Cecily, looked wistfully around as they came out of the administrative building. "I guess the Deans' and Laymans' big dream of growing this place into a major resort dimmed during that time."

"They had some struggles." Rhea saw no point in stressing just how difficult some of those struggles had been. "However, rich Northerners still wanted to come to the mountains, especially as the national park became more established. And by the forties and fifties, more middle-class families began to travel here for vacation weeks. They liked that the assembly was near the park— and yet quiet and scenic. Many of these families come back year after year to Laurel Springs."

Ralph McMahan, who had been quiet, suddenly perked up at that comment. "Our family has been coming here for vacations for over fifteen years. We've stayed in different cottages over that time, but our favorite is Two Gables on West Camp Road."

"Oh," gushed Mrs. Reeves. "We're only two doors down from you in Redbud Cottage."

Rhea loaded her visitors into the tram now. She'd drive them from the assembly grounds around the lake, with stops at the old Tritt and Gilliland cabins and the cantilever barn, then up to Gold Mine Springs below High Ridge, where historic photos and artifacts told of the gold-mining days in the Smokies. On the route back, she'd stop the tram so her visitors could see the gazebo and boat dock beside the lake and then give them a tour of the old one-room school-house as a finale.

"Got room for two more?" a voice behind her asked.

Rhea turned to see Carter and his son, Taylor, walking up to the tram. She ground her teeth but offered them a pasty smile. "Of course, but wouldn't this be old hat to you, Carter?"

"Maybe." He grinned at her. "But not to Taylor. He's never taken the tour."

She saw Taylor's bright eyes watching her with childish enthusiasm.

"Well, climb on," she said, introducing them around as they did.

She put the tram in gear and headed down the

meeting grounds driveway to connect with the main Assembly Road. Rhea continued her tour talk with less ease now. Having Carter on board made her nervous.

He and Taylor had climbed into one of the front seats where no one else wanted to sit, and Rhea could sense Carter's presence close behind her. She could also hear Taylor's excited questions and comments.

"This is just like a little train, Dad. And Rhea is like the conductor, isn't she?"

He was a cute little boy, but Rhea churlishly didn't want to like him or get to know him better. However, despite her own misgivings, his sweet, eager disposition—and nice manners—quickly stole the hearts of the tour group.

Furthermore, at every stop, Carter tossed out extra comments about Laurel Springs to entertain Taylor, old memories or cute stories, which soon mesmerized the visitors on the tram. Naturally, Taylor told them how his dad had grown up here, which opened up a spate of questions Carter was only too eager to answer.

"My dad and Rhea learned to swim right there in this lake," Taylor told his captivated audience when they stopped at a pull-off beside Laurel Springs Lake. "And my dad can swim all the way out to the raft in the middle of the lake and back."

Mrs. Reeves giggled. "I'm not sure I could do that anymore."

Like most six-year-old children, Taylor bubbled with questions on the tour route. The grown-ups found his questions charming, but Rhea, the one expected to answer, found his questions annoying, especially with Carter watching her with barely suppressed mirth the entire time.

At Gold Mine Springs, Rhea finally lost her temper as the group climbed up the short trail to High Ridge to see the old Sutton cabin.

Taylor had asked why the old springs, spurting out from the rocky ledge in a small falls, were called Gold Mine Springs. Before Rhea could answer, Carter jumped in to reply. "The name comes from the fact that settlers hoped they might find gold here in the Smokies' streams like the gold being panned in the mountain streams out West."

"Did they really find gold here in the Smoky Mountains?" Taylor asked.

The tourists looked first at Rhea and then at Carter, not sure who should answer.

Rhea gave Carter an insipid smile. "You know, I think it would be nice if Carter did the rest of the tour. After all, he grew up here, just as I did, and I'm sure he'd enjoy offering his account and memories."

He turned questioning eyes to hers and Rhea sent him a tight-lipped, challenging look. She hoped he fell flat on his face. After all, he hadn't been here for nine years.

Carter's eyes flashed back at her in challenge, and then he turned to the group with enthusiasm. "I rode this tour a million times with Sam Dean, Rhea's father, when I was a boy. It will be my pleasure to do the rest of the tour."

He directed the group up the steps to the door of the Sutton cabin and then turned to put a finger over his mouth. "If we're all real quiet we might hear the ghost of Jonas Sutton rattling around in the cabin."

The group gasped.

His voice dropped dramatically to a whisper. "Rumor has it that he still roams this part of the mountains and walks through his old cabin."

Carter opened the door carefully. "Jonas was a prospector in the 1800s. He panned with his brother on a claim down in Dahlonega, Georgia, and after his brother's death, returned and panned here at the springs on Rocky Creek and at a stake on Porters Creek in Greenbrier."

He led the group into the cabin with confidence, acting as though he'd been here only yesterday. Rhea seethed. Granted, the old cabin had hardly changed a whit, with the same dented gold pans hanging on the walls and the same spade and shovel leaning against the fireplace. The furnishings still included a battered table and chairs, a rocker by the fireplace, a few tin dishes and personal items on a rough sideboard, and an iron bedstead draped with a faded quilt.

But Rhea had added a display table in the cabin with artifacts under glass inside it—plus old photos on the wall above it.

Spotting the new table right away, Carter walked over to study it covertly while he talked about the other simple furnishings in the room and reiterated how harsh life was for mountaineers in the 1800s.

"Jonas Sutton was murdered here in 1850." He pointed toward the fireplace. "That dark stain on the floor in front of the fireplace is thought to be a blood stain from where his body was found."

Cecily gasped and jumped back from the spot.

Kent laughed. "Who killed him?"

"Authorities never found the murderer. Legend has it Jonas was killed to learn where he'd hidden his gold stash. Whenever he got liquored up, he foolishly bragged about all the gold he was savin' for his old age."

Ralph McMahan picked up one of the battered gold pans to study it. "Did the murderer get the gold?"

"Rumors from that time say no. Family and friends said Jonas would have died before he told where he'd hidden it—and most think that's exactly what happened."

Several in the group looked up in interest. "Was the gold ever found?" Cecily asked, wide-eyed.

Carter shook his head. "No, and no one is really sure if Jonas ever really had much gold. Still, those who panned around Dahlonega, Georgia, found some big stashes. And there are accounts that say Jonas went over to pan a stake around Franklin one year, too. Gemstones were found in that area—rubies, amethysts, emeralds, garnets, topaz." He smiled at the group. "It's an unsolved mystery in this area that still gets talked about."

He raised his eyebrows and grinned at Rhea before artfully drawing the group's attention back to the display area. "Two decades before the California gold rush in 1849, a major epidemic of gold fever descended on the streams, creeks, and riverbeds of the Blue Ridge and Smoky Mountains. The amount of gold found in the Smokies was limited, but an industrious man could pan two dollars a day in gold, an excellent business in those hard times."

Carter pointed to several quartz rocks in the display case sporting gold veins in them. "Most gold was found in quartz veins like this. Sometimes, when you are hiking in the mountains, you can find quartz pieces similar to these—some with bits of gold or copper running in them. However, most gold was panned from rivulets and brooks in the mountains."

He discussed a rough map of the area and an old rifle and knife in the display case and then pointed to a small collection of gold pieces in a tin box. "Prospectors had different names for the gold pieces they found. Small bits like these—

large enough to pick out of the pan with one's fingers—were called 'pickers.' Bigger pieces, which could weigh up to several ounces or pounds if a prospector was lucky, were called 'nuggets.' Gold pieces larger than nuggets were rare in this area."

Carter turned to the group. "Most of the gold in the Appalachian region was found along a forty- to fifty-mile-wide belt going through East Tennessee, North Carolina, Georgia, and Virginia. You can still prospect for gold in the Smokies— but you need a gold prospecting permit from the ranger station to do it."

Kent leaned forward with interest. "Do people still find gold in the Smokies?"

"Some people still do, Kent, and a few tourist venues capitalize on this by offering sites to encourage tourists to pan." Carter grinned. "Generally, these locations stock a little gold or a few flecks of gemstones in the panning areas to make their tourists happy."

McMahan considered this thoughtfully. "With gold having seen a 20 percent increase in value lately—and with the price of gold now up to nine hundred dollars an ounce, it might be worth getting out the pans again and hitting the streams." He laughed. "I read that some professional panners make sixty to eighty dollars a day panning around the Appalachian region. That's not bad money while you're having a little fun."

The college kids began to talk enthusiastically about doing a panning expedition as Carter led the group out of the cabin and back down to the tram.

To her increasing irritation, Carter led the rest of the tour with equal aplomb and success. Rhea only barely kept her anger in check. She had no idea how he'd learned so much about gold mining in the area or how he remembered so much about Laurel Springs history after all these years. She could have kicked herself for handing the tour over to him.

In addition, Carter shared personal memories as he led the rest of the tour, memories Rhea didn't want to remember. His eyes found hers often as he shared these old stories.

At the elaborate gazebo by the lake, he talked about how couples often danced there in the moonlight. "When you're in love," he said softly, "you make your own music."

Rhea felt color rise in her cheeks. She and Carter had danced in the gazebo many times at night to music from a transistor radio, or to no music at all, just for the chance to be close and to hold each other. She focused her eyes out toward the raft built in the middle of the lake to avoid looking at Carter.

"There's the raft my dad can swim to." Taylor pointed toward the raft in excitement. "My dad said he and Rhea used to skinny-dip here at night sometimes when no one could see and they'd swim out to the raft."

The group tittered and passed knowing looks to one another. Rhea thought she would die on the spot. This certainly didn't help the professional image she was trying to maintain.

"We were very young then." She smiled at Taylor. "About your age."

Carter moved closer to her as they walked up the path back to the tram. "We weren't *always* small when we skinny-dipped," he whispered.

She jerked away from him in annoyance.

At the old one-room schoolhouse, the last point on the tour, Carter finally turned the tour graciously back over to Rhea. "I'm going to let Rhea close out the tour for you here at the school," he said. "She knows more about the history of the Laurel Springs School than I do— especially since it was her great-grandmother, Rhea Ansley Dean, who restored the log school-house and taught classes for the local children."

He smiled at Rhea. "Rhea often dresses in costume and teaches classes here to show outsiders what school was like in the 1800s. You should stop by when her school hours are scheduled and sit in to sample the experience."

Rhea, embarrassed and surprised at the compliment, stumbled over her words for a few minutes as she settled back into the tour discussion. She talked about the history of the school as she led her visitors through the log building, and then she drove the group back to the old meeting grounds, where the tour had begun.

Several in the group had established friendships by the time the tour ended. And the college kids were full of plans to go panning for gold, to take both hikes to the old cemetery areas, and to hike up High Ridge behind the Sutton place to catch the Lower Mount Cammerer Trail inside the Smokies park boundary.

"Thanks for letting us take your tour." Taylor offered his hand to Rhea in a surprisingly adult manner.

She shook his hand. "I hope you had a good time."

His eyes shone. "I did. And Dad's going to take me and Beau swimming next and then Grandpa's going to let me ride with him on his tractor."

"That's nice." Rhea tried to smile again, but the strain of the day was wearing on her.

"I *love* Laurel Springs," Taylor enthused. "And me and Beau are getting to be the bestest friends. Just like you and Dad were." He paused. "Dad says we're probably going to stay here to live and not go back to California." His eyes shone. "We're going to build our own house where the Costner cabin ruins are. That's on Low Ridge not too far from your house. You told us about that place today, remember?"

Rhea nodded. She felt sick. The site of the

Costner cabin ruins had always been a favorite tryst spot for her and Carter. They sat against the old rock chimney on the hillside many times planning how they would build a house there one day.

She felt Carter's brown eyes probing hers and busied herself collecting weekly schedules from off the tram seat. Then she studied her watch.

"I need to go now." Rhea attempted another smile. "I'm supposed to work in the store this afternoon for a few hours to cover for Jeannie, and before that time I need to do some work in the office."

She turned toward the administrative building.

Carter's voice started behind her. "See ya later. . . ."

"Don't finish that, Carter." She turned to frown at him, knowing the next words would be *and love you forever, Rhea Dean*. "The past can't be recaptured. You need to keep that in mind."

She strode off then, but she could feel his eyes following her.

Chapter 6

Carter's thoughts centered around Rhea for the rest of the afternoon. It was proving more difficult to get back into her good graces than expected.

He took Taylor swimming in the lake and

decided the old swim raft should definitely be replaced. The deck boards felt loose, and it shook so much on its worn foundations that it was downright dangerous. The big gazebo needed its roof replaced, the boat dock needed a total rebuild, and some of the canoes looked decrepit.

It saddened Carter to see how run-down many areas of Laurel Springs had become. He'd taken Taylor to see the administrative building and the old church after Rhea stalked off. Arriving late, they'd missed that part of the tour. The furniture and equipment in the ad-min building looked archaic, and the broad front porch of the long building seemed to be listing to one side. Carter scowled. The paint had even faded off part of the exterior of the church—a sorrowful sight to see. A stained-glass window in the church was broken and boarded over, and the old Scripture over the doorway had faded almost to oblivion.

He mumbled to himself as he walked through the assembly grounds, adding continual notes to the notepad tucked in his shirt pocket. Was the place this run-down when he left? Or did it just seem worse after so many years away?

Leaving Taylor to ride the tractor with his grandpa, Carter decided to walk through parts of the assembly grounds he hadn't closely studied yet. He'd seen most of the historic areas on the tour earlier, so he walked up the Assembly Road toward the covered bridge now, wanting to check out the cabin and campsite roads.

He stopped and laughed out loud when he spotted a familiar weathered signpost at the junction of the East and West Cabin Roads. The top sign read "Thisa Way," while the bottom sign said "Thata Way."

"Shoot, I remember when I had this sign made," he said out loud to himself. Rhea had made a joke one day about trying to decide whether to go *Thisa Way* or *Thata Way,* and he got a guy in high school shop to make the street sign.

He felt pleased to see it still standing.

Carter sighed. How could Rhea walk around this place every day and not think about him? Their memories lived in every nook and corner of Laurel Springs. He ran a hand through his hair. It's why he could never come back when Judith was living. It would have driven him crazy to be here.

He started down the West Cabin Road, looking at the resort houses on either side of the paved lane. They all looked shabby. He scribbled notes as he walked, letting the old familiar names of the cabins comfort him—Hemlocks, Redbud Cottage, Leaning Oak, Hickory House, the Magnolia—still in the same soft colors of green, pink, gray, nut brown, and white.

Carter paused, noting sheets of blue plastic covering part of the roof of the Magnolia. He walked around the house and found a downed pine tree lying by the side of the house. A storm had obviously felled it right across the roof. With the house showing a gloomy look of disuse, Carter guessed the damage had been done months earlier—but never repaired. He marked it as a priority.

As he walked on down the road, he continued reading the signs in front of the houses alternating on either side—Wayside Way, Two Gables, Bluebird Stop, Sweetgum, Crow's Nest, Summer House, and Mockingbird Hill—again all in a soft array of complementary colors.

Carter turned to start back up the street, savoring the sights of the picturesque cottages he so loved and enjoying the lyrical sounds of Little Cascades Creek tumbling over the rocks nearby.

Crossing the main road to East Cabin Road, he found the resort homes there equally derelict. Again he enjoyed reciting the names of the cabins as he walked, much like he and Rhea had done in singsong tones so many times as children, "Creekside Cottage, the Highlander, Pink Lady, Beech Grove, Dream Catcher, Four Seasons, Fox Den, Summerwind, Chestnut Place, Azalea House, Crescent Moon, and the Dancing Bear."

He stopped to make a note that the Crescent Moon desperately needed new shutters and then detoured off the road to walk closer to the Dancing Bear. He and Rhea had painted and decorated this one themselves. A sweep of memories washed over him as he thought back. *I wonder if that old set of car pictures is still on the bedroom wall.* He tried to peek in the window but found the curtains drawn.

Annoyed at the memories, Carter headed back out toward the Assembly Road again. Maybe when he started fixing up Laurel Springs, Rhea would come around. He hoped so.

Carter walked through the covered bridge and then explored the West and East Camp Roads beyond the bridge. They paralleled the cabin roads on the other side of the creek but were set up for tent and RV camping.

There weren't many campers using the sites, and Carter could hardly blame them. All the camp-sites needed to be cleaned up and resurfaced, and the grills needed replacing. He stuck his head into one of the bathhouses. "Yuck," he said out loud. "These bathhouses need to be totally remodeled, too. They're archaic." He wrinkled his nose. "They smell musty, too."

Knowing Rhea was working at the store this afternoon, Carter started up the road in that direction. If he kept putting himself in her face often enough, maybe he would break down that stubborn will of hers in time.

His lips narrowed in determination. Carter prided himself on his ability to rise above challenges and to maintain optimism in the face of discouragement. He certainly needed both of these traits with Rhea Dean right now.

A new wave of nostalgia washed over him as he walked up the porch steps of the Laurel Springs Market a short time later. Vintage tin signs still hung on the wall, battered wooden chairs lined the long porch, and the same old table with the checkerboard painted on top still sat in the corner. Heading inside through the rusted screened door, Carter could hear the soft chatter of local customers and the whine of country music on the radio. The vintage Coke machine that opened from the top still stood by the door, and the wood shelves in the store spilled over with the same mix of store goods and local crafts. A cluster of tables nestled near the back wall by the deli counter, and, amazingly, the ancient metal cash register was still ringing up sales.

A group of children sat eating ice cream cones at one of the tables, and Carter could hear Estelle's voice and Jeannie's over the din of the radio and the chatter of the kids. He looked around for Rhea and saw her, at last, propped in a corner, with Marshall Sutton leaning all too close to her.

A familiar rush of jealousy flashed in his veins as he pushed his way to the back of the store. Marshall Sutton had always nourished a yen for Rhea.

Carter saw Jeannie's expression of surprise as

he knocked over a chair on his way through the deli area.

"Hi, Carter," Jeannie called.

Hearing Jeannie's words, Marshall turned his way. "Well, Carter Layman." He didn't hold out a hand in welcome. "I heard you'd come back for a visit." He propped an arm proprietarily against the wall beside Rhea.

Rhea glared at Carter, eyeing the chair that had clattered to the floor.

Carter slid an eye over Marshall's sharp gray suit, starched shirt, and neatly knotted tie. His hair, as always, was cut army short to his head and his dark eyes were not friendly.

From his mother's letters Carter knew Marshall had become quite successful in the banking industry.

"I guess from the suit that you must still be working at your daddy's bank." Carter knew his tone sounded condescending, but he hardly cared.

Marshall's mouth tightened, and his eyes narrowed. "I'd say you'd know how that is— working for your *wife's* daddy like you do."

Carter felt his right hand clench into a fist. He'd never liked Marshall Sutton, and looking at him now, he knew that hadn't changed.

He studied the arm leaned too close to Rhea against the wall. "Is Marshall bothering you, Rhea?" he asked softly.

Marshall smiled at Carter in answer—a sly

smile. "Rhea and I have been dating for the last six months, Carter. Perhaps you didn't know that?" He straightened his tie carefully. "But, of course, it's hardly your business anymore what Rhea does, is it?"

Carter's eyes slid to Rhea's in question. She lifted her chin and put a hand on Marshall's arm. "I need to get back to work, Marshall. But I'll see you Friday night."

He put a hand over Rhea's, but his eyes connected to Carter's when he replied. "Yes. I'll see you then. Wear something pretty. We're driving into Knoxville for the symphony."

Carter's eyes followed Marshall as he walked away. In another day and time, he'd have gone after him and beaten the crap out of him in the parking lot. He'd certainly done it before.

Jeannie Ledford broke his concentration by coming up to throw herself in his arms. "Carter Layman, you big heartbreaker. Why haven't you been by to see me?" She leaned back to let her gray eyes dance into his. "Billy Wade says he's seen you *twice* now, and I haven't gotten to see you once."

Carter relaxed, looking into Jeannie's pixie-cute face. "Well, you're seeing me now, Jeannie. How has life been treating you?"

"Just fine," she answered. She looked him up and down. "And you still look as handsome as I remember."

"That's the honest truth," added Estelle Denton, coming around the counter to give Carter a hug of her own. "Lord, Son, how long has it been since I laid eyes on you? You've grown from a scruffy country boy into a fancy, slick city man. Real polished and fine-looking."

"Now, Estelle, Carter was always good-looking," Jeannie said.

Another throaty voice chimed in. "And he was always one the ladies chased after."

Carter turned to see Marion Baker leaning against one of the soda tables. She gave Carter an appreciative glance.

"Hello, Marion." Carter nodded her way.

"I hope you're going to be around for a while to spend some time with your old friends. *Some* of us would really enjoy that." She twisted the end of the long necklace that fell into the deep cut of her shirt. It drew attention automatically to the large bustline Marion had always been famous for.

Carter heard Rhea snort.

Marion heard it, too, and looked in her direction. "I'm real pleased, Rhea, that you and Marshall Sutton are an item just now. It gives some of the rest of us a chance to know Carter in a way we never could before."

Carter let his eyes rove over Marion simply to vex Rhea. There was no doubt that Marion Baker was still a good-looking woman.

Seeing his glance, Marion took out a small business card from her pocketbook. "Here's my card," she said. "You call me sometime. I'm in the real estate business, as you can see, and you'll note that the name is Marion Baker again." She made a little pout. "You might have heard I married and became Marion Cruse for a time but my marriage didn't work out. I took back my maiden name." She paused. "So, I'm single again at the moment."

Carter tucked the card in his shirt pocket while watching Rhea stomp over to the register to ring up a customer sale. He grinned. He'd always loved riling her up.

After Marion left, Carter sat down at one of the soda tables to catch up with Jeannie and Estelle. Rhea kept busy the entire time, but Carter knew she could hear their conversation. The Laurel Springs Market was hardly a large store, and sound carried. He and Rhea had listened in to all the local gossip in times past often enough.

"That vandal caused more trouble on the assembly grounds last night," Estelle announced. "Have you been hearing about that, Carter?"

Carter leaned forward. "What happened?"

Estelle shrugged. "Oh, nothing much this time. He broke out a window in the old Gilliland cabin."

He thought back. "I didn't see that this morning when I went on the tour with Rhea."

"It was in the back bedroom," Rhea put in. "We didn't go in there."

He focused on her. "Why didn't you tell me about it?"

She rolled her eyes. "I didn't know you even *knew* about the break-ins. After all, you don't live here anymore."

He glared at her before turning back to Estelle. "Did anybody see the person who broke in?"

"A couple of the boys swimming in the lake last night said they saw someone on the back side of the lake near the cabin. But it was dark. And they didn't think anything about it until Billy Wade walked around inquiring today, shortly after Hiram found the broken window."

"Was the window the only damage?"

"Well, now that's odd." Estelle pushed her glasses back up her nose. "Hiram said it looked like someone might have pried up some of the old floor boards. And there was a lot of stuff moved around."

"Like someone was looking for something?"

Estelle shrugged. "Maybe. But what would anyone expect to find in that old cabin? There's only a few sticks of furniture in the whole place and nothing of value there."

"It's curious, isn't it?" Jeannie leaned her elbows on the table. "You'd think as run-down and beat-up as this whole place is, that no one would bother coming here to do their thieving.

They could go down the road to the Cobbly Knob resort and golf course where all the folks with money stay."

"This is a nice place, too," Rhea said defensively.

Jeannie waved a hand. "Oh, you know what I mean, Rhea. Don't get testy. You've said about the same thing yourself before."

Carter frowned. "Well, I don't like the idea of someone skulking around the grounds at night. I think Billy Wade should put a padlock on the entry gate and start locking it at night."

Jeannie giggled. "You must have read Billy's mind. He drove into Newport to the hardware store today to buy one."

"Good." Carter stood up, looking toward the door. "I'll go see if he's come back and I'll help him put it on." He glanced toward Rhea and scowled. "Rhea, you, your mother, and grand-mother live alone. I don't like the idea of some-one breaking into houses and climbing into windows at night."

Rhea crossed her arms in irritation. "Don't you worry about Mother and Nana and me. We manage just fine. And if I remember correctly, the only person I ever recall climbing into our windows uninvited at night was you, Carter Layman!"

Carter chuckled remembering that as he walked down the main Assembly Road, eating one of Estelle's fried pies and looking for Billy.

Chapter 7

Rhea hated that she'd let Carter rile her up again. That dang man. She noticed Jeannie and Estelle exchanging knowing looks after Carter left, too.

She took a damp cloth over to clean off the table where the children had dripped their ice cream cones and righted the chair Carter had knocked over.

"Carter sure was mad to see Marshall in here cozying up to you," Jeannie said, unable to resist making a comment.

Estelle laughed, pushing a hand through her short, curly hair. "Yeah, it seemed almost like old times to see those two ready to duke it out again."

Rhea busied herself picking up trash on the floor without making a reply, glad to notice Estelle soon busy helping another customer.

"You're avoiding answering me," Jeannie said, at her elbow now.

"Maybe because I don't want to talk about this." Rhea crossed her arms and turned to frown at her friend.

Jeannie shook her head. "I can't figure you out sometimes, Rhea Dean. Never mind what went on between Marshall and Carter here today, what I can't figure out is why you're going out with Marshall Sutton at all." She wrinkled her nose.

"He's so full of himself—and so intense. He always looks like a *GQ* magazine."

Rhea bristled. "What's wrong with being serious or dressing well?"

"Oh, come on, Rhea." Jeannie rolled her eyes. "We all used to laugh at Marshall in high school, with his neat, button-down shirts always tucked in and that briefcase he carried to school."

"Maybe Marshall was simply showing an early maturity." Rhea lifted her chin. "He manages one of the Cosby Bank branches now and he's very respected in the community."

Jeannie snorted. "Yeah, and he makes sure you know it, too! He's the biggest bragger. He went on and on when he came in here today about the boat he'd just bought, pointing out how prestigious it was and being sure he told us how much he paid for it so we'd be impressed." She shook her head. "He always does that—as if how much he spends on something reflects on his worth in some way."

Rhea wanted to argue, but there were some aspects about Marshall that unsettled her, too, despite the fact that they'd been going out over the last months. "It's not as though there are a lot of hot choices for dates around Cosby," she said at last in a surly tone. "And *you* told me last year I needed to date more."

Jeannie headed back to the counter to help Estelle with the customers. "Well, I didn't have

Marshall Sutton in mind when I made that suggestion, you can be sure."

Rhea headed over to the register in a few minutes as she saw that Jeannie and Estelle needed her help.

"Howdy, Rhea," said Caleb Dorsey, the sound man for the Gabes Mountain Band, moving over to the register. "I got a bunch of lunch orders for you to ring up for the band."

"Is the group practicing at the church today?" Rhea asked, taking the bags and tickets from Estelle and starting to ring up the totals.

"Yep." Caleb smiled. "I left them working on a new number Leroy wrote. I think they're going to try it out at service on Sunday before singing it at the festival over in Bryson City on the Fourth of July weekend." Caleb hadn't inherited the musical talents his father, mother, and brothers shared in spades, but he excelled at handling the sound-board and setups for the group.

After Caleb and the other customers let themselves out, Estelle sat down on a stool behind the counter. "We've been busy as beavers today. Thanks for coming in to help out, Rhea, especially while Jeannie had to take Beau to the dentist earlier."

"Yeah, I appreciate that," Jeannie added, cleaning up the sandwich counter while she talked. "It's slowing down now and you can head on home if you want."

"How'd the dentist visit go for Beau?" Estelle asked.

"Terrible." Jeannie frowned. "Beau didn't want to open his mouth for the cleaning and he bit the dentist. I was just *so* embarrassed."

Estelle laughed. "He's a lively one, that Beau."

"Where is he now?" Rhea asked. "With Nana?"

"No, Mary Jane is keeping him." She grinned. "He and Taylor Layman have struck up a fast friendship. They want to be together about every minute possible to play. I'm even letting Beau spend the night tonight. The boys are so excited about that."

"That's real sweet that them boys have become such fast friends," Estelle said. "Beau was needing him someone about his age to play with."

"Yeah, and I'm getting Billy Wade to take me out to dinner and a movie tonight since Beau is spending the night with Taylor." She paused thoughtfully. "You know, that little Taylor is the nicest, most polite boy. I sincerely hope his goodness wears off on Beau."

"Mary Jane says the boy is too serious and adult by half." Estelle brushed some crumbs off her apron. "She told me he's had a hard time these last years, being mostly with adults and having to watch his mother die. She hopes Beau's carefree, fun-loving nature will wear off on Taylor."

"Well, maybe they'll find a compromise."

Jeannie laughed, but her eyes slanted toward Rhea.

Rhea watched Estelle and Jeannie give each other a thoughtful look then, realizing they were thinking about Carter and his earlier visit once more.

She took off her store apron. "I'm going to head on out now. I need to run by the office and do some paperwork before I go home." She didn't want to take a chance that they'd start probing her again about Carter—or Marshall.

Rhea slipped out the back door when she left and took the shortcut leading through the campground and across the creek to the ad-min building and her office, hoping to avoid any sight or sound of Carter Layman again. She hated herself for all the feelings Carter stirred up in her after all these years. And she felt furious at herself for having them.

At home later, over dinner, she felt relieved that her mother and Nana Dean kept up a steady stream of conversation. She didn't feel sociable, just stressed and anxious. Having Carter back was proving to be very difficult. Every day, Rhea resolved to go on with her life and not be affected by Carter's return, and every day, he managed to turn up to irritate and embarrass her in some way.

Tired and confused over the events of the day, she went to bed early with a book, trying to think how she was going to handle Carter being around

Laurel Springs continually. And worrying even more about how she would handle him staying on permanently—if he actually did.

A scratching sound outside her window awakened her shortly after she dozed off. Rhea listened intently. It sounded like someone was on the roof, scrambling around! Her breath caught in her throat as she remembered the incidents with the vandal recently. Rhea sat up in bed, heart racing a mile a minute now, as the sounds grew closer. She looked frantically around the room to see if she could locate a weapon. As her eyes spotted an old softball bat in the corner, she crept out of bed and padded quietly across the room to pick it up.

"I hope you're not planning on using that on me," a familiar voice said with amusement from outside the window.

Rhea turned around, in annoyance now, to see Carter pushing her bedroom window the rest of the way open to climb in.

"What *are* you doing here? You scared me to death!" She seriously considered hitting him with the bat but then put it down, her thoughts moving in a new direction.

She wore nothing but a short, silk nightshirt with spaghetti straps, and Carter's eyes were already roving over her in a way that sent Rhea scurrying to the closet to hunt for a robe.

He chuckled. "The view from the back is as

good as the view from the front. You always did wear the sexiest nightclothes, Rhea Dean." He sat down on her window seat and made himself comfortable, just like he'd done so many nights in the past when they'd been young. "It was always one of your little surprises. You dress mostly in tomboy clothes or homemade jumpers and dresses your Nana makes but you wear sexy nightclothes and underwear. I always loved that —visualizing skimpy black panties and a bra covered in lace lurking under your frayed jeans shorts and old T-shirts."

"I do not wear black underwear!"

"No, but you wear pretty colors." He gestured to a pink bra draped carelessly over her bedpost.

Rhea snatched it up to stuff it in her underwear drawer, while pulling on a short silk robe—the only one she could find. She wished it were longer and less scanty, like one of Nana Dean's thick, floor-length chenille ones. She sat down on the bed, covering up her bare legs with a quilt.

"For the second time . . . what are you doing here, Carter?" She crossed her arms and scowled at him.

"Just stopping by to visit." He stretched and grinned at her. "You were the one who all but invited me to stop by this afternoon."

"I did not!"

He propped his long legs on the bed nearby. "Sure you did. You said you remembered me climbing into your window—and all but implied that you, your mom, and Nana would be safer because I'm around now to do just that again."

"I said no such thing!" He was always twisting her words around. "I said you were the only person I could remember who climbed into our windows uninvited."

He shrugged. "Same thing."

"It is not!" Rhea heaved a sigh. "Carter, we are not kids anymore. It's been nine years since you were home last. And it's totally inappropriate for you to be climbing in my bedroom window."

His lips twitched. "Rhea, it was always totally inappropriate that I climbed into your bedroom window—or that you climbed into mine—but we always did it anyway. Seems like we had some of our best talks at night, me sitting in your window-sill, or you curled up on my other twin bed."

She felt her annoyance rise. "And your point is?"

"We need to talk, and I thought this might be a good place and time."

"I don't think we have anything to say that hasn't already been said."

"Well, I disagree." He got up and began to wander around her room, picking up things and examining them distractedly along the way. "We need to get along, Rhea."

She crossed her arms and frowned at him. "And maybe I don't want to get along."

"I've seen that." He picked up a bottle of her Jean Naté from the dresser to sniff at it. "But you need to make more of an effort to change your viewpoint in that area. I'm working hard to rebuild our friendship. You need to do the same."

"Hmmmph." She punched at a throw pillow. "I guess you'd call taking over my tour today and coming into the store and insulting Marshall Sutton your way of trying to rebuild our friendship."

He turned to her with a cocky smile. "It was *you* who gave the tour to me, with that nasty little challenging look of yours, acting like I wouldn't know what to say, when I grew up here the same as you."

She hated it that he was somewhat right. "I thought you'd decline politely and take the hint to back out on interfering in the tour so much."

Carter shook his head. "You always were competitive, and I never have been able to resist your little challenges. You should have known exactly what I'd do." He walked over to tweak her cheek and then leaned his face in intimately toward her neck.

She slapped him away.

He sat down on the bed. "You still smell the same, Rhea Kaden Dean. Citrusy, lemony, and musky like the Jean Naté you've worn since high school. And there's another heady smell that's just totally you in the mix—a sweet and sultry scent that's your own unforgettable essence."

He leaned toward her again, nostrils flared, his voice growing husky. "I always so loved it."

Rhea tried to stop her pulse from beating faster at his words, from noticing that he still smelled like she remembered, too, of woodsy English Leather, minty toothpaste, and the strong male scent that defined him.

He leaned closer to trace a hand over her shoulder and down her arm. "You're even more beautiful than before. And more exciting to be near. Have I told you that?"

A protective fear clutched at her heart, and she pushed his arm away. "Get off my bed, Carter," she said between gritted teeth.

He hesitated.

"I mean it—or I'll call out for Mother."

Carter rolled his eyes, got up, and went over to stretch out on the window seat again. "Far enough away, Rhea?"

"Only back in California will be far enough," she shot back, pulling her quilt up to cover the chill she felt.

Carter shook his head. "I don't intend to go back. I've told you that."

She hugged a pillow to her. "I'm sorry to hear it—once again."

Irritated at her remark, he got up to wander around the room again, picking up her pictures to look at them, poking in her jewelry box, looking at the books on her shelf. "I remember the year we read every one of those Zane Grey Western books. Don't you?"

He picked up a yellow topaz ring. "I gave you this birthstone ring for your sixteenth birthday, too. It took me six months to save up the money."

She felt like throwing her pillow at him.

Rhea crossed her arms. "Why did you insult Marshall today? That sort of behavior will not help you and I to get along."

"He didn't offer his hand in greeting. Purposely held it back." He ran a hand through his hair. "And I thought he was edging too close to you. Bothering you."

She glared at his back. "And what's that to you if he was?"

His eyes flashed as he turned around to face her. "Are you really dating him, Rhea?"

"And shouldn't I date people? You dated other people. You even got married. You started a new life and a family. Should I just sit here as if time stood still?" She spread her hands in exasperation. "I've dated a lot of people in the last nine years. And, yes, I'm dating Marshall Sutton right now. So what? He asked me out after we ran into each other at a Christmas party and we've been seeing each other now and then since."

He took a step toward her, his eyes dark. "Are you intimate with him?"

Rhea felt her face flush. "That is none of your

business, Carter Layman. Nor is whom I date. You have *nothing* to say about my life in that area, do you hear me?"

He turned to pick up a book from her desk. She watched him flip through the pages, collecting himself. Rhea remembered this diversionary technique all too well.

"I've never liked Marshall Sutton," he said at last. "I always felt there was something off in him."

"How ridiculous." She fumed. "That's only old high school prejudice talking. Marshall was a bit of a nerd then and some of us made fun of him. But he's gone on to become a respectable member of the community. I think he just always exhibited more maturity than the rest of us."

"Maybe." Carter turned to study her. "But he isn't right for you. Surely you know that."

She bristled. "And who do you think is? You— now that you've decided to wander on home since your wife died?"

He walked toward her, angry now. "You've got a mean tongue, Rhea Dean. And you don't know anything at all about my relationship with Judith, how we courted, why we married, how she suffered with ALS and how hard that was on Taylor and me."

"Well, poor you!" She threw the pillow at him now. "So what should I have done? Stayed your pen pal through all those years? Let you tell me about how much you loved your wife in your letters or how good she was in bed?"

He strode over to the bedside, sat down, and grabbed her arms, bringing his face close to hers. A muscle twitched angrily in his jaw. "One day you'll let me talk with you about all this. So you'll understand."

"I don't *want* to understand. Do you hear me?" Her voice shook. "I don't want to know about it." Rhea felt the tears threatening. She put her hand up to push him away, but he caught her hand instead and wrestled it behind her, bringing them even closer.

Rhea heard his breathing escalate and saw his eyes darken just before his mouth descended on hers.

She was caught immediately in the passion and intensity that always raged between them. Rhea's head spun with the impact. His warmth and scent enveloped her. She let him wrap her closer, let his kisses deepen, reveled in the feel of his hands in her hair, on her back, tracing soft patterns down her arms. Why did it have to be Carter who still made her come alive like this? Who made her weak with wanting and dizzy with desire? Whose kisses electrified her senses? Whose fingers brought alive every place on her skin he touched?

Rhea's heart cried even as her blood raced. How could he have left her? How could he have loved and kissed and shared himself with someone else? Hurt her so deeply and married another woman?

Rhea felt Carter's hands slipping under her nightshirt, touching her bare leg above her knee. What was he doing? He feathered breathy kisses over her neck in a way she didn't remember, making her shiver in delight. It registered painfully with Rhea that he'd grown more artful. He'd never done this when they were younger.

Words of passion slipped out of his mouth—tantalizing words—but they sounded unfamiliar, too. Where had he learned these things? Who had taught him all these new moves? They'd learned loving together as children, exploring innocently at first and then with more passion and wonder later. But with all their explorations, they'd never made love. It wasn't right—and they had never gone there. Instinctively Rhea knew where Carter headed now. And they had not learned this game together. Carter had learned this with Judith.

She stiffened. And began to push and pull away.

"No, Carter. No." She struggled under him.

"Oh, Rhea." His words were husky and raw. "Don't push me away. It's been so long. I have missed you so much, been so lonely for you."

She pushed his face away from hers and glared at him. "You had Judith. You haven't been lonely. You've had no need to lie alone at night."

His dark eyes looked down into hers, and he smiled one of his slow, sensual smiles at her.

"Judith said it was your name I called out the first time."

Furious now, she pushed Carter off onto the floor. "How dare you tell me something like that? How dare you!" She slid out of the bed and stomped around to kick him as he started to get up. "Did you think it would please me to hear that? Well, it doesn't, do you hear? It makes me feel sick and angry."

Carter's eyes were heated now, too. "Watch yourself, Rhea Dean. You're always so quick to judge without knowing all the facts. It's not one of your nicer traits."

"And it's not one of your nicer traits to climb up into my window and to try to seduce me with all your newfound skills learned with another woman. Don't you have any shame? Have you lost your morals? Don't you have any respect for me anymore—when you claim to still care so much about me?"

Surprise touched his face as he stood up to face her. "You haven't been with anyone else," he said at last, slowly shaking his head.

A gradual, smug smile spread over his face. "I just assumed you would have after all this time. . . ."

She kicked out at him again. "Get out of my bedroom, Carter Reagan Layman. I'm sick of you and all of your games, do you hear? And I wish you'd never come back! You're turning my life upside down and making my days a wreck. I hate you!"

Carter threaded his hands through his hair, his eyes studying her thoughtfully. "It will all come right, Rhea. You'll see."

She shook her head, tears threatening somewhere deep inside.

He reached out a hand to brush back a wisp of hair from her face, but Rhea backed away from him as his hand lingered on her face.

"Go home," she said between clenched teeth.

He nodded and started toward the window. "I didn't mean to come on too strong or to disrespect you. But feelings have always escalated so fast between us. They tend to override my reason."

She stood there, hugging her arms tightly around herself, not wanting to hear his words or to make a response. He was right that passion had always escalated between them rapidly like fireworks, consuming them and wrapping them in a whirlwind of feelings. Spiraling them into a wonder of sensory ecstasy.

Her heart wrenched inside her. Had it been the same for him with Judith, she wondered? She wanted to weep as the thoughts came to her. Thoughts she could never put into words or ask. But thoughts that tormented her.

"There has never been anything like the wonder of you," Carter whispered to her before he opened the window to climb out.

She glared at him, hating how he'd always been able to pick up on her thoughts. Even after all this time, he still knew her all too well.

He dropped out of sight onto the roof, but his voice called out softly from below the window. "See ya later—and love you forever, Rhea Dean."

Rhea slammed down the window on his words and then crawled into her bed to finally weep with outrage.

Chapter 8

Carter heard Rhea slam the window as he climbed from the roof into the branches of the oak tree growing beside the Dean house. Dropping to the ground, he followed the well-worn path through the back property, skirting under the trees out of sight of the house until he met the Deans' drive. After walking a short distance down Dean Road, he turned right on an old settlers' road, following it through the woods to a pathway angling left beside an old fence line.

Usually he turned at this point to follow the grassy, rutted lane below Low Ridge that led over to the Layman farm. But tonight he hesitated. He checked his watch. He'd tucked Taylor and Beau in bed, both worn out, before he left for Rhea's. He could take time to climb up Low Ridge to the old Costner ruins—and he wanted more time alone to think.

A full moon helped light his way, and Carter quickly found the crumbling stone walls and big rock chimney of the old Costner house, built long ago by early settlers to the mountains. Smiling at the familiar sight, Carter climbed over the foundation to the chimney. He sat down on the old hearth, leaned his back against the chimney, and savored his recent memories of being with Rhea.

He lifted his shirttail against his face. The scent of her still lingered—that citrusy, sweet smell unique to her. Even after his walk, the excitement from being with her still stirred his body. No one had ever affected him as Rhea Dean.

After they'd fallen in love, they used to sit here, at the Costner cabin ruins or higher on Rocky Knob, and plan their future. Carter wondered if he still had a chance to make those dreams come true. He wasn't sure.

Rhea held just cause not to want him back. But she hadn't married through the years. Carter learned tonight she'd not been with anyone in intimacy since he left either. He grinned in the dark. She hated the fact she'd revealed this piece of information to him.

Carter shifted against the fireplace to kick a pinecone into the night in irritation. That dang, stubborn pride of hers always reared up. He shook his head. He'd have his work cut out for him getting past that.

Behind him, Carter heard an unexpected noise.

He sat up—alert, listening. It might just be a raccoon or night creature scurrying in the brush. But an uncomfortable premonition caused him to stand, trying to see more clearly in the darkness around him. All the talk of vandals probably made him prickly.

Suddenly, he felt a presence behind him. Before he could turn, a hard blow whacked the back of his head, dropping him to his knees. As searing pain lanced through his consciousness, Carter struggled to lift his head. He glimpsed the dark shape of a man retreating into the night shadows just before darkness enveloped him.

A short time later, he surfaced to find Jinx, his Airedale mix, licking his face and barking out a happy greeting. He tried to focus his thoughts. Where had the dog come from? Carter felt momentarily confused as he felt the rough ground beneath his head and wondered where he was. Then he remembered being hit from behind. He must have passed out.

Carter reached out a hand to pet the dog and then saw his father and grandfather climbing over the rock wall toward him.

"Are you all right, Son?" his father asked with concern, squatting beside him.

Carter struggled to sit up. "I think so. Someone hit me from behind."

Wes Layman examined the back of his head. "That's a right nasty blow. Looks like you got hit with a good-sized stick or something. Who did this?"

He shook his head, feeling a little dizzy when he did. "I don't know. Whoever it was sneaked up on me. I only saw a shadow of the person retreating before I fell."

"Well, here's the weapon." Grampa Layman brought a thick stick over for them to examine. A little blood still decorated the side of it.

Wes held a finger in front of Carter and began to move it back and forth. "Can you follow this, Carter?"

Carter nodded.

Grampa chimed in. "What's your full name, your date of birth, and where you went to school?"

Carter grinned, knowing they were checking him for signs of concussion. "Name's Carter Reagan Layman, born April 6, father Wesley Dodd Layman, mother Mary Jane Reagan Layman. I went to Smoky Mountain Elementary School, Cosby High School, and Cogswell Polytechnical College in Sunnyvale, California. Majored in Game Design and Development."

Grampa punched Carter's arm, pleased with his response. "Just checking, boy. Just checking."

Carter, who'd been knocked out in childhood antics and in high school football, knew how potentially dangerous a hit to the head could be.

"How long were you out?" Carter's father studied him with concern.

Carter tried to remember. "I don't think long. And I don't have any nausea or amnesia. How bad's the bump?"

"You'll have a nasty goose egg there for a day or two." He parted Carter's hair, studying it. "But there's not much blood or breaking of the skin." He moved around to look at Carter. "Think your Grampa and I can help you stand?"

Grampa scratched his head. "It's a mighty long walk home, Wes."

Carter looked up in surprise. "Did the two of you walk in?"

"Yeah." His father grinned. "Followed the dog as best we could. He set up to howling and scratching at the back door a while ago. Taylor woke up and told us Jinx always did that when something happened to anyone in the family. The boy insisted we let the dog out and told us to follow him. He was real scared when he learned you were out of the house. Cried to come with us."

Carter ruffled the big dog's ears again. "Well, aren't you the fine hero tonight, Jinx?"

The dog woofed softly and pushed his head affectionately against Carter's chest.

Carter frowned, thinking of his son and remembering his father's words. "Taylor's afraid something might happen to me like it did to his mother, Dad. He has nightmares of me dying sometimes."

"Poor kid." Wes shook his head.

Carter rummaged in his back pocket and pulled out his cell phone. "Call Mama and let Taylor and her know I'm all right. Beau, too; he's spending the night and probably worrying right along with Taylor."

Grampa put a hand on Wes's arm. "Ask Mary Jane to drive the car over here to bring Carter home. It's too far for him to walk."

"I can walk." Carter tried to stand but found himself surprisingly unstable on his feet.

Grampa watched him. "See? And tell Mary Jane to call Ellie to come over to check Carter out."

Carter put a hand against the rock chimney to support himself. "Ahhh, Dad. Don't make Aunt Ellie get out this late. I'm okay. I just need a minute."

"It's only ten at night." Wes looked at his watch. "She and Rice will still be up." He put an arm out to support Carter. "It's either call Ellie and let her check you, since she's a registered nurse, or your Grampa and I will have to haul you into the hospital emergency room in Newport."

Knowing this was an argument he couldn't win, Carter acceded. Ellie, his mother's sister, and her husband, Rice, lived nearby in Cosby. They weren't traveling with the Gabes Mountain Band this weekend, and they wouldn't mind coming. Also, Carter knew it would frighten Taylor if he went to the hospital for anything.

He rubbed a hand over his head while his

dad made the call. "She's on her way," Wes said.

Carter looked through the darkness at the rocky, unpaved roadway leading up to the Costner ruins. "Well, at least we can walk down to meet them at the paved road. It's hard to drive up this rutted settler's trail."

With his father's and Grampa's support, they started toward the road.

An hour later, Carter lay in the twin bed in his old childhood bedroom, an entourage of his family hovering nearby.

"I think the boy's going to be all right," his Aunt Ellie pronounced, closing a battered black medical bag she'd brought with her that once belonged to her father. Ellie frequently tended to the mountain people in the area who sometimes couldn't afford—or simply feared—the doctor. Her father had done it in his generation, and Ellie did it in hers.

Taylor turned anxious eyes toward Ellie. "Is Dad *really* going to be okay?"

Ellie tousled the boy's hair. "Sure thing, Taylor. Your dad's seen a lot worse blows than this one in his lifetime. He just got the back of his head bruised and needs to rest." She took the ice pack off Carter's head and handed it to Taylor. "Why don't you go downstairs and put some fresh ice in this for your dad? Think you could do that?"

"Yes, ma'am." Taylor jumped up, pleased to have something to do for his father.

When his footsteps receded down the stairs, Ellie looked at Carter.

"You've got a right smart bruise on the top of your head, Carter. You did black out briefly and you experienced some difficulty with balance— so you could have sustained a mild concussion. Mostly for Taylor's sake, I'm not going to send you to the hospital to be more thoroughly examined. But I'll be wanting someone to wake you up every couple of hours to check to see if everything's all right through the night."

She looked at Wes, Mary Jane, and Grampa Layman. "Could you three take shifts coming in here to check on him?"

They agreed, and, after mumbling his complaints, Carter concurred, as well. He knew Taylor would get unnecessarily upset if he went to the hospital. The last time Judith went in, she didn't come back.

Ellie checked the bruise on Carter's head a last time. "Put ice on this to keep the swelling down. Do it for about twenty minutes every hour until you fall asleep and again at the wake-ups in the night."

She picked up her medical bag. "I've cleaned the skin breaks, and no wood debris from the stick is in the wound now." She patted Carter's shoulder. "You be a good boy, stay in bed to rest tomorrow, drink plenty of fluids, and take Tylenol if you have headache or pain."

She gave him a kiss on the cheek. "You're lucky

this wasn't worse—that he didn't whack you on a more vulnerable part of your head."

Ellie turned to her sister. "Is the sheriff still here, Mary Jane?"

Carter's mother bit her lip. "No, he got all the information he needed from Carter earlier. Now, he's gone over to the Costner ruins to see if he can find any traces of who attacked Carter—footprints, scraps of clothing, or anything else."

"Well, good." Ellie frowned. "It's one thing to have a little vandalism around Laurel Springs, but it's quite another when people start being attacked. I don't like that."

Carter fingered his head. "I think I simply surprised him and he panicked. He probably didn't expect to see anyone at the old cabin ruins at night."

Mary Jane put her hands on her hips. "And what in the world do you suppose he was doing up there anyway? There's nothing but old rocks and a chimney at the end of that old woods lane."

Wes looked thoughtful. "Maybe he was only passing by the place on his way to someplace else. The old ridge path runs by there."

Grampa sat down on a chair near Carter's bed. "Still, it's not a good thing to know there's someone hanging around Laurel Springs who would hurt someone like he did Carter. If God hadn't been gracious, he could have been seriously injured."

"Yes, God was taking care of him." Carter's mother put a hand over her heart.

Carter made no comment. There hadn't been much of God in his life through the years in California.

Later in the night, he realized this fact even more as he heard the sounds of his Grampa praying by his bed.

"What are you doing here, Grampa?" Carter asked into the darkness.

His Grampa chuckled. "What does it sound like I'm doing, boy? Praying for you before it's my shift to wake you up and see if all's well."

Carter felt uncomfortable. "Well, I'm okay."

"Your head's okay." He handed Carter a fresh ice pack to hold on the bruise. "But your heart's not okay."

Carter frowned at him. "Are you going to preach at me, Grampa? Seems like you ought to save up your preaching for tomorrow morning's church service."

"I've got plenty to spare." His Grampa chuckled.

Carter took a drink of water from the glass on the bedside table and situated the ice pack on the right side of his head. "How long have you been here?"

"Long enough," Grampa Layman said, leaning back in the plaid bedroom chair. "Certainly long enough to see that things aren't well with your soul."

Carter closed his eyes. He was in for it now. Grampa possessed a strong gift for discerning the hearts of people—and evidently the Lord had shared a revealing talk with Preacher Layman during his prayer vigil.

"I don't suppose we can avoid this talk?" He shifted the ice pack on his head slightly.

Grampa shook his head. "No. I'm accountable to give you what the Lord gave me."

Carter looked around the familiar room, waiting. In the moonlight filtering through the window, he could see the rough beamed ceiling, the old fireplace, the familiar hunter plaid bedspreads, the car prints on the walls, and the shelf full of sports trophies and model cars he'd assembled and painted as a boy.

"You used to pray a lot in this room," Grampa said, seeming to follow his eyes around the room.

"Those were innocent days." Carter sighed.

"And now you don't feel worthy to pray." Grampa's words were soft. "You're having a hard time forgiving yourself for your mistakes. And you're mighty angry at God."

Carter made no comment.

"Oftentimes we go off on our own, make our mistakes, bear our consequences, and then get ourselves annoyed with God for the way things turn out. We pull away from the Lord and then seem surprised when things don't get much better."

Carter pushed at his pillow with annoyance. "There's a lot you don't know about my life in the years since I've been away."

The old man crossed his ankle over one knee. "And there's a lot I do. God has a way of keeping me informed about things. You need to forgive yourself for things in the past, Carter. And you need to forgive Rhea."

Carter snorted. "Rhea? It seems to me Rhea Dean needs to forgive me. She's outright told me she hates me now."

"Yeah. Rhea has some of the same problems herself that you're dealing with." He paused thoughtfully. "The both of you have bitterness, unforgiveness, and resentments you haven't let go of. They've taken root and gone down deep into your souls. It's going to take a serious decision and some hard work to root them out—on both your parts."

He leaned toward Carter. "Do you know studies show unforgiveness is unhealthy to human life? Even setting all the Bible knowledge aside that exists, research alone proves that unforgiveness and bitterness harbored in a life can create psychological and emotional stress. They can cause headaches, digestive problems, anxiety, depression, cognitive disorders, and increase the risk of heart disease, cancer, and stroke." He ticked off the consequences on his fingers.

Carter took the ice pack off his head and

plopped it down on the tray by the bed. "You're making me regret teaching you how to search on the Internet when you came out to California, Grampa—and for giving you that new computer, too."

Grampa laughed. "The same technology that can be a tool for the devil can be a fine tool for the Lord. It sure has helped me in getting my sermons together."

A space of quiet filled the room.

At last Carter said, "What have I not forgiven myself for?"

"You know the answer to that, Son. There's no need to ask me."

Carter considered this. "How can I get Rhea to forgive me? I want to make things right with her. But she's still so angry with me."

"She's hurt, boy. And she's afraid. When you've loved and been hurt, you're afraid to let yourself love again. When you've trusted and had your trust shattered, you're fearful to open the door to potential pain again." He paused. "It's going to take time to rebuild love and trust."

He laid a hand on Carter's arm. "Think of it this way. Let's say you've built a house—but then a destructive storm tears it down. You don't just say: *'House be built'* after it's broken down into a shambles—and then wham!—there's the house all whole and rebuilt again. No. It takes time and conscious effort to rebuild the house. Brick by brick. Little by little. Just because you remember how the house once was, and how pretty it was, doesn't mean it can ever be exactly the same again either. The destructive forces of nature—and the forces of sin and wrong—incur their toll. It takes time to rebuild—and it takes love."

Carter heaved a deep sigh. "Are you saying there's no hope?"

"Never. I *never* suggested that. Where there's love, there's always hope." His eyes found Carter's. "Have you asked Rhea Dean to forgive you, Carter?"

He bristled. "I've told her I want to be friends again."

"Son, you and I both know you want more than that. But that's not what I asked you."

Carter closed his eyes. "I guess I haven't offered that request as fully as I might have."

"Well, it might be a place to begin." He leaned over to put a hand on Carter's knee. "And another might be in praying a prayer—here and now—to get you back in a right place with God. You ready to do that, Son?"

Carter nodded, a lump forming in his throat.

Grampa's familiar voice began to flow over him, healing in its familiarity and in the Spirit it carried. "Father God, Carter comes to you tonight—a boy come home again to his birthplace and a boy longing to come back into right fellowship with you. Welcome him home again into your love and heart tonight, Lord. Hear his prayers asking for your love and forgiveness. Hear his prayers yearning to draw nigh unto you. Meet him here as he pours out his heart before you, and before me as his witness, and draw him back into the circle of your care and love."

The healing words flowed over Carter like warm honey. He soon added his own prayers into the quiet of the night and gradually began to feel the heaviness around his soul lighten. The Spirit of God touched him in the room of his childhood—and Carter's faith and relationship with the Lord became renewed.

When Carter's mother came into his room in the early hours of the morning to check on him again, she said, "Your Grampa and you have been praying in here."

He gave her a curious look. "Why do you say that?"

She smiled at him and leaned over to kiss his forehead. "I can still feel the presence of the Lord lingering."

Carter nodded, closed his eyes, and slept peacefully.

Chapter 9

Rhea walked into Laurel Springs Church on Sunday morning with a sense of dread. She considered feigning sick, just to avoid seeing Carter Layman again after last night. However, she quickly found out, as Pastor Layman gave the announcements and prayer requests, that someone had attacked Carter the night before.

Her humiliation paled beside the news. He could have been killed! Rhea leaned forward to catch the details—a hit on the head, not hospitalized, home recovering, going to be all right. She sighed with relief as Carter's grandfather finished the account and requested prayer for Carter's continued recovery. He also asked for everyone's help in finding the individual, or individuals, responsible for the attack and for the repeated cases of vandalism at Laurel Springs.

Rhea wrestled with her mix of feelings throughout the service, made worse by Pastor Layman's sermon on the topic of unforgiveness. He even presented research on how bitterness and unforgiveness could cause mental anguish and health problems—and explained that without repentance and resolution, continuing to harbor resentment and unforgiveness could interfere with an individual's spiritual relationship with the Lord.

Well, great. Rhea found it difficult meeting Pastor Layman's eyes as she shook hands with him at the church door. She kept wondering if he'd directed the sermon toward her.

After service, she brooded through lunch while her mother and Nana Dean talked, trying to decide if she should visit Carter. She desperately wanted the details of what happened—despite the awkward feelings between them.

Nana gratefully helped resolve her indecision. "If it's okay with both of you, I'll serve strawberries with whipped cream for our dessert today —so I can send that chocolate cake I baked yesterday over to the Laymans'. I feel awful about what happened to Carter."

Lillian looked up from the Sunday paper she'd started to read. "That's fine with me." She glanced toward Rhea. "Could you take it, Rhea? I promised Nana I'd drive her to the Walmart in Newport after lunch to pick up fabric for her new quilting project. It's hard to find time to get over there during the week."

"Sure, I'll take it over, Mother."

Considering what to wear later, Rhea decided to keep on the long jumper she'd worn to church. It was, admittedly, a little old-fashioned with its quilted bib-top—but Rhea favored the simple, old-time garments Nana created. They seemed in character with the history of the assembly grounds, and, quite frankly, Rhea liked the idea of having on a long skirt that covered her legs after last night.

She carried Nana's cake out to her old Volkswagen and carefully tucked the carrier into the front floorboard. She patted the car fondly as she walked around to the driver's side. Just before her sixteenth birthday, Volkswagen had reintroduced the Beetle, and Rhea's dad, feeling sentimental and extravagant, bought one to surprise her. Rhea still loved the old car, bright yellow in color, the paint dulled only slightly over the years. Plus, it was paid for in full and ran like a top.

Dutchie wove all around Rhea's legs, begging to go along, so Rhea let her jump into the backseat for the short trip. When Rhea stopped the car in the Laymans' driveway, the large Airedale mix that Rhea remembered from the day Carter arrived bounded off the porch, barking.

Taylor, playing in the front yard, came over to hold the dog's collar as Rhea let Dutchie out of the VW. "You be good and stop barking, Jinx." He shook a finger at the dog. "These are friends."

The dog obeyed, surprisingly, and Taylor smiled brightly at Rhea while Jinx sniffed Dutchie out in a friendlier manner.

"What's your dog's name?" Taylor asked.

"Her name is Dutchess, but we call her Dutchie for short. She's a Border collie mix."

Dutchie woofed a small greeting to the larger dog and wagged her tail.

Taylor's mouth dropped open. "Wow! This is the Dutchie in Daddy's *Time Traveler* games. Jinx is in them, too. Did you know your dog is famous, Rhea?"

"I guess I didn't." She smiled. "I don't play video games much."

"Well, Daddy's games are all great." He puffed out his chest in pride. "His *Time Traveler* games with Jinx and Dutchie are going to be made into animated movies." His face dropped. "The games are too hard for me to play at six, but I'll be able to watch the movies." He brightened again. "They're going to be G-rated."

"I see." Rhea knew very little about Carter's games. She'd purposely avoided reading about them or locating any of them to play.

"Jinx and Dutchie are making friends. See?" Taylor petted one dog after another. "They like each other."

Satisfied that the dogs presented no problem, Rhea opened the car door to get the cake.

"Ummmm. Is that for us?" Taylor's eyes lit up. "I like chocolate."

"Well, I'm sure Mary Jane will let you have a piece." Rhea carried the cake into the Layman kitchen.

Despite her problems with Carter, Rhea had refused to allow those difficulties to interfere with her relationship with Mary Jane and Wes Layman. She grew up visiting in their home, and they were like a second family to her. They all experienced awkwardness at first when Carter married, but after that, they made an effort to move on as before. Or at least somewhat as before, with the major focus of their conversations no longer centered around Carter and his life in California.

Mary Jane turned from her job of putting the clean lunch dishes away to give Rhea a hug. "Hey, you sweet thing."

She took the cake from Rhea's hands, taking the top off the carrier and sniffing with appreciation. "Oh, Carter will be pleased with this. One of Nana's chocolate cakes."

"Can I have a piece, Mamaw?" Taylor danced up and down around the kitchen.

She gave him an indulgent smile. "Sure. I'll cut you one right now."

"How *is* Carter?" Rhea asked.

"He's still got a large pop knot on his head, but he's okay." She cut a large piece of cake and put it on a glass plate, holding out the plate to Rhea.

She smiled. "Why don't you go up and say hello to him and take him a slice of Nana's cake? He could use some company. We're having trouble keeping him in bed like Ellie wanted today."

Rhea hesitated. It would seem ungracious not to take the cake up.

Taylor pulled on Mary Jane's skirt. "Will you walk me out to see the baby chickens after I eat my cake?" he asked. "We can look for eggs, too."

Mary Jane smiled at Rhea. "Taylor is still fascinated with all the aspects of farm life just now." She ruffled the boy's hair. "We'll go right after you eat your cake."

Carrying the cake, and the glass of milk Mary Jane poured, Rhea started toward the stairs.

Mary Jane's voice followed her. "We put Taylor in the little guest room, so you'll find Carter in his old room. You know the way."

Rhea did, but she'd managed to avoid Carter's room all these years, not wanting to confront old memories. She found herself hoping Mary Jane had totally redecorated.

The door to Carter's room stood open, and Rhea felt a moment of déjà vu seeing him propped up in bed with a laptop computer on his knees. Even in high school, he'd been a gamer, always on the computer or squatted in front of the TV with a controller in his hands.

His room looked exactly the same, too. The old hunter plaid spreads covered the twin beds, the same classic car prints hung on the walls, and Carter's old sports trophies, school pictures, and carefully assembled model cars still cluttered his desk bookshelves. It hurt to look around.

She sighed, and the sound caused Carter to glance up. A slow smile lit his face, and Rhea's heart clutched.

"Come to visit the sick?" He wiggled his eyebrows, catching sight of the cake. "Come closer, Little Red Riding Hood, and bring me that fine cake you're carrying."

She frowned at him, walking over to set the glass of milk and the cake on a tray angled by his bedside table.

He laid the laptop to one side and picked up the cake eagerly. "This is Nana Dean's famous chocolate cake, isn't it? Did you ever find out what her secret ingredients are that make this cake so delicious?"

Rhea grinned despite herself. "She still won't tell. Mother says she's written the recipe down and put it in a safety deposit box."

"Figures." Carter chuckled. "Sit down." He gestured to the small easy chair close to the bed. "I'll be glad of some company. It's driving me crazy to be in bed." He rolled his eyes. "But Ellie threatened the hospital if I didn't rest for one day."

She sat down, aware that Carter's eyes scanned over her slowly as she did, lingering over the dress.

A faint smile played on his lips. "Did Nana make your dress?"

Rhea bristled. "There's *nothing* wrong with this dress."

"Did I say there was?" Carter cut off a chunk of cake with his fork. "I always liked your clothes. You know that. They're distinctive."

Rhea considered this, wondering what sort of wardrobe his wife, Judith, possessed. It was probably stunning. She'd sneaked glimpses of her once in a magazine of Jeannie's that spotlighted the lives of the rich and famous.

"How was church?" Carter asked, after wolfing down his cake in four or five bites.

"Fine. Everyone was concerned about you."

He drank down several gulps of milk. "What did Grampa preach about?"

Rhea hesitated, feeling a small flush start up her neck at the remembrance of that sermon. She tried to make her voice sound light and casual. "I think it was about unforgiveness or something—you know, forgiving people their trespasses and that kind of stuff."

Carter choked on a swallow of milk and started laughing.

Rhea scowled at him and stood up to leave.

He waved a hand at her. "Private joke, Rhea. Sit back down. I'm not laughing at you, so don't get mad."

Carter leaned back against the pillow and closed his eyes. "Grampa came to sit with me in the middle of the night and preached a sermon to me along that line." He opened his eyes and looked intently at Rhea. "I needed that sermon and the prayer time after. I haven't stayed close to God like I should have. It was a different life in California. . . ."

His voice drifted off for a moment, and he closed his eyes once more.

Rhea watched him pick at the bed covers and pop his knuckles. She knew he had something on his mind. He always fidgeted when he did.

His eyes found hers at last. "I need to ask you to forgive me. I did betray you and I married someone else. I broke promises to you and I wasn't faithful." He blew out a long breath, seeming to be glad to get the words out.

She sat, watching him.

"So. Will you forgive me?" He reached out a hand for hers, but Rhea crossed her arms defensively, pulling back into her chair.

Flustered at this turn of events, she considered how to answer him. "Carter, it's easy to listen to those sermons in church about forgiving seventy times seven like Jesus told Peter to do in the book of Matthew." She twisted her hands in her lap. "I can *say* I forgive you because it's the right thing to do, but my heart still hurts inside and I can't just forget what happened, even if I do say I forgive you."

He thought about that. "Well, it's a start, don't you think—just to try to forgive?" He sighed. "I want to say I forgive you, too, Rhea, for not coming when I needed you, for making me feel you didn't care, for making me believe you loved Laurel Springs more than me."

Her eyes popped open. "You thought that?"

Carter nodded.

She shook her head, puzzled. "But you knew my

father had a heart attack and then died. You knew I was the only child, and that only Mother and Nana were left to do the work."

He gave her a patient look. "Rhea, I'm an only child, too. And you and I both know my parents, my Grampa, your mother and Nana Dean—and the hired help—could have successfully kept Laurel Springs going for a few years while we were in school."

Rhea didn't like this line of thought. She set her jaw stubbornly. "You weren't here, Carter. You don't know what it was like."

"No, I wasn't."

Carter sighed and picked up his laptop. "Hey. Check this out, Rhea." He typed in a phrase and then pulled up a screen.

Rhea put a hand on one hip with exasperation. "You're going to change the subject—just like that?"

He shrugged. "It seemed like we'd accomplished about all we could with it. And I don't want to fight." He gave her a pleading look. "I want to try to be friends again."

She avoided a response.

In the quiet, Carter put a hand up to his head and winced.

The movement instantly caught her attention. "Are you hurting? Are you all right?"

He rubbed his head. "Every now and then I get a twinge. I got a pretty good whop last night."

Standing up, she walked over to examine his head. She parted his hair with her fingers and felt the huge knot where he'd been struck.

Rhea sucked in a breath. "What happened?"

"I stopped by the Costner ruins on my way back from your house. I wanted to think." His eyes caught hers, and she realized she stood too close.

Stepping back, she sat down in the chair again.

He grinned at her, recognizing the defensive move for what it was.

"Tell me what happened," she insisted.

He rubbed his neck. "It's a short story. I sat down in front of the old chimney in the dark. After a while, I remember shifting around, kicking at a pinecone, making some racket in the quiet." His voice trailed off. "Just afterward I heard some noise in the brush. I thought it was probably a raccoon or another critter, but I stood up to look around and see."

Carter put a hand to his head. "I suddenly felt a presence behind me. Before I could turn around, I got whacked soundly and knocked unconscious for a few minutes."

Rhea leaned forward. "Did you see anyone?"

He shook his head. "Before I fell, I saw a man dressed in dark clothes fleeing into the brush, but that was all."

"You're sure it was a man?"

"The shape and height were wrong for a woman.

I'm almost sure it was a man, and the clothes I glimpsed looked like those of a man." His eyes met hers. "He wore that ski mask I've been hearing about. No one wears a ski mask in the summer, Rhea."

She threaded her hands through her hair. "Then it probably was the same vandal people saw at other times." She bit on a nail. "But why do you think he attacked you?"

"I've thought about that." He scratched his forehead. "My guess is I startled him. I don't think he expected to find anyone at the cabin ruins that late—just sitting in the dark. Maybe when I kicked at the pinecone, he heard me. When I stood up, he probably panicked. He realized I might see him, possibly recognize him, or that I might pursue him."

Rhea snorted. "That's an understatement. You definitely would have pursued him if you'd seen him and you know it."

"Well, I didn't get the chance." He sounded annoyed and rubbed his head again. "He hit me with one heck of a stick, too. Ellie said he could have seriously injured me if the blow had been to the side of my head or lower on the back." His eyes narrowed. "I don't like the idea of having someone that dangerous lurking around Laurel Springs."

"Me neither." She straightened the items on his bedside table distractedly. "What can we do?"

"Not much. Be more careful." He pushed at the

pillow behind him to straighten it. "We changed Hiram's hours so he can guard the gate from close to midnight every night. And Billy Wade and Dad are trading shifts each night to drive or walk around the grounds to check things. There's not much else we can do."

He heard her sigh. "Don't worry. The vandal might have been scared off by this incident. This could be the end of it."

"I hope so."

"Here. Let's think about something else." Carter turned his laptop toward her. "Take a look at this YouTube clip about the future of gaming."

Rhea smiled. Carter seldom liked to focus on gloom and doom for long. He patted the bed beside him. Curious, Rhea came over to study the computer screen.

Carter pointed to the image in front of them. "This is a clip about Project Omega, the new future for video gaming. There's no controller required. It's going to be a whole new way to play video games by voice, hand motions, body movements." He gave her one of his white-toothed grins. He'd never worn braces, but his teeth were toothpaste-commercial perfect, like so many things about him.

Rhea moved her eyes to the screen, where Carter had activated the YouTube demonstration. He talked over the onscreen voices. "This new aspect of gaming gets the participant off the couch and into the game even more than we're seeing now." He pointed to the ongoing computer action. "See, a person can drive a race car with their hand movements without a controller, or send a soccer ball down the field by kicking it with their own feet, or even play game shows by pressing an imaginary buzzer in their lap."

He laughed. "It's great, isn't it?" He punched her like old times. "Here, you'll love this part. See how this girl can pick a dress and actually view how it will look on her as she swirls and turns in front of the television screen?"

"However do they do that?" Rhea felt amazed at what she saw.

Carter laughed again. "It's too technical to readily explain, but it's going to revolutionize the whole industry of gaming." He clicked off the YouTube video. "Quest is in on the cutting edge of this. We've got games already in the works that will debut when the new EOne system comes out to support them."

He grinned. "Our programmers have a Grand Prix race ready to market and I've been pre-viewing parts of an undersea game we're publishing with mermen and mermaids in it."

She got caught up in his enthusiasm. "How will a sea game be interactive like the examples we saw?"

He made excited arm gestures. "You'll be able to swim and turn, fight off octopi and jellyfish, dive or paddle with your arms to get over or around obstacles. It will be great!"

Rhea watched the animation in his face. "You really love doing this, don't you?"

"Well, sure. And it's exciting to be on the cutting edge when something new is coming out."

She remembered Taylor's comments about Dutchie and Jinx earlier. "Did you really put Dutchie in one of your video games?"

He looked at her in an odd way. "Haven't you ever *looked* at the *Time Traveler* games, Rhea?"

She shifted her eyes from his. "No. You know I've never been as much into games as you."

"No, but you used to enjoy them." His fingers tapped the keyboard thoughtfully, and she heard him sigh. "You've just avoided the whole thing because of me, haven't you?"

Rhea hesitated, not wanting to answer. Finally, she said, "I've been busy, Carter."

His reply was soft. "I see."

He closed the laptop slowly, and Rhea found herself feeling like a heel. This was the world he loved and worked in, and she'd totally avoided following his progress in it since he married simply from bitterness and anger. Not wanting to see his games or think of him. She'd even hated the gaming industry many times for drawing Carter away from her. For taking him to California. For leading him to Judith.

The words of the morning's sermon flashed

across her mind, convicting her again. She winced inwardly. Perhaps she'd carried her resentments a little too far.

Rhea hunted for words to soothe the situation. "Listen. I'm sorry I haven't watched your games." She twisted her hands in her lap. "It was spiteful of me."

The quiet in the room stretched for a long time before Carter answered softly. "It's okay, Rhea. I think I understand a little."

She hated to look up and meet his eyes. Once she'd been the biggest supporter and encourager of his dreams. She studied all his early boyhood game ideas, adding her enthusiastic suggestions to his as he inventively created each imaginary plot or character. She'd thrilled and celebrated with him when the concept of his mountain adventure game helped him win a scholarship to the design college in Silicon Valley.

In his first year at school, he'd called, written her letters, and e-mailed her continuously about his new school and all he was learning. She remembered his excitement when his mountain adventure concept was translated into a real video game for Quest. The next summer, he hadn't been able to come home to Laurel Springs because the game, *Mountain Quest*, was nearly ready to come out. She knew he'd created several other adventure games after that, but she didn't even know the names. Billy Wade owned all of them and talked about them often, but she'd never paid much attention.

Guilt washed over her. "I'm glad your games became a success. I've seen them at Billy Wade and Jeannie's. Billy Wade loves them, especially the one about finding gold."

He watched her with sad eyes now.

An understanding suddenly flashed in Rhea's mind. "It was while creating the game about gold that you learned so much about gold mining here in the Smokies, wasn't it? Like you shared on the tour?"

He nodded. "We named it *Gold Quest*. I do a lot of research while creating a new game. It's sort of like writing a book. The developer or lead designer comes up with a premise for a game, writes the story line, backstory, and script to tell the narrative. He sketches the characters, good and bad, develops the conflicts, and the levels of play. Extensive research comes in at several stages in the process of developing the game's setting, characters, sound effects, and even regional voices—to make it realistic."

His mind seemed to drift to another place. "Then the developer collaborates with the programming team as they work for about a year to bring the game to life three-dimensionally." She watched a smile drift across his face. "Alvin Johnson, the young man from Ohio who won the other scholarship with Quest, became my main teammate."

A memory flashed back across Rhea's mind. "Alvin was the one you roomed with near the college, wasn't he? The one who became such a good friend to you?"

He looked her way, seeming to come back to himself. "Yes, Alvin and I developed a strong friendship learning the gaming business, through our studies in school, and through our ongoing work with Quest as work-study scholarship recipients. Alvin's gift is programming, mine developing. We were chosen by Morgan Benton with those dual talents in mind." His fingers played on the laptop keyboard restlessly. "Alvin and I made *Mountain Quest* come to life that first year, then *Gold Quest* and *Cave Quest* over the next years. After graduation, we both stayed with the company and created the *Time Traveler* games together. We're still a team."

It was obvious Carter missed him. Rhea remembered hearing so much about Alvin that first year while Carter lived away. It dawned on her for the first time what Carter might have given up to come back here. Why had he done that? He was rich and famous. He had new dreams to pursue now, probably better than his old dream to fix up Laurel Springs—a broken-down assembly grounds in a rural backwoods area of the Smokies.

Not wanting to voice these thoughts, Rhea shifted the conversation to another area of Carter's interest. "Tell me about the *Time Traveler* games that have Dutchie and Jinx in them, the games that are going to become movies."

He smiled at her. "Better than telling you about them, I'll show you." He closed the computer and started to swing his bare legs out from under the bedcovers.

"Whoa!" Rhea put out a hand. "You're supposed to rest in bed today. I'm not going to have you climbing out of bed on my shift, so that I get in trouble with your mother."

He stuck his legs back under the covers with reluctance. "Okay, you win." He sighed. "But you'll have to walk down the hall to Taylor's room to find the *Time Traveler* games I want to show you. I think they're on his bookshelf."

Carter grinned. "If they're not on the shelf, dig around in his room. They might be under a pile of stuffed animals or crammed under a bunch of picture books. Taylor isn't always the neatest kid. And Beau spent the night last night. The room might be a little messy."

"Takes after his dad, huh?" Rhea avoided his swat as she started out of the room.

He laughed. "I've got a game console, TV, and controllers in here. I can show you a glimpse of what Dutchie and Jinx look like on the game screen when you get back."

The old guest room down the hall had been converted into a charming little boy's room, filled with airplanes, cars, books, and toys. Rhea walked around the room, looking for the *Traveler* video games.

She found them at last, crammed under a thick book on top of an old maple desk that had been in the Layman house for years. Moving the book, Rhea's attention was captured by the words *Photo Album.*

Taylor bounded into the room just then. "Hi, Rhea. Dad said you were here looking for the *Traveler* games. Did you find them?"

She nodded as he walked over beside her. "That's my photo book," he told her, grinning with a white-toothed smile much like his father's.

"Wanna see my mom and our house in California?" He flipped open the photo album on the desk before Rhea could answer.

"That's me when I was born." He pointed to a photo on the first page. "And that's my mom holding me. And there's Dad."

He flipped another page. "Here's my Grandaddy Benton and there's the Benton house where we lived all the time I was little."

Rhea suppressed a smile. He talked as though six was terribly old.

"There's my mom all dressed up for a party." Rhea looked down at a photo of a sleek, beautiful woman, her perfectly coifed hair parted in the middle and tucked behind ears studded with glistening diamonds.

A pain welled around her heart.

"She was real pretty, wasn't she?" Taylor's voice softened. He sighed. "I miss her and my Grandaddy Benton."

Rhea searched for something to say. "That's a big house." She looked at the gigantic, palatial home spreading at the end of a long drive.

"Yeah, it's *huge.*" He grinned. "It's so big we lived in one whole part of it and hardly ever saw my grandaddy unless we wanted to. I think our part was called a wing—you know, like on an airplane."

"I see."

Taylor flipped pages in excitement, pointing out pictures of him growing from baby years to school age, drawing her attention to happy photos of him and his dad playing in the yard and having good times together. Rhea noticed after a while that the pictures of Taylor's mother grew less frequent. In one, she lay in bed, looking pale, books and drawings scattered around her.

"That's one of the last pictures of my mom she'd let us take. She was working on her clothing designs. She drew ladies' dresses and things. Lots of shops carried her stuff after they got sewed up." Taylor put out a finger to touch her picture. "She started getting really sick after this." He sighed. "I don't remember her much at all except sick."

Rhea struggled to find something to say. "That must have been hard."

He nodded and heaved a very grown-up sigh. Then he flipped to the end of the book.

"This is our new house. Dad bought it after Mom died and we moved there." His finger touched a simpler white bungalow, old-fashioned and homey in design compared to the elegant Benton mansion. "He said we needed a change and a place of our own."

Rhea studied it, not knowing what to say.

"It's near the beach and we can walk down a couple of streets and be at a park right by the ocean. Jinx likes to go there and run." He looked up at Rhea with an engaging smile. "I like it there, too."

Rhea picked up the *Traveler* games. "We'd better be getting back to check on your dad."

He skipped ahead of her back to Carter's room.

The next half hour was a small nightmare as Rhea listened to Carter and Taylor tell her with enthusiasm about the *Time Traveler* games they previewed for her on the television screen. The dogs in the video games did look like Dutchie and Jinx, even in animation.

Carter pointed at the beginning scenes of one of the games. "The basic plot in the *Traveler* games is about two humans who move through time to impact lives and change the future. While time traveling, they can shape-shift—as needed—into their dog counterparts." Carter directed her attention to a dark-haired man on the screen.

"This is mild-mannered Jacob Farley, who has his own investigative agency, but kind of like a Superman character, he possesses another unknown identity."

Taylor pointed to a woman character with enthusiasm. "That's Dinah McNabb, Jacob Farley's assistant and his girlfriend." He looked at Rhea. "She looks kind of like you."

"I see that." Rhea pasted on an interested smile, but her thoughts were back in Taylor's room with the photo album.

After an appropriate interval, Rhea rose, trying not to seem too eager to leave. "I really need to get back home now. Thanks for showing me the games. The dog really does look like Dutchie. I'll have to tell her she's a famous celebrity and will soon be a movie star."

Taylor laughed and chattered as she prepared to go, but Rhea noticed Carter watching her carefully now.

"I'm going to be fine, Rhea," he said, misinterpreting her anxiousness.

She tried another smile. "I'm sure you are and you be sure and rest." She picked up the cake dish and the empty milk glass to carry back down to the kitchen.

"Thank Nana Dean for the cake." Carter reached out a hand toward her, but Rhea edged out the door, avoiding his touch.

Loading Dutchie into the car and escaping from

the Layman house at last, Rhea let the held-back tears spill over. How could Carter find her attractive at all after being married to such a beauty? Privileged and gifted—an established clothing designer from what Taylor said.

Rhea looked in the car mirror. "I must look like a dweeb in comparison." She sniffed. "And that mansion Carter lived in! I heard he married into a wealthy family, but I had no idea! How tame and shabby everything here must look after a life like that."

She swiped a hand over her eyes. "Surely Carter will never stay here—even if he said he might, not with all that to go back to."

As she cried her way home, Rhea couldn't decide whether having Carter leave again would be a blessing or another sorrow.

Chapter 10

Carter's head healed quickly, and by Wednesday he was on his way back to California. An unexpected meeting had been called in regard to the *Traveler* movie in the works, and Morgan said the studio wanted Carter in the mix. He'd brought Taylor since Morgan wanted so much to see him.

"Bring Taylor. Martha and Pickett miss him," Morgan had said gruffly. Carter knew he hated saying how much he missed the boy himself.

Martha and Pickett Oslo lived on the Benton estate and managed Benton's large house and grounds with consummate ease. The pair had been like surrogate grandparents to Taylor since his birth, keeping Taylor while Carter worked and watching after him through the years when Judith had been too ill to tolerate his exuberance.

Taylor sat in a window seat of the company jet now, flying one of his toy airplanes into a landing on the windowsill. "Grandaddy Benton said Martha is making me peanut butter cookies."

Carter looked up from his papers to smile at his son. "Your favorite, huh? Martha knows what you like."

"Yeah, she's nice." His voice sounded sad.

"Do you miss living in California, Taylor?" Carter laid down the pile of papers he'd been looking through to direct his attention to his son.

Taylor shrugged as he crisscrossed two airplanes in flight.

"Not as much as I thought I would." He turned candid eyes to Carter and smiled. "Laurel Springs is neat—just like you said. I really like it."

He turned troubled eyes toward Carter now. "We are going back, aren't we, Dad?"

"Sure. We're just flying out to California for some meetings."

Taylor landed the two planes on the pull-down tray in front of him, making whooshing landing sounds.

"Your grandfather is looking forward to seeing you, Taylor." Carter watched him, wondering what was on his mind.

"I know." He sighed. "He tells me all the time how I'm his heir and tells me all the stuff I'll need to do one day." He taxied the planes across the tray. "Papaw Wes and Grampa Layman just let me play."

Carter's eyes widened, always surprised at the insight his son seemed to possess about the adults around him. "And that's good?"

He gave Carter a patient look. "I'm only six, Dad."

"I see."

"That's one of the reasons I like Laurel Springs so much. I can just play with Beau and be a kid."

Carter frowned. "I think you're saying you don't always have to be Morgan Benton's grandson there."

Taylor laughed. "Nobody even knows who Morgan Benton is in Cosby, Dad."

Carter sighed. "And that's kind of nice, isn't it? Less pressure and less expectations."

"For you, too, Dad." Taylor picked at a scab of poison ivy on his arm. "You seem more happy at Laurel Springs. You laugh more." His eyes flicked over Carter. "And you don't have to wear suits and stuff."

Carter looked down at the elegant, tailor-made suit he wore and the perfectly polished lace-up shoes. "You don't think I look good in suits?"

Taylor rolled his eyes. "Sure you look good. You're just more relaxed and have more fun when you don't have to wear them all the time and stuff."

"Oh." Carter bit back a smile.

"When are we going to start our house?" Taylor drove a miniature service truck over to work on his landed airplanes.

"Actually, a surveyor came yesterday. We're getting things started." He grinned at Taylor. "But won't you miss your grandmother's cooking once we move?"

"She only lives a mile from where our house will be and I can ride my bike down anytime. She said so." He launched another plane into the air.

Pausing it in midair, he added, "We won't get servants or anything at Laurel Springs, will we?"

Carter lifted a brow in question.

"Nobody else has servants and stuff. Beau doesn't. His mom cooks and cleans for them. And Mamaw cooks for Papaw Wes and Grampa Layman." Taylor crinkled his nose. "It would be weird to have servants at Laurel Springs."

Carter considered that. "I guess it would."

"Beau asked if we were going to build a big mansion or something because we were rich, but I told him we were building a regular type house." He turned his gaze toward Carter. "We are, aren't we?"

Carter's eyes returned to the papers in front of him. "You saw the drawings and the blueprints, remember? It's a country plan—exactly right for Laurel Springs." Distracted now, he picked up a pencil to work on a change for a character drawing before him.

"Do you think you might get married again, Dad, so I'd have another mother?"

Dropping the pencil, Carter turned to stare at Taylor. "What brought that on, Son?"

Taylor shrugged and drove his airplanes around on his tray, avoiding Carter's eyes. "Well, Beau says you used to really like Rhea and that you and Rhea were going to get married once."

"And?"

A short silence followed.

"Is this bothering you, Taylor—what you heard?"

He looked up with questioning eyes. "Is it true, Dad?"

Carter considered what to say. "You know Rhea and I were best friends growing up and it's true Rhea and I became sweethearts later. We talked about getting married a long time ago."

Taylor nodded.

Carter tried to return to his paperwork, but he found his attention diverted now. In exasperation, he put the pencil down to look out the window at the bank of clouds they were moving through.

"I like Rhea. You don't have to get mad."

He turned to find his son studying him with wise eyes.

"Rhea's really nice, Dad. I showed her the pictures of our house and of my mom and Grandaddy Benton when she was in my room the other day."

"Ahhh." A lightbulb came on in Carter's mind. So that's why there had been such a change in Rhea that day, and that's why she'd avoided him since.

Carter almost laughed, thinking what Rhea must have thought of the huge Benton estate house and all the intimate family pictures collected in Taylor's book. Judith created it for him, so he would have visual memories of her and of his early life.

"She thought Mom was really pretty."

"I'm sure she did." Carter smiled to himself, imagining what Rhea thought of Judith in some of her designer dresses. She reeked elegance and class—and had been a truly gifted woman.

Taylor dropped his eyes. "Mom told me once she thought you would get married again. She said it would be all right with her. She wouldn't be mad or anything. And she told me to be nice about it."

"And so that's what you're doing?" Carter watched him. "Being nice about it because you think I'm interested in someone?"

He wrinkled his brow. "No, I was just letting

you know it would be okay with me. And letting you know I like Rhea." He crossed his arms. "She's not the same kind of beautiful Mother was—but she's . . ." He stopped, searching for the right word. "She's sexy."

He looked up and grinned. "She's pretty and sexy—and maybe that's better than just beautiful." He wiggled his eyebrows.

Carter frowned. "Now where did you hear talk like that? And what do you know about sexy?"

Taylor rolled his eyes. "I may be only six, Dad, but I'm not stupid. I watch TV too." He looked thoughtful. "Besides, men watch Rhea. You should go after her again, Dad. Estelle said lots of men have asked Rhea to marry them. She told Jeannie you were lucky Rhea was still single when you came back."

Kids were listeners. He and Rhea had always known everything that was going on in the adult world by just sitting around and listening.

"Well, I'll keep your advice in mind, Taylor." Carter tried to keep a straight face while he said it.

He got more advice from Alvin later that night. Al had come out to the bungalow to hang out with him and Taylor after their meetings were over. The two young men sat in the den now, shoes off, feet up on the coffee table, their attention half focused on a football game. Taylor, after the long flight and the afternoon with his grandfather, had crashed—and was upstairs asleep.

Alvin dipped a nacho into the cheese dip on the coffee table. "Great dip, man."

Carter punched Alvin affectionately. "It doesn't take a culinary degree to mix Velveeta cheese and Ro-Tel tomatoes."

They munched in silence, focused on a tight play in the game.

"How are things going with Rhea Dean?" Alvin asked candidly as the halftime ensued.

"Not as well as I would have liked." Carter filled him in briefly. Then he laughed. "My six-year-old son told me I ought to make a move on Rhea while we were flying over today. He says he thinks Rhea is sexy."

Alvin almost choked on a chip. "Taylor said that?"

Carter nodded his head.

"Well, maybe the problem is that you've made a few too many moves without enough romancing." He crossed his arms. "You know you gotta do the romancing stuff with women."

He looked at Carter. "Have you asked her out on a date? Taken her to the movies or on a picnic or out to eat? Given her flowers? Bought her some special gift? Don't you white boys know nothin'?"

Carter groaned. "Man, the way things have been going with Rhea, she'd probably slam down the phone if I asked."

"Well, then you need to get sneaky. Find a way

to get her to spend time with you without it feeling like a date—but let it turn out to be a date. Find ways to be sweet. Don't leap on her every ten minutes." He swigged down a long swallow of IBC root beer from its brown bottle. Alvin was a connoisseur of bottled root beers. "That's how I got Felicia Denita Brown to start seeing things my way."

He flashed a white smile at Carter. "She is one sweet woman, Miss Felicia Brown."

Carter had heard Alvin talk about Felicia at length and met her before he went to Laurel Springs. "She's too good-looking for you, Brother—and too nice."

Alvin laughed. "Do you think Taylor would say she's sexy?"

"Far be it from me to know the mind of a six-year-old. You'll have to bring Felicia around and ask him." Carter scooped up dip with a nacho and popped it into his mouth.

"I might do that. How long you going to be here?"

Carter frowned. "I'd planned to stay through the weekend originally, but Morgan's putting pressure on me—so I think I'll go on back Friday after the morning meeting at Quest."

"He still thinking he can talk you into staying here full time?"

Alvin walked through to the kitchen to find another root beer.

"Yeah, he keeps coming up with a new pressure tactic. He's got a good, strategic mind; I just wish he'd channel it in another direction."

Alvin laughed. "You can't blame him, Carter. You're the best designer Quest has ever had. He'd be a fool, just in a business sense only, not to work to keep you here."

"I'm going to continue to stay on with the company." Carter scowled. "It's not as though I've quit."

"Well, sure, Bro—but it's not the same." Alvin punched his arm companionably as he sat back down with his root beer. "Even for me. I miss you, too."

Carter smiled at him. "Back at you, Al. But I need to be at Laurel Springs right now. Maybe later I can spend more time here. Not get so much pressure from Morgan." He paused, his smile fading. "He's even putting pressure on Taylor, you know. I don't like that."

"Trying to get the boy to persuade you to come back?" Alvin turned to him with interest.

"That—and he puts pressure on Taylor to start thinking like an executive, to focus on his future with Quest and all the Benton businesses." Carter clunked his root beer bottle down on the table in irritation. "The kid's only six. He's not ready to start running a dynasty."

Alvin blew out a breath. "It was a blow to Morgan when Judith died like she did. He once said he figured she'd have a bunch of children one day to keep the line going. You know."

"Yes, I know. It must be hard on him. But Taylor's been through a hard time, too. He needs a season not to be so serious—to just be a kid. To get to do the things all boys do." Carter gnawed on a thumbnail. "He deserves that."

"Yeah." Alvin's attention shifted back to the TV as the game restarted. "Just don't the two of you stay away too long. And maybe bring Rhea out here with you next time."

"That would be a fiasco!" Carter snorted.

"I don't think so." Alvin shot him a glance between the game action. "She's never been out here. Never been anywhere from what you told me. You own a nice house here near the beach." He gave Carter a pointed look. "And, as a critical point, your former wife never lived here. You told me yourself you bought this house thinking Rhea Dean might like it."

He nodded.

"So in time, this place can become your second home." Alvin shoved a hand into the nacho bag to get out a few more chips. "You guys can come here for long vacations—and work trips—when Laurel Springs is in its slack season." He grinned. "Or when you've hired and trained more staff to cover things. Rhea Dean may find she sort of likes the good life herself once she samples a taste."

Carter thought of that throughout the evening as they watched the game. He had thought of Rhea when he chose the bungalow-style house set back from the road on a shaded lot.

Later, after Alvin left, Carter slipped in to check on Taylor before he went to bed. He found him bundled in a hump under the covers, surrounded as usual by a pile of stuffed animals.

"Dad," a soft voice called as Carter started to slip out the door.

"Just checking on you, buddy." He walked back over to Taylor's bed and leaned over to give his son a kiss on the forehead.

Taylor sighed deeply. "Dad, I can't remember Mom very well anymore. Grandaddy Benton is always saying 'remember when she did this when you were two' and 'remember when you and Judith did that when you were three' . . . but I don't remember."

He turned his face up to Carter's, and the light from the hallway showed Carter a track of tears. "I feel real bad that I don't remember but I never tell him. I don't want him to think I'm bad." He sniffed.

Carter patted his knee. "You're a good boy, Taylor. And you need to know that no little kids remember much before they are four or five years old. Psychologists call it infantile amnesia; that means your brain isn't developed enough to hold memory like it will later in your life."

"But I remember some things."

"Everyone has some random memories of their preschool years but they don't have the focused memories they will have in their school years later on." He rubbed Taylor's leg. "A lot of times small children have seen pictures and heard stories so many times about their baby and toddler years that they think they remember things they actually don't. I know some stories like that about my young years—ones that have been told to me again and again."

Taylor chewed his lip. "What I remember most is Mom being sick. Not being able to walk or run. Needing to have Martha or her nurse dress her and feed her. I remember running around the yard or climbing in the tree and seeing her sitting in her wheelchair." He hesitated. "I felt guilty a lot of times because I wasn't sick and could run and play."

Carter leaned over to kiss Taylor again. "I felt that way, too, buddy. It seemed wrong to be able to live my life in a normal way when your mother was so sick—and when I knew she was dying."

Taylor slipped a hand into his. "A person shouldn't have to die when they're young."

"No."

Anguished young eyes looked up at his then. "You won't die, will you, Dad? Promise?"

Carter tucked the covers around Taylor. "I don't plan to die anytime soon, Taylor. Most people live long, rich lives, like Grampa Layman and Nana Dean. I expect to do the same." He squeezed Taylor's hand. "But no one can *promise* another person they won't die. It's something we can't totally know."

Taylor sighed. "Okay."

"Listen, Taylor, I can talk to your Grandaddy Benton, if you'd like. He may not realize all small children don't remember the past well. He doesn't mean to be hard on you." He paused. "He's hurting, losing his only child. It helps him to remember all the good times."

"I know." Taylor pulled a lop-eared stuffed dog closer to him. "He cries sometimes. Martha says he's mad and angry that he couldn't find a way to save Mom, even with all his money."

"Martha said that to you?"

"No." Taylor shook his head. "I heard her say that to Pickett."

"I see." Servants talked and children listened unobserved. "Listen, Taylor, I was going to stay through the weekend, but I think we might fly on back home on Friday after my Quest meeting if it's all right. We won't be able to go to the zoo, but maybe we can plan to go somewhere special around Cosby."

"Okay." Taylor's voice brightened. "That will be cool."

Obviously Taylor wasn't very upset to leave early. Carter tucked him in again and stood up to leave.

"You know, Dad, I think I'm going to ask Grandaddy Benton to take me to the zoo tomorrow. He said he might take off work to spend some time with me. We could have a good time and talk about the animals." He hesitated. "It might help him to get his mind off Mom, don't you think?"

"Yeah, I think that would be great, Taylor." His boy had turned out to be such a nice kid. How had that happened amid all the tragedy he'd experienced?

Carter turned at the door. "How would you like to take a hike over near the Cosby Campground this weekend? Go up to Hen Wallow Falls? Maybe cook hot dogs outside afterward at the campground?"

"That would be cool!" His sudden grin flashed in the dim light. "Maybe we could take Rhea. You could tell her I want her to go if you're scared to ask her."

Carter grinned. "Yeah, I might do that, Taylor."

Chapter 11

After Rhea's Sunday visit to Carter, she purposely avoided him for the next several days. She heard through Nana and others that he'd recovered. From the schoolhouse one day, she saw him drive by, laughing with his son, and on another occasion she secretly spied on him and Taylor as they swam in the lake. It was cowardly, but she needed breathing space.

At the office on Monday, she shamelessly googled the name Judith Benton Layman and studied every piece of information about her. She learned about the Benton family's vast wealth and enterprises, Judith's elite schooling, her studies in design, and the business she created and worked with until illness made her unable to work. She saw the names of the wealthy, privileged men Judith had dated and noticed that even after her marriage the press always included Judith's maiden name in any coverage. To her surprise, there was seldom mention of Carter. Even after their marriage, society pictures of Judith only occasionally included Carter as her escort.

Of course, a lot of wealthy women still maintained a great deal of independence after marriage. She frowned as she expressed the thought. And Carter still attended school during the first years of their marriage and worked at Quest. He probably had little time for social events.

Researching Carter's life, she learned about the development of his career, read about games he'd developed, and found online trailers of some of his latest games to view. However, neither his social life nor his marriage were highlighted often in the online articles and news clips she found.

Mostly, as an afterthought, journalists would add: *Carter Layman is married to the heiress Judith Benton, whose father, Morgan Adelman Benton, the current head of Benton Electronics, started Quest Corporation.*

Previously Rhea had avoided learning anything about Carter's life, now she felt she needed to be armed with all the facts she could find. She didn't want any more shocking surprises. Dealing with Carter proved difficult enough without continually bumping into information from his past that shook her self-control and defenses.

Tired from bookkeeping and indoor office tasks, Rhea took her sack lunch out to the front porch of the ad-min building. She wanted to see the sunshine and breathe the summer air.

With surprise, she saw scaffolds set up against the church and a group of painters and laborers hard at work on repairs. Carrying her lunch with her, she walked over to see what was going on.

Grampa Layman came out the front door as she came across the drive. He waved at her before he turned to talk to one of the workmen.

"The front doors here are to be stripped and restained." He gestured. "We want to try to keep the original color, too."

"Yes, sir," the man said. "We ought to get the first coat of paint on the exterior today and have the interior repainted and dry before Sunday service. We're also scheduled to clean all the stained-glass windows, repair the broken one, and then let Mattie Brownlow carefully repaint the Scripture over the door when we're done. She's good with that restoration sort of stuff."

When the man left, Grampa gestured to Rhea to sit down on the stone bench by the porch. "Sit and talk to me a spell while you eat your lunch, girl. I could use to sit and rest myself."

Rhea sat down and dug into her lunch bag to pull out a second sandwich half. She offered it to Pastor Layman. "Here, want the other half? Nana always packs too much lunch for me."

"Don't mind if I do." He took the sandwich eagerly. "I got tied up here with the workmen and haven't made it home for lunch."

"I'll share." Rhea smiled, spreading her food items out on her lunch sack between them.

She sniffed the air. "It's great to smell fresh paint."

"Yep, that it is. And it's a blessed thing to see the old church getting such a face-lift." He took a small sweet pickle out of a Ziploc bag and popped it into his mouth.

While munching the pickle, he gestured above them. "Mattie Brownlow, the historical expert hired to help with some of the restorations around here, has found us a bell steeple to put back on the top of the church."

"Really?" Rhea opened a bag of chips to hide her astonishment.

"Yes, indeed. She researched old records and found a description and an old photo showing what the original steeple looked like. It got destroyed when a flat-line storm hit Cosby back in the 1930s. Storm took half the roof off, too." He grinned widely. "I didn't think I'd ever live to see the day we'd get a bell steeple back on the church."

Rhea looked up toward the square-topped steeple, remembering how she and Carter once dreamed of finding a bell tower to replace the one pictured in ancient, grainy black-and-white photos of Laurel Springs. She frowned at the memory.

"What's that frown for, girl? Isn't it a blessed thing for the church to have herself fixed up like this?"

"Of course." She offered Grampa a bright smile. She'd called Pastor Layman simply "Grampa" since she was only a small girl.

He studied her. "You're troubling over the fact that it's Carter's money that's doing all the fixing, aren't you, girl?"

Rhea dug out a pickle for herself and avoided his eyes. "I'm happy the church is being repaired and restored. How could I not be? It's the church I was raised in and I love it."

"And?"

She gave up. "And, yes, it's hard seeing all my old dreams being fulfilled by Carter's money."

Grampa dug into the bag of brownies now, ready for dessert. "I'm reminded in all this of how Joseph was sold down into Pharaoh's land to become prince so he could help his people."

Rhea snorted. "Carter was hardly sold into slavery in California, Grampa. It's hard to see how those two stories relate."

"Oh, I see similarities." He munched a bite of brownie, thinking. "When Joseph's brothers bewailed all they'd done, Joseph said: 'Don't be grieved . . . for perhaps God sent me before you to preserve you a posterity in the earth.' God has a way of working things out for good, Rhea. And a lot of good is coming from Carter's time in California."

"Hmmmph." Rhea fished another sweet pickle out of the bag.

A workman came to direct a quick question to Grampa before he continued, "Carter's back in California. Did you know that, girl?"

Rhea dropped her pickle to the ground in surprise, and then bent over to retrieve it.

"Don't eat that now; it's soiled," he told her unnecessarily.

He put a hand on her knee and patted it. "Your reaction told me something I was wondering on, Rhea Kaden Dean. You still have feelings for Carter."

She started to deny it, but Grampa's probing eyes forced her to say the truth instead. "I don't *want* to have feelings for Carter, Grampa."

He shook his head. "I'd hoped that message on unforgiveness on Sunday might help you to let go of old resentments and bitterness toward Carter. It's not healthy to harbor feelings like that."

She crossed her arms. "Listen, Grampa, I know Carter is your grandson and that makes this awkward, but even if you forgive, it isn't all that easy to simply forget." She set her jaw, trying to think what to say. "You loved Gram, your wife, Edith, a lot, didn't you?"

"Still miss her every day." He gave Rhea a misty smile filled with memories.

"Well, what if she'd gone off and married another man when the two of you were pledged . . . and then wandered back here nine years later—widowed and with a son, how would you feel?"

She watched his eyebrows lift.

"You see?" She shook a finger at him. "It's easy to tell someone else how to feel—but it's harder to live it."

"I see your point, girl." He ate another of the brownies, thinking.

"Still, the past is the past, and the present is the present. I loved Edith Ann Costner. I still remember the day I first met her when we weren't but fifteen. Prettiest little thing I ever saw. It's hard for me to imagine loving anyone again like I loved Edith Ann."

He tapped a finger on his chin. "I reckon it might have been hard for me to get past her choosing another instead of me. But if later on she got free, and if God hadn't brought another partner to me in the meantime, I'd probably go after her all over again."

Rhea sighed. "Here, Grampa, you finish up any of the rest of the lunch you want. I've got to go meet Jeannie to clean cabins."

Fortunately, one of the workmen came to ask a question, giving Rhea a chance to slip away without getting into more conversation with Grampa Layman about Carter.

Rhea soon learned Carter's visit to California would be brief. Billy Wade said he'd gone for a business trip in relation to the *Traveler* movie—now in early production stages. Taylor went along to see his grandfather. Rhea gnawed a fingernail thoughtfully and wondered how often Carter would be running back and forth between two worlds.

"It's none of your business," she told herself in the mirror Friday night as she got ready for her date with Marshall. "You'd be smart to focus your attentions on Marshall Sutton. He lives here in the valley; he'll *stay* here in the valley. He's safe and solid and sensible—just the sort of person you need in your life."

Rhea twirled slowly to watch the black skirt fan out around her knees. With the black satin skirt, she wore a white silk blouse and a lavishly sequined black vest. She and Marshall were going to the symphony—and dressy black and white was always an appropriate choice.

Hearing Marshall's car drive up, she put quick, finishing touches on her hair, pinned up for tonight, and grabbed the clutch purse she'd chosen. Marshall's eyes lifted in appreciation as she came down the stairs.

"You look fantastic," he said as he led her out to the car.

"Thanks. You look good, too."

He did, dressed in a black suit, crisp white shirt, and neatly patterned tie. Rhea smiled at him, purposing to put away thoughts of Carter tonight and to have a good time.

They ate dinner at Chesapeake's, an elegant, classic downtown restaurant in Knoxville. It had a quiet, tasteful atmosphere, and they talked of local happenings while attentive waitstaff made their meal even nicer.

"I liked your new column in the Newport paper." Marshall lifted a wine glass to her in tribute. "You wrote about the history of the Carver Apple Orchard and I learned things I didn't know about it."

Rhea smiled with pleasure. "I enjoyed doing that piece. In fact, I've found writing my *Now and Then* column to be a genuine pleasure these last years."

"It was a lucky day when the newspaper hired

you." He put butter and sour cream on his potato while he talked. "How did that happen?"

Rhea sprinkled bacon bits and chives on her own potato, thinking back. "I was a student at Walters State Community College. I took a journalism class as an elective and one of our projects was to write and submit an article or piece to a newspaper."

She stopped to take a bite of her prime rib. "All I really knew very much about was local history, so I invented a column idea and wrote a short history about Laurel Springs for it. I sent it to the editor—not expecting much—and he decided to print it." She shrugged. "People liked it and the editor asked if I'd write a few more. The rest is history, I guess. I've been writing a weekly column for the paper ever since."

"Don't diminish it, Rhea. You do excellent work." He smiled at her again, and Rhea decided this was becoming a very nice evening. It felt good to be appreciated for her writing, and Marshall was making a distinct effort to make this evening special.

Knowing he would warm to the subject, she asked him how he was enjoying the new boat he bought. He entertained her then with lake stories, especially with an amusing one of teaching his nephew to water ski.

"I'd probably fall flat on my face, too." Rhea laughed.

His eyes met hers with warmth. "You know, I'd enjoy teaching my own children to ski one day. My mother says it's past time I married."

Rhea dropped her eyes. "You're only twenty-six, Marshall."

He laughed. "*You're* twenty-six and have a birthday in September. I turned twenty-seven in January."

"Oh, I didn't know." Rhea felt sorry she hadn't acknowledged Marshall's special day in some way.

He shook his head indulgently. "Don't feel bad for not knowing. We'd just started dating then, Rhea. But maybe for your birthday we can do something special." He paused. "Like having a party to celebrate our engagement."

Rhea's breath caught in her throat, and she put a hand to her heart.

Marshall cocked his head to one side. "Have I surprised you, Rhea? I thought you'd know how I feel about you by now. That it would be inevitable where my thoughts might be traveling."

She searched for some words in response but didn't know what to say.

Marshall took one of her hands and patted it. "I find you very beautiful, Rhea, and very desirable. I think you and I would suit well in marriage. I hope you will think about it. Obviously, I've surprised you too much with my proposal for you to give me an answer now."

Rhea worked a smile onto her face. What should she say? "It's a lovely offer," she said at last.

Marshall grew more possessive as the evening wore on. He found more ways to touch her than before—settling her into the car, walking into the theatre where the symphony performed. In the dark of the theatre, he found her hand and held it.

The orchestra performed Gershwin favorites that night. Rhea admittedly loved it. A guest pianist added sparkle, and many of the tunes, like selections from *Porgy and Bess*, were toe tapping. Other old favorites, like "I've Got a Crush on You," brought a smile, and the finale of *Rhapsody in Blue* drew the audience eagerly to their feet.

She and Marshall talked about the performance with pleasure all the way home. He had bought season tickets to the symphony as soon as he learned Rhea loved to go. She sighed inwardly as they pulled up in the driveway. Why couldn't she fall in love with Marshall Sutton? Or was love really necessary for a good marriage?

In the darkness of the car, Marshall pulled her toward him for a good-night kiss. Rhea tried to throw herself into it. But no sparkle occurred, no rush of warm feelings. No rising passion. Perhaps passion was overrated, too.

Rhea suddenly felt Marshall's hand begin to fondle too close to her breast. She tried to pull away, but he held her in a tight grip, his other hand pressed firmly behind her back. She felt his breath grow hot on her neck and began to panic.

"I don't want this, Marshall." She brushed his hand off and tried again to pull away.

Angry eyes met hers. "How will you know if we're compatible if you never let me near you, Rhea?" He gripped her arm and leaned in to kiss her with ferocity now.

Rhea kicked at him and pushed away more forcibly. When Marshall backed off in irritation, she opened her car door and made a sprint for the front porch.

As she looked frantically for her key, he came up behind her. "Don't be angry with me." His voice was soft now. "I didn't mean to scare you. I just have strong feelings for you that are hard to control sometimes."

He turned her around to face him, smiling at her now. "We had a nice evening, didn't we?"

Wary, Rhea nodded, not wanting to say more.

"We'll have more. And you think, Rhea, about what we talked about at the restaurant. I'd really like to buy an engagement ring for your birthday." He patted her cheek fondly, like he would a child's.

Rhea felt like smacking him. How dare he talk to her like she was the village idiot?

"Good-night, Marshall," she said, struggling to offer him a polite smile before she let herself in the door.

Rhea tiptoed up the stairs, slipped into her

room, and leaned back against her bedroom door with a deep sigh. What a night!

"Have a good time?" a voice asked, startling her.

Her eyes widened to see Carter sprawled in the window seat, his feet propped up on her bed.

With resignation, she walked over to drop her purse on the dresser.

"Yes, as a matter of fact, I did."

He raised an eyebrow and smirked, and Rhea wondered if he'd watched them in the driveway from the window.

"You look very beautiful." His voice softened now, and Rhea turned to see him eyeing her with appreciation.

She felt her heartbeat quicken. "Don't start with me, Carter."

He smiled. "How was Gershwin?"

Her mouth popped open in surprise. "How did you know we heard Gershwin?"

He crossed one of his long legs over the other. Carter wore shorts, and Rhea could see the dark hairs on his legs that tickled her legs when he drew her close.

"It's easy to check the Internet to see the symphony schedule. And I heard Marshall say that's where you were going tonight."

His white teeth flashed in the light from the bedside lamp. "You've always liked Gershwin. Me too." He started humming softly and then began singing stanzas of "Embraceable You"—one of her favorites.

Before she could collect herself, Carter got up and began to whirl her around in a waltz, still singing an improvisation of the lyrics.

Rhea stopped dancing and pulled away with reluctance. "You look like a gypsy, like the words in the song, with that dark hair."

He snatched a silk rose out of a vase on her dresser and put it in his teeth, continuing to dance around.

Giving in to the joy of the moment, she laughed, pushing at him playfully before she sat down on the bed to pull her strappy sandals off.

"Want me to do that?" Rhea looked up to see Carter's eyes watching her legs.

"No. Definitely not."

"You sure?" He started to improvise again from Gershwin, teasingly twisting the lyrics of one of the song's romantic lines.

Rhea threw a pillow at him, but she caught herself snickering as she did it. "You're impossible, you know that?"

"Only with you, Rhea." He sat back down in the window seat, studying her thoughtfully now. "You know, I'm jealous Marshall took you to Gershwin instead of me."

Rhea thought about the past evening and all that happened with Marshall and frowned in annoyance.

"Anything you want to talk about?" Carter asked.

"No." She shook her head emphatically. The last thing she wanted to do was talk about Marshall with Carter!

Changing the subject, she said, "I thought you wouldn't be back until next week."

"Taylor and I came back early."

"I see." She went over to the dresser to take the earrings out of her ears and to unclasp the bracelet on her wrist. Rhea could feel Carter watching her, and it vexed her how her blood churned even when he simply sat in the room. She didn't need this.

"Carter, I really can't deal with another scene tonight," she said before she thought. "I'm tired and I want to go to bed. Will you leave?"

"Sure." To her surprise, he stood and pulled up the window so he could climb out. "I just dropped by because I wanted to ask if you would go hiking to Hen Wallow Falls with Taylor and me tomorrow."

Rhea hesitated, surprised.

"I know you have to do the tour in the morning but I thought we could go right after lunch." He gave her an appealing look. "Taylor asked if I would invite you. He wants you to come."

"*Taylor* wanted to invite me?" She gave Carter a suspicious look.

He lifted his hands. "No kidding, it's the truth.

He likes you." He grinned at her. "He said if I was scared to ask you, then he would."

She giggled. "He really said that?"

"He did." Carter laughed, but then his face grew serious. "Taylor had sort of a bad time during our visit in California. Memories troubling him. Some difficulty with Morgan, his grandfather. I cooked up the idea of this hike as a way to cheer him up, and he said he wanted you to come with us."

He paused. "It would mean a lot to me if you would say yes—for Taylor's sake."

Rhea unbuttoned her vest, slipped it off, and hung it on a hanger. Carter watched her and waited for her answer.

He walked over closer to her where he could look into her eyes. "Whatever has happened between us, Rhea, it isn't Taylor's fault. He's just a little kid, caught in the middle—a good, sweet boy who's been through a difficult time—wanting desperately to be happy again." He sighed. "I wish you could look at him and not see Judith."

Rhea bristled. "That's really not fair. I don't dislike Taylor."

His eyes studied hers. "But you've held back from really enjoying him like you do most kids. I've watched it."

She felt remorseful at his words.

He obviously saw the change in her face. "Taylor hasn't picked up on it," he assured her.

"But I have. That's why I'd really like you to say yes to this."

"You'd stoop to emotional blackmail to get me to go?"

He shrugged, lifting his hands, but a smile tugged at his lips.

"Oh, okay, I'll go. You and Taylor can pick me up here at one. That will give me time to do the tour, change clothes, and get a bite of lunch before we leave."

He grinned, swooping in to kiss her on the mouth before she could stop him, swirling her around in his arms.

Rhea swatted at him with one hand but her other hand crept, against her will, into Carter's hair to draw him closer. Why was it only Carter who made her blood hum like this? Why not Marshall?

He leaned back to look down into her eyes with a cocky grin. "I kiss better than Marshall, don't I?"

She shoved him away in annoyance. "Go home, Carter."

He laughed as he walked over to the window to climb out. "I'll see you tomorrow at one."

As he slipped out of sight over the windowsill, she turned to start unbuttoning her skirt.

"Rhea?" She heard his voice from the tree by the roof.

"What?" Rhea went over to the window to lean out where she could see him.

"He's not right for you." His face looked serious. "I'm not just saying that because I love you, but because he's wrong for you in every way. He'll make you unhappy. I don't want that."

With that, he dropped down from the tree to stride off through the yard under the trees.

Rhea stood there, a hand to her throat. Had he just said "I love you," and if he did, whatever did he mean by it?

Weary with too many emotions in one evening, Rhea turned back into her room to get ready for bed. As she slipped into sleep, she dreamed. In her dream she danced to old Gershwin tunes, first with Marshall and then with Carter, until the changing of partners and the pace of the dancing grew so frenzied it woke her.

And then she cried.

Chapter 12

On Saturday morning, Carter sat on the screened porch behind his parents' house reading the newspaper and drinking a second cup of coffee. His mother rustled around the kitchen, cleaning up from breakfast, and he could hear the quiet hum of conversation between her and his father. His Grampa, eager to see if all the work at the church was complete, had left after a quick snack.

Carter looked out under the big oaks, where

Taylor and Jinx played a game of fetch with a ratty tennis ball. It felt good to hear Taylor's happy laughter again, mixed with Jinx's exuberant barks.

He flipped through Friday's newspaper after studying the Saturday morning edition. He'd missed several days being away in California. He needed to start catching up on local happenings again, to start meshing back into the community.

His eyes slid over the local news items—new bank branch opening, local teacher given an award, rockslide slowing traffic on a section of the Foothills Parkway. Flipping the page, he started reading one of the local columns about the Carver orchards and the Carver's Applehouse Restaurant. Carter scanned the history of the orchard with interest, enjoying the account of Kyle Carver starting the orchard by hand-grafting and planting apple trees in his cornfield in the 1940s. Now the orchard of over forty thousand trees sat on seventy-five acres, with 126 varieties of apples.

He remembered that old gray barn on the hill filled with a wide variety of apples in season—plus fruit pies, apple butter, and apple cider. He used to love to go eat the breakfast special with eggs, grits, biscuits, gravy, and apple fritters at the Applehouse Restaurant. He'd have to take Taylor there one morning—and to the sweet shop across from the barn afterward.

Enjoying the article and the journalist's writing style, Carter scanned to the top of the column for a name. *Rhea Kaden Dean,* he read. "What!" Carter sloshed his coffee out of his cup in surprise.

He looked again. There was no mistake. Rhea's name appeared right under the article title.

Carter carried the paper into the kitchen. "There's an article in Friday's paper by Rhea." He held it out toward his mother. "Did you and Dad see it?"

His mother looked up at him abstractly. "Oh, of course, Carter. We always read Rhea's Friday column."

He pulled the paper back and studied it again. "You mean, she's been writing a column in the paper for some time. Why didn't you mention it?"

His mother spread marmalade on a biscuit. "I'm sure I mentioned it to you at some point or other. Rhea's been doing that little column for about seven or eight years now." She took a bite of the biscuit. "You probably just forgot."

His father picked up the conversation they'd been having before he interrupted, about picking sweet corn later in the day and whether they should freeze or can it this time.

Carter walked back to the porch and read the article again. It was very well written. He prided himself on knowing Rhea as few did, and here was a part of her he was completely unacquainted with.

Curious now, Carter walked across the backyard to the main barn to locate the old woodbin where his parents piled newspapers for recycling. After digging through the bin for other Friday editions of the *Newport Plain Talk*, Carter carried several past editions back to the porch with him.

Rhea called the column *Now and Then*. It seemed to focus on local places, bits of history, and old-time arts and crafts. He found an article on beekeeping, one on the history of the railroad into Newport, another on early mountain customs, and one on waterfalls. He settled in to read the latter one. In it Rhea clarified the difference between a cascade and a waterfall and talked about several falls and cascades around the area, while tucking in historical information and charming descriptions.

"Well, I'll be danged." He laid down the article, shaking his head with wonder. He remembered Rhea writing in diaries with little keys as a young girl and working on the school annual and newspaper in high school, but he could never recall her talking about wishing to write more seriously.

There's more to how this came about, that's for sure, he thought.

Taylor banged open the screened door to come in, Jinx slipping in behind him before the door shut again.

"When are we going hiking, Dad?"

Carter laid the paper down. "After lunch. I told you. Rhea has to do the tour this morning."

"I forgot." Taylor slumped down in a chair and reached for the glass of juice he'd left on the table earlier.

Carter leaned forward, putting his elbows on the table. "Listen, sport, I need to remind you about our rules for this hike. You have to promise to mind the rules or we might not go."

"I know, Dad." Taylor rolled his eyes. "Be safe, be polite to Rhea, don't eat anything on the trail like mushrooms or wild stuff, don't get in the water with your clothes on, and don't whine."

Carter grinned. "And don't go more than a few yards ahead of us on the trail, like when we walk on the beach. It's important that you keep us in sight."

Taylor nodded over the top of his juice glass.

"It's a two-mile hike to the falls, Taylor. The hike in gets a little steep in a couple of places, but the walk out is easier."

"I can do it, Dad. Don't worry." He grinned. "We walk more than that lots of times."

"Yeah, I know, but walking in the mountains is different from walking for miles on a flat beach."

Taylor nodded, and then with the quickly changing interest span of a six-year-old, Taylor switched topics. "Can I go over and play with Beau for a while this morning until he and his dad have to go to football practice?"

"Sure. Call Beau and see if it's all right and I'll run you over."

A few hours later, at 1:00 p.m., Carter pulled up in Rhea's driveway to pick her up for the hike. He found her sitting on the front steps, ready and waiting.

"Hi, Rhea!" Taylor called.

"Hi, back." Rhea walked over and let herself into the front seat of the car. She looked around appreciatively. "You sure it's safe to take this vintage convertible over to the Cosby Campground area? You'll have to park and leave it for a couple of hours."

Taylor answered, leaning across the front seat. "It's okay. We take it everywhere." The boy sat back and buckled up as Carter began turning around in the driveway.

Carter's eyes slid over Rhea as he drove back down the Deans' driveway. She wore dark green khaki shorts, a white T-shirt, and hiking boots. The golden tan of her legs glistened in the sun, and she'd tied her rich honey-brown hair in a ponytail for the hike. Her cheeks still held a pink tinge from being in the sunshine earlier with the assembly tour.

He loved having her sit beside him in his car again. It brought back a sweep of happy memories.

"How'd the tour go?" he asked.

"About the same as usual." As the car gained

speed around the lake, she took the ball cap she'd been carrying and put it on her head, tucking her ponytail into the back.

It took less than twenty minutes to drive from Laurel Springs down Highway 32 into the Cosby Campground area. They parked at the picnic grounds, made a pit stop at the campground bathrooms, and then found the Gabes Mountain Trail leading to Hen Wallow Falls across the road.

"Look, Dad, Rhea's got a waist pack like me."

Without waiting for an answer, Taylor asked Rhea, "What's in your pack, Rhea?"

"A water bottle, tissues, ChapStick, a hiking map, and a small towel." She turned to smile at the child. "What's in yours?"

He grinned back. "Water, some snacks, and a boat to play with at the falls. Dad has all the rest of our stuff in his big pack."

Rhea raised her eyebrows at Carter.

"I have all the basics for a hike, plus a towel and a change of clothes for Taylor." He chuckled. "You can never tell with six-year-olds around water."

Rhea laughed as they settled into a single-file arrangement heading up the trail, Taylor enthusiastically leading the way, Carter next, and Rhea at the rear. They talked happily as they walked, enjoying the balmy summer day.

"Gabes Mountain Trail winds up through a wooded valley between Round Mountain and

Snake Den Mountain in its early miles and then winds up and over Gabes Mountain," Carter told Taylor.

Taylor squinted up the trail ahead. "Are we going that far?"

"No. We're only hiking 2.2 miles to the falls."

"Is that far?" Taylor obviously didn't have much concept of distance yet at six.

"It's far for a six-year-old if you remember we'll need to hike the same distance back."

"Two and two is four and some more makes it almost five." Taylor turned around to grin. "Five miles is far, isn't it?"

Carter nodded, and Taylor romped ahead up the trail.

Carter turned to smile at Rhea. "Taylor asks a *lot* of questions."

She smiled back. "I'm used to Beau. Don't worry. He can't ask more questions than Beau does."

He turned back to watch the trail ahead, happy to be having a day with Rhea. In their teens, they'd hiked all the trails near Cosby, Greenbrier, and Deep Creek, and then explored farther into other areas of the mountains.

"I wonder how many times we hiked this trail when we were younger?"

"More than I can remember," she answered. "Our parents brought us here the first time when we were little, and later we often hiked it on our own."

"There's a bridge up ahead over a creek!" Taylor shouted as they found the first log bridge on the Gabes Mountain Trail.

A mile up the trail they found another. "This is Crying Creek," Carter told Taylor as they walked across the creek.

"That's a funny name." Taylor wrinkled his nose. "How come it's called that, Dad?"

He shrugged. "I'm not sure."

Rhea answered. "An old legend tells that when two brothers were on a bear hunt in this area, one accidentally shot the other in the dark here."

Taylor's mouth dropped open. "You mean he shot him dead?"

"Yes." Rhea nodded. "It was an accident, of course, but a sad one. So that's where the name 'Crying Creek' came from."

"Tell me another story." Taylor dropped back to walk with Rhea.

"Well." She stopped to think. "The waterfall we're going to is called Hen Wallow Falls. The waters of Hen Wallow Creek slide ninety-five feet over eighteen levels of beautiful gray sandstone rocks to fall into a pool before swirling and continuing downstream. Ruffed grouse, or wood hens, used to roll, or wallow, in the dirt or dust not far from the falls. I guess it was funny to watch— so someone named the creek and falls Hen Wallow. Many of the creeks, mountains, ridges, and trails have funny names in this area, like

Camel Hump Mountain, Rowdy Ridge, Sinking Creek, and Rich Butt Mountain."

Carter listened to the melody of her voice. She was always researching this place she loved so much. He remembered now how she'd always loved the stories and legends of the mountains.

"Look! What's that stuff like corn growing at the base of that tree?" Taylor ran over and pointed to it. "Is this a flower, Dad?"

"It's called squawroot. It's a plant."

Taylor squatted down to look at it. "So how come it's not green if it's a plant?"

"I think it's a parasite or something, lives off the nutrients of other plants, like this oak tree here. It doesn't use chlorophyll or need sunlight, so it has no green color."

"Your dad's right." Rhea squatted down beside Taylor. "Its odd-sounding name, squawroot, comes from the fact that its starchy root used to be a food used by the Indian women."

Taylor studied the plant intently. "How come this one's browner?"

"Squawroot turns brown as it matures and starts to look more like a pinecone than an ear of corn," she explained.

"Yuck. I don't think I'd want to eat this." Taylor made a face as he stood up. "It looks like it would taste gross."

Rhea laughed and stood up, too. "I don't think I'd want to eat it either." She started to wrap her arm around Taylor's shoulder but then drew back.

Carter saw a slice of discomfort cross her face.

He sighed. She was thinking of Judith again.

Taylor bounced on up the trail, and he and Rhea fell in line behind him. The day was warm, but the deep shade of the woods trail kept them from getting too hot as the trail started to climb.

After approximately two miles, they turned right on a side spur to the falls. As Carter remembered, a steep path worked its way down to the bottom of the waterfall. At the base of the falls, they gladly settled on boulders to rest and to look up at the long spill of water streaking down over the rocks in several shining rivulets.

"Is this a cascade or a waterfall?" Carter asked, remembering Rhea's article on the subject.

"Mostly a cascade, since most of the water flows over rock." She pointed. "There are several places where the water falls free from the rock in small waterfalls. But this isn't a long plunge water-fall, where the water falls vertically down to a pool, and it isn't a horsetail, that spreads out and falls to a pool below. It mostly cascades over rock."

"Dad and I saw a really big, long waterfall out in California." He looked at Carter questioningly, trying to remember the name.

"It was Vernal Fall at Yosemite on the Merced River. It falls about three hundred feet."

"Wow." Rhea's eyes widened.

"It's cool." Taylor chimed in. "The mist from it sprays you when you get near it and sometimes you can see rainbows in the mist." He turned to Rhea. "Have you ever seen it?"

She smiled. "No. I haven't ever been out West or to California."

"No kidding?" Taylor took off his waist pack to take his small water bottle out. "You'll have to come with us sometime when we go. You can fly in our jet with us. There are lots of cool things to see in California."

Leaning over to skim his hand in the cold water, Taylor asked, "Can I wade in the water, Dad? Please? I'll take my shoes and socks off and be real careful not to fall in." He pointed. "I can wade over in that part by the bank where it's shallow."

Carter nodded, and Taylor let out a whoop. He soon had his shoes and socks off and had climbed over several rocks to shinny down to the shallow pool by the bank.

"It doesn't take a lot to make a kid happy, does it?" Carter glanced over to Rhea and smiled.

"No. Those are wonderful carefree years." She took off her own boots and socks and stuck her feet into the cold water. "But wading is fun at any age."

Agreeing, Carter pulled off his own boots to drop his feet in the stream, too.

Chapter 13

Rhea watched Carter wince as he stuck his feet into the chill mountain water. She gave him a cocky smile. "Did you forget how cold the water is here after being in sunny California?"

He flipped a handful of water at her in retaliation.

Risking trouble, she splashed water back at him defiantly. Battle flashing in his eyes, he started to kick another swath of water her way, but then paused, eyeing Taylor thoughtfully. "We'd better not get anything started with Taylor around." He sighed. "It would be just the excuse he needs to dunk himself in the stream."

She rolled her eyes. "Ah. The responsibilities of fatherhood."

Carter didn't respond at first, watching his son digging in the shallow edge of the stream. Then she saw a smile touch the edge of his mouth. "Taylor has been the greatest joy of my life, Rhea." His voice dropped to a husky tone, and Rhea felt her heart turn over at the love in his tone.

As if on cue, Taylor, with a joyous face of discovery, held up a shiny red salamander. "Look Dad! It's a red lizard!"

"That's a salamander, buddy."

Taylor looked doubtful. "Is it, Rhea?"

She smiled at the boy. "Yes, it is. It looks like a lizard, but it's a Sonnini, a black-chinned red salamander. This is the 'Salamander Capital of the World,' here in the Smokies. At least thirty species live in these mountains."

Taylor turned the wiggling salamander over curiously. "Way cool. He does have a black chin. And black spots, too."

He studied the creature on his hand and then let it go, gently dipping it back into the water.

Rhea was impressed. "He has a kind heart, your boy," she said to Carter.

"Yeah, I can't figure out how he turned out so good." He grinned at her. "He didn't get that sweetness from me."

"From his mother?" She asked the question tentatively.

Carter frowned. "I doubt it." He got up to jump the rocks to get closer to the waterfall.

Taylor splashed over to join him, and Rhea watched the two of them talk and interact. The love and affection between them was evident, and it touched her in some deep place to see their two dark heads bent over in intense concentration studying a mayfly on top of the water.

If they had married, Taylor might be her child. The thought hurt.

After enjoying the falls, the trio hiked back down the trail to the Cosby Campground. As they retrieved their cookout supplies from Carter's car and sought out a picnic table and grill, they heard singing coming from the pavilion.

Taylor pointed. "Look. Some people are singing over there."

Rhea walked closer to see around the trees and smiled. "You're right. Let's drive the car closer to the pavilion and maybe we can listen to their music while we cook our hot dogs."

Carter reloaded the items they'd gotten out and drove the car nearer the covered picnic area. Taylor bounced out of the car as soon as it stopped.

"Taylor, this is the Gabes Mountain Band." Rhea started introductions as they drew closer and greeted the band. "They play bluegrass and gospel music. They sing at our church at Laurel Springs and at many festivals and events around the Appalachian area. They've been traveling a lot lately, but we're glad to see them home again."

Carter smiled and stepped in. "Some of these folks are relatives of ours, Taylor. The older man there with the cowboy hat on is Jim Reagan, my mother's father and your maternal great-grandfather on the Reagan side of the family."

Taylor's eyes grew wide as Jim walked over to shake his hand. "Hi, Mr. Reagan. What should I call you since you're one of my grandfathers?"

Jim laughed. "How about Pop Reagan? That's what my other grandkids call me."

"Okay." Taylor nodded, studying the shiny banjo around Jim's neck with interest.

Carter continued the introductions. "Ellie Reagan Butler here is Pop Reagan's daughter and my mother and your grandmother Mary Jane's sister."

"You're the nurse," Taylor said. "You came to take care of my daddy when he got hurt."

"I did." Ellie leaned across the dulcimer on her lap to give Taylor a buss on the cheek. "And you were a good help to me."

"I'm Rice Butler, Ellie's husband," a salt-and-pepper-haired man said, nodding at Taylor while he picked a few random notes on his mandolin. "The girl there is our daughter, Teresa. She's not formally in the band, but she sings a little with us from time to time."

Teresa, with her curly, jet-black hair the color of Carter's, smiled at Taylor with fondness. "I've been wanting to meet you," she said. "And I'm thrilled to see you again, Carter." She threw her arms around Carter and hugged him fiercely. "You've been gone way too long."

Rhea watched Taylor's eyes shift to the last band member, an older gentleman with a short, snowy white beard, strumming out a soft melody on his guitar. "I'm Clyde Dorsey," he said. "Leroy, here, playing the big double bass, is my son." He gestured toward a tall young man with glasses, his rusty-red hair tied behind his neck with a leather string.

Introductions over, Carter asked, "Have you guys eaten supper?"

Ellie shook her head. "No, but we're going to pick-and-sing a little longer and then go get a bite up the road. It was such a nice evening, we decided to practice out-of-doors instead of in the church."

Carter grinned. "Well, if you'll pick-and-sing and entertain me while I fire up the grill, you guys can eat with us. I've got two packages of hot dogs in the cooler, a big tub of homemade slaw, a couple of cans of chili to heat, plenty of buns, two bags of chips, and all the makins for s'mores after."

Ellie grinned, looking around at the group. "Hard to beat that offer. Tell you what. You start cooking and we'll get to practicing and work ourselves up an appetite."

A few minutes later, Rice started the group into a lively rendition of "Over in the Glory Land." Taylor perched on a rock by the pavilion to watch the group with fascination, while Carter and Rhea walked back to the car to unload the picnic supplies.

"Did you really bring enough food for six more people?" Rhea hissed at him as he opened the trunk. "If not, I'll run up the road to the market while you start the charcoal."

He flashed her a wide smile. "You really think I'd let you drive this vintage car?" Carter patted the car fondly. "Not a chance. I don't think you've ever driven anything but that old bug of yours, some farm trucks, and the assembly tram."

Her anger flared at his remarks, and her jaw set.

He leaned over to give her a kiss on the cheek. "I'm only teasing, darlin'. Don't get your dander up."

She jerked away, hoping no one had seen. "Don't do that!"

"Why not?" He loaded her arms with picnic supplies and a large basket.

"Because everyone knows I'm dating Marshall." She shifted the items in her arms to distribute the weight. "It might make people talk to see you pecking me on the cheek like that."

He chuckled. "No telling what they'd think if they'd seen some of the other times."

Rhea frowned at him. "Be nice." She peeked into the bags to check on the food Carter had brought.

He shook his head. "Don't worry about the food. I ran by the market this morning and Estelle packed everything for me. You know how she is. She insisted on doubling everything I asked for."

Rhea laughed. "Well, that explains why you have so much. Estelle thinks everyone needs an army of food for any occasion."

"Anyway, there should be plenty." He hoisted a big cooler from the trunk and balanced a bag of charcoal on the top. "I'll start the charcoal, if you'll fix up the table and get all the stuff out."

"I'll be glad to." She skipped down the path with her arms full, enjoying the wonderful music filling the campground.

The day and the evening were practically perfect. Rhea, Carter, and Taylor enjoyed the music of the Gabes Mountain Band for several hours after dinner, too, eventually singing along to old favorite tunes.

Pop Reagan put down his banjo as twilight began to fall and delighted Taylor with a little old-time clogging. Teresa joined in and then taught Taylor a few steps. Getting into the spirit of the evening, Leroy and Teresa and Carter and Rhea paired off to show Taylor a sample of square dancing to "Turkey in the Straw" in a four square while Rice did the calling. Rhea hadn't square-danced in ages, and it felt wonderful to swing through the familiar steps and patterns again.

After they loaded the picnic remains and said good-byes, Taylor fell asleep in the car almost immediately.

"The day wore him out, didn't it?" Rhea glanced fondly over her shoulder at the child curled up on the backseat.

"Yeah, he had a good time." His eyes caught hers briefly. "Thank you for coming."

"I had a good time, too. Thank you for asking me."

It was the truth, and there seemed no point in denying it.

She saw Carter's smile in the gathering darkness.

"We're getting along better now, aren't we, Rhea?"

Rhea met his eyes as he paused at a stop sign. "We got along well today."

He chuckled. "You won't give more than an inch, will you?"

"I've learned to be cautious with you, Carter."

They drove in silence, enjoying the cool of the evening until they rumbled into the covered bridge. Carter slowed the convertible to a crawl and then stopped in the darkness.

"A penny for your thoughts, Rhea Dean." His voice sounded soft and husky in the darkness, with only the sounds of the stream tumbling under the floor of the bridge.

"If I had a penny, I'd put it through the crack and make a wish." She had no intention of telling him her thoughts or how her heartbeat had escalated as they entered the dark of the old bridge.

He fumbled in his pocket, found a penny, and put it in her hand. "Remember our old game? If you can lean over the side of the car and get the penny to go between the cracks on the first try, you get your wish. Think your aim is still good?"

She saw his grin even in the darkness. "We'll see," she said, leaning over the side of the car. The penny dropped neatly through a large space between two boards, splatting into the water below.

"What did you wish?" he asked as she turned back around to face him with a smug grin.

"Maybe I wished Marshall Sutton would propose."

He grabbed her arm, almost hurting her. "Don't tease me."

"Ouch." Rhea complained, pulling his hand off her arm. "And how do you know Marshall Sutton hasn't already proposed?"

"I don't. Has he?" His voice was low and dangerous.

"Actually, he has."

"And you said?" He drew out the words.

She tossed her head. "I wasn't ready to give an answer yet."

"The answer is no." Carter pulled her into his arms and kissed her fiercely, his hands wrapping her tight against him so she wouldn't pull away. As if she could, with past memories swirling in the darkness of all the times they'd kissed here before.

Their emotions climbed as their kisses grew sweeter, but Rhea put a finger to Carter's lips as he moaned in pleasure. "Shhhh. We'll wake your son and have more explaining to do than either of us are ready to offer to him."

He drew back with obvious reluctance, heaving a long sigh before he put the car back into gear and started to drive out of the bridge. "We're not finished with this, Rhea Dean."

She wisely made no reply.

They drove around the lake to Rhea's house, saying little, letting their feelings cool down.

As Rhea started to get out of the car, Carter's hand snaked over to grab hers. "You wanna leave your window open tonight?" His voice was teasing in the dark.

"No." She snatched her hand back. "I'm tired. We've had a big day. And I want this day to end on a good note, not with a fight and quarrel later."

He laughed softly. "It wasn't fighting and quarreling I had in mind." He caught her hand again. "I loved being with you today. I loved watching you laugh and lie back on that rock in the sun. I loved seeing you across the table from me, smiling and talking over a meal, entertaining everyone with your warmth and congeniality. And I loved seeing how tender and kind you were to my son."

Rhea's heart caught in her throat.

His white smile flashed in the darkness. "Do you know what Taylor said about you?"

"What?" She felt wary asking.

"He said his mother was beautiful . . . but that you were pretty *and* sexy."

Rhea gasped. "You made that up!"

"I didn't." He laughed. "He's right, you know."

"That I'm not beautiful like his mother?"

Carter blew out a breath in annoyance. "How

200

did you miss the best part of what I said?" He paused. "Get this straight. There is no comparison between you and Judith Benton Layman, Rhea. And you should never set yourself beside her in your mind and see yourself wanting in any way."

She crossed her arms. "Hmmmph. Comparing us is like comparing Elly May Clampett of *The Beverly Hillbillies* with Sophia Loren."

Carter laughed, annoying her. "Now, there's a picture. But certainly not an accurate one. However, even if it were, I like Elly May better than Sophia."

He reached out to snatch her hand again as she uncrossed her arms to reach for the door handle. "Never think you're not beautiful, gifted, and exciting, Rhea Dean. No one compares to you. No one."

She left her hand in his for a moment, caught in the web of his words.

"You always were good with words, Carter," she said at last, taking her hand from his and letting herself out of the car.

Rhea heard the Benz purr into motion as she opened the front door.

"See ya later—and love you forever, Rhea Dean." Carter's words floated tantalizingly into the darkness as he drove away.

She shook her head in exasperation and, once again, wondered at how freely Carter seemed to toss out the word 'love' to her. She'd believed his words of love totally once before and what had it gotten her? Only pain and betrayal.

I wish he'd be more careful of throwing words out so freely that are supposed to be eternal, using them so casually and airily. Doesn't he realize how hard it is for me to believe and trust those words again? she thought.

She blew out a sigh and started up the stairs to her room.

Carter wanted to be friends. Maybe that wasn't unreasonable to consider. They'd enjoyed a good day today. Perhaps she could try more to let friendship develop and just hold off the elements she was unsure of.

Chapter 14

Summer slipped by swiftly, as it always seemed to do at Laurel Springs during the heavy tourist season. The months proved busy ones for Carter. The assembly grounds bustled with changes, and the ongoing improvements had already increased tourism and caused many visiting families to reserve vacation times for next summer.

Carter and Rhea formed a tentative friendship through the summer weeks. Even though they experienced occasional slips into intimacy, they never exhibited any of these feelings in front of others. . . . If people noticed anything other than a renewed friendship between the two, they seldom commented on it. Rhea continued to date Marshall Sutton, to Carter's annoyance—and Marion Baker tracked Carter down so often in public places that people started speculating about whether something was "going on" between them.

At times Carter believed he was making real progress with Rhea, while at other times he felt frustrated and unsure of where he stood with her. Dang girl. He wanted to marry her, not play some secret cat-and-mouse courtship game with her.

He pondered these thoughts one night as he sat on the back patio of Jeannie and Billy Wade's house. The girls—Rhea and Jeannie—worked together in the kitchen getting dinner together. Billy Wade was on the phone, and Carter sat outside to keep an eye on the boys, who were playing in a tree house Billy had built in the backyard.

The boys' childish chatter drifted across the yard, making Carter smile. Beau and Taylor had formed a strong friendship over the summer. Carter liked watching his boy contented and carefree now, riding his bike happily around the lake road, helping his grandparents on the farm, doing odd jobs about the assembly grounds with the tourists, learning to swim strongly enough to make it to the raft in the middle of the lake.

Snapping shut his cell phone, Billy Wade came

out the back door, followed by Rhea and Jeannie. "Another place has been hit by the vandal," he groused, slumping into a metal lawn chair.

"Tonight?" Jeannie asked, coming out on the porch to curl up on the glider beside Billy while Rhea settled herself into an old rocker, propping her long legs up on a side table.

Billy frowned. "No. Hiram thinks it probably happened last night. But he didn't discover the damage until he made his rounds tonight. It took place behind the old Gilliland cabin at the springhouse."

"That's funny." Jeannie made a face. "Someone already broke into that cabin earlier in the summer. Wonder why they came back to bother that old springhouse again after all this time?"

Jeannie blew a wisp of short, frosted hair out of her face. "I just don't understand any of this at all. We've had random break-ins all summer long and they don't seem to make any sense. Nothing is ever taken."

"I know," agreed Rhea. "And the sheriff says there have been instances of vandalism in other areas nearby."

"Like over at the Tritt and Gilliland cemeteries." Jeannie wrinkled her nose. "Ew. Someone dug up some places around some of the graves."

"It seems obvious that this vandal, or group of vandals, is looking for something." Billy Wade kicked at a stick on the patio in annoyance. "But what? Rhea, is there an old story about some Dean or Layman ancestor burying a string of pearls or some valuable artifact we don't know about?"

Rhea laughed. "If there'd been something valuable buried here by one of the Deans or Laymans, they'd have dug it up a long time ago and cashed it in during the lean years."

"Maybe it's only someone nutty." Jeannie slipped her feet out of her flip-flops. "I mean, there are a lot of crazy people out there that do all sorts of things that don't make sense. Like those sick people who set fires."

Rhea laughed, a throaty sound that always made Carter's blood stir. "Well, thank goodness we're not dealing with an arsonist. I'd rather have some loony digging holes around the place than setting fires!"

"Eventually, he'll slip up and leave a clue and we'll find him." Carter let his eyes slide up over Rhea's bare legs.

"I hope so." Billy Wade followed Carter's eyes thoughtfully and raised his eyebrows at him with a grin.

"Guess what?" Jeannie changed the subject.

"What?" Rhea answered, obviously glad to let talk of the vandals go.

"Estelle saw Marshall Sutton and Marion Baker driving out of the parking lot of the Shady Grove Motel last night." She turned a mischievous glance to Carter. "I hope that doesn't upset you hearing that, Carter."

He laughed. "Believe me, it would be a relief to hear of Marion setting her sights on anyone else around here but me." Carter saw Rhea frowning. "However, your news might upset Rhea since she and Marshall are still going out together."

"Oh, pooh." Jeannie waved a hand in the air. "Marshall Sutton is not in any way right for Rhea. For the life of me I can't figure out why the two of them are still dating."

"Excuse me." Rhea kicked at her playfully. "Keep in mind that I'm sitting right here, Jeannie. Perhaps Marshall and I are dating because there's an attraction between us."

Billy Wade cleared his throat. "Nothing personal, Rhea, but Jeannie and I never have much liked Marshall Sutton. I'm sure that influences our thinking."

"Yeah." Jeannie giggled. "I just cringe to think of us having to be nice and host Marshall for dinner someday because the two of you have gotten engaged or married or something. Yuk."

Rhea looked at her in surprise. "Would that be so bad?"

"Oh, come on, Rhea, you know it would." She crossed her arms in exasperation. "Even you try to figure ways to get away from him when he comes in the store. You know it's true! Whyever do you keep dating him?"

"Yeah, Carter's a lot more fun to be with," Billy Wade said, sending a look Carter's way.

Jeannie grinned. "That's the truth. It's been fun the evenings we've gotten together this summer —just like old times."

Carter watched Rhea's eyes flash in irritation as she looked from Billy Wade to Jeannie. "Well, I guess I'll have to look around and find someone to date that the Ledford committee likes better."

"Oh, don't get mad now." Jeannie punched at her playfully. "You didn't like Tucker Glenn, that guy I started dating one of the times Billy Wade and I broke up, and you didn't hesitate to say so."

"You dated Tucker Glenn?" Carter laughed out loud at the thought.

Billy Wade laughed, too. "Yeah, that little weasel moved in quick as a snake when Jeannie and I had one of our fusses."

Rhea looked at her watch and frowned. "I really need to get home," she said. "I have to get up and do the tour in the morning. And I promised to help Nana set up and get ready for her quilting demonstration before that."

Carter's eyes moved to the tree house to where the boys played. "Are you sure it's all right if Taylor spends the night here? I can take him on home if you think it would be too much."

"No." Jeannie waved away his concerns. "I already promised them and Taylor's no trouble."

"Yeah, it's fine," Billy added. "I'll drag them

both out of the tree house in a few minutes and get them cleaned up for bed."

Carter stood up. "Then I'll walk Rhea home."

"I know the way, Carter." She gave him an annoyed look.

"Awww, let the man be a gentleman." Billy Wade sent Rhea a grin.

Rhea rolled her eyes and stood up in resignation.

After saying their good-byes, Carter and Rhea started the walk home down the Assembly Road.

As they neared the covered bridge, Carter reached over to take Rhea's arm. He liked the looks of the long expanse of dark bridge ahead. "You didn't seem overly upset about Marshall being seen with Marion."

Rhea jerked away and stalked ahead of him. "Don't start with me, Carter Layman. What Estelle saw could have been anything. Marshall works in banking, Marion in real estate. They might have been simply working together."

Carter laughed. "Yeah. I'd say they had a workout at the Shady Grove. You may be right."

She gave him a dirty look and then took off running. "Bet I can beat you to the other side of the bridge!"

Carter took off after her. Even given a late start, he was still unable to let any dare from Rhea slip by him. Neither of them had ever been able to pass up a dare between them, no matter how foolish—often getting them in a peck of trouble over the years.

Rhea beat him by a stride and turned to give him a grin before sauntering on down the road.

"Cheater," he said, following along behind her. He owed her one now.

When they got to the split in the road, Carter took her arm again. "Come down and see what the workers did to the gazebo today."

"It's dark." She balked, looking down toward the lake.

"It's not that dark. Come on." He practically hauled her down the bank to the large white gazebo by the banks of Laurel Springs Lake.

"Oh. How nice." Rhea smiled with pleasure as they climbed the steps into the graceful, hexagon-shaped structure. "You had the benches built back around the sides."

"Just like in the old picture." He knew it would please her. "And I had the floors redone—better for dancing." Carter tried to take her in his arms to dance around the large space, but Rhea pulled back, walking over to the rail to look out over the lake.

"It's hot tonight," she said to cover for the flush on her face.

"Yeah, it is." Carter grinned. "Think I'll go skinny-dipping like we used to." He started unbuttoning his shirt.

Rhea's eyes flew to his.

He lifted his eyebrows. "I dare you to go, too, and I'll race you out to the raft." He threw out the old taunt as he pulled his shirttail out of his shorts.

Carter watched Rhea hesitate, struggling with old memories. As kids they would strip off their clothes in a flurry to see who could swim out to the raft the fastest. Later, of course, they only stripped down to their underwear.

"Don't you dare take all your clothes off." She watched him unbutton his shirt with a frown.

"I'll stop at my skivvies. But you're a double-dog coward if you won't race me. I raced you through the bridge." He grinned at her in challenge.

He saw her consider his dare as he pulled off his shirt, and then, in a familiar flurry, they were both ripping off their clothes and shoes to see who could get to the water first.

Rhea dived off the dock moments after Carter. He heard her strong strokes behind him and then saw her gaining on him as they swam furiously out into the dark water.

It was over four hundred yards to the raft, almost a quarter mile, and they were both winded as they reached the ladder almost at the same time, Carter just a few feet ahead of her.

"You had a head start," Rhea complained, panting as she uttered the words.

Carter brushed the water out of his eyes and

shook his hair, sending sprinkles of water over Rhea.

She scooped up a handful of water and sent it his way in retaliation. A small water fight ensued, both of them soon laughing and Carter binding her arms behind her back so she couldn't pummel him with water again.

And then it hit. The sizzle. The passion. One of those wonderful moments. Blood rushed through Carter's veins, and he had his mouth on Rhea's before he knew what he was doing. She kissed him back with fervor, looping her arms around his neck to stay afloat in the water.

Carter wrapped a leg through the ladder for support and moved his free hands over her water-slicked body, pulling her tight against him, almost skin to skin.

Remembering she was innocent, he carefully kept his hands from exploring and touching as they yearned to do. But he reveled in the feel of her against him, always the perfect fit to him.

Concerned about the rising level of their passion, he chuckled against her mouth. "I think there's a little more of you up above than I remember, Rhea Dean." It was hard to ignore her breasts heaving against his chest and, even in the darkness, he could see the white mounds of them pushing above her bra in the moonlight.

His words had the desired effect, and he felt her struggle back, loosening the grip of her arms around his neck. But her pulling away only gave him a better look down the length of her body, even in the dark, and before she could sputter a reply, he took her mouth again, plunging them under another time. There had never been another woman who made him feel like Rhea Dean, and kissing and hugging in the dark water was unbelievably sexy.

"This is heaven, Rhea," he said at last in a husky voice, raining soft kisses down her face, over her closed eyes and cheeks.

She gave a little whimper as his hands traced soft patterns down her back and over her arms. Yielding sweetly to her emotions, Rhea pressed herself against him more tightly, finding his mouth again with her own, leading the way this time.

It was all Carter could do to hold himself together, to keep himself in check from taking more intimacies.

"Tell me you love me," he said at last in a whisper beside her ear, his mouth raining kisses down her neck.

He felt her tense.

"You know you love me, Rhea." He looked down into her eyes in the dark, reveling in the feel of her chest heaving against his. "Why can't you admit it? Say it out loud?" He kissed her softly and then held her face in his hands. "You know I love you. Let's quit pretending it isn't true."

Something in her eyes shut down then, and she drew back from him. Carter felt her pull her resolve back together.

"Race you back," she said suddenly. She pushed off the raft and headed back toward shore before he had time to stop her.

Carter bit off an expletive before starting after her.

She was out of the water before he got to shore this time, pulling her T-shirt back over her underwear and slipping quickly back into her shorts.

He stood in the doorway of the gazebo, watching her dress. "How are you going to explain your wet clothes?"

She shrugged. "Tell the truth. That it was hot and I took a dip."

His voice grew quiet. "But you won't add that you took a dip with me, will you?"

She didn't answer.

"Rhea, we can't keep denying what we feel for each other. And we can't keep playing games with everyone we know, pretending that we're only friends."

She gave him a defiant look. "We *are* only friends."

He shook his head as he started to pull his shorts back on. "Rhea Dean, we are much more than friends."

"There's an attraction, I admit." She sat down

on the gazebo bench to lace up her tennis shoes.

"Well, at least you admit that." He slid his arms into his shirt and sat down beside her.

"Look at me." He reached over to lift her chin so he could look into her eyes. "I have loved you all my life and I still love you. I don't want to just play games with you. I want you to be a part of my life."

"I don't want to hear this." She stood up and started sprinting down the steps of the gazebo.

"Dang it, Rhea." He slipped his feet into his loafers and started after her. Hearing him behind her, she ran. It took him a while to catch her and whirl her around to face him.

Panting, he asked her, "What do you want of me, Rhea Dean? Tell me."

She shook her head and gave him an anguished look. "I don't know. I don't know."

In annoyance, he leaned his face close to hers, to where she had to look into his eyes. "Well, you let me know when you figure it out."

Then he stalked off down the road. He heard her following after him, but he didn't turn around.

They walked in silence to the turning at the road to Rhea's house.

"I'll let you find your own way down the driveway to your house," he said, breaking the silence.

She stood watching him, and he could see the display of confusing emotions playing across her face. How could she not know how she felt about him?

"Is it because you can't forgive me for what happened?" he asked at last. "That I married Judith?"

He watched the pain flash over her face and knew that was it.

Carter sighed and shook his head. "We need to talk about this sometime. Really talk."

She crossed her arms defensively. "I don't want to talk about it."

"I know, and that's part of the problem."

A small puddle of water had started to gather where she stood. He looked down at it in amusement. "You're leaking."

"So are you," she said, smirking, and drawing his attention to the trickle of water running down his legs and onto the ground.

"I guess we'd better call it a night."

She nodded as both of them let their eyes rove over each other one last time. "Thanks for walking me home."

Rhea turned to start down her driveway but then glanced back with a grin. "I almost beat you, Carter Layman—and would have if you hadn't gotten a head start."

He grinned at her. She wanted the evening to end on a less emotional note. So did he.

Carter wiggled his eyebrows at her. "I hope the lake water comes out of that pretty lavender underwear." He hooked his thumbs in his pockets. "You always did have the sexiest underwear."

"Well, I can't say the same for you." She tossed her head as she headed down the drive. "If I'm not mistaken, there was a Mickey Mouse print on your jockey shorts."

He laughed, turning his steps back toward the lake road toward home. "Taylor gave them to me for my birthday."

"A likely story," she added.

"Night, Rhea," he called back, smart enough not to add his usual good-night call this time.

Chapter 15

Rhea woke the next morning with a splitting headache—and she never got headaches. Her neck felt stiff, and she'd slept fitfully. In all honesty, every time she got around Carter Layman for any length of time, she tossed and turned at night. Wretched man.

She made an effort to be pleasant while she helped Nana Dean tighten and straighten the quilt in progress on the quilting frame. Rummaging in the old pie safe, she took out an assortment of Nana's booklets and packaged quilt patterns that she sold after her demonstrations.

"What's this quilt pattern?" she asked, smoothing her hands over the partially completed quilt on the frame. She knew she'd acted grumpy and moody most of the morning—and Nana deserved better.

"It's called Bleeding Heart." Her grandmother ran her hand over one of the patterned squares. "A fit name to go with your mood today, I'd say."

Rhea scowled at her grandmother. "And what's that supposed to mean?"

"Just that it's no secret, at least to me, that your heart's pining after Carter Layman and you're denying your heart ease."

"My heart is *not* bleeding over Carter Layman." Rhea crossed her arms in irritation. "I've already been through bleeding over him quite enough in the past. I have no intention of going there again."

"Hmmmph." Nana offered a soft little laugh. "Despite your words, your *heart* hasn't gotten the message your head is telling it."

Her eyes narrowed. "Now don't start reading things into my spending a little time with Carter. We're just friends."

Nana sat down in a caned chair beside the quilting frame, starting to look for her thimble, needle, and thread in her sewing basket. Pushing her favorite metal thimble onto her middle finger, she looked up at Rhea thoughtfully. "I haven't said anything before this, Rhea Kaden Dean, because I figured even a person as stubborn as you would figure it out—given enough time. You still hold a place in your heart for that boy, no matter what you say."

Rhea turned to look out the window. "I don't want to care for Carter, Nana. Surely you can understand why."

"I understand you got hurt in the past, but time goes on. Often we get a second chance for happiness in some areas." She threaded her needle with white thread, knotting off the end of her thread neatly.

Out the window, Rhea watched several ladies coming up the cabin pathway to attend Nana's quilting demonstration. Going toward the door to open it, she gave her grandmother a defiant look. "I don't want to be a *second* chance or a *second* choice, Nana."

She ushered in the arriving guests before Nana could reply. Then with a small wave of her hand, she slipped out to head toward the ad-min building at the assembly grounds to lead her Saturday morning tour.

However, not thinking about Carter Layman proved more difficult than escaping from Nana Dean. Everywhere Rhea drove the tour tram, something reminded her of him—the new bell tower above the church; fresh pavement on the lake road; bright red canoes at the dockside replacing the battered, leaky ones; the shiny new roof on the gazebo. It wasn't fair that Carter had accomplished all this in so short a time, become the local hero, when she'd worked and slaved so hard all these years keeping the place up, keeping everything going. And for what thanks?

In a foul mood, Rhea strode into the ad-min building after the tour ended, planning to work on her column for next week's newspaper. At the doorway to her office, she stopped in shock. Every surface lay covered in drop cloths, and a workman she'd never met stood on a ladder painting her walls!

Anger flaring, Rhea stomped down the hall to her mother's office, waiting in a fury until she saw her hang up the phone. "What is that man doing in my office, Mother?"

Her mother lifted an eyebrow at her. "The one painting?"

"Yes!" Rhea crossed her arms in irritation. "I don't recall asking anyone to paint my office, and I'll just bet this is Carter Layman's doing. Taking charge, pushing his way in and initiating things, without even discussing the plans with anyone. Well, I've just about had it with him taking over and making changes around here without soliciting my opinion once. He had no right to paint my office, and choose the color, without even asking me."

Her mother leveled a hard glance at her. "Sit down, Rhea," she said in that no-nonsense, authoritative voice of hers, pointing to the chair across from her desk.

Reluctantly, Rhea slumped into the chair.

Her mother studied her quietly, making Rhea squirm in the lengthy silence. Rhea had time to note her mother's short salt-and-pepper hair, her mannish face with no makeup, her trim figure and tailored clothes. Rhea certainly looked more like her father.

"I think I have suggested to you on more than one occasion that you need to learn to curb that temper of yours. I also have frequently advised you to take time to get all the facts of a matter before you fly off the handle and react."

She tapped a pencil on her palm, weighing her next words. "I've had my resentments against Carter from the past, I'll admit, but your criticisms of him just now are unwarranted."

Rhea leaned forward, feeling her anger flare again. "Yet you do admit there's a man in my office painting. Was I asked about that? Did I even get any choice in the paint color for my own office?"

Her mother shook her head slowly. "I personally gave the order to have your office painted, Rhea—not Carter. If you recall, it was you, yourself, who complained, only this winter, that the walls in your office 'looked nasty,' to quote your own words. You slapped a paint chart on my desk and told me specifically that you wanted your walls painted Pacific Blue when I could find enough money for some interior paint. I recall you being in rather a snit about it, said you'd paint the office yourself and do the vestibule and the library, too, if I'd only get the paint."

She opened the drawer and took out the paint chart, passing it across the desk to Rhea. "If you'll walk through the building, you'll see that all the rooms you suggested are being repainted —and in the colors *you* chose. I thought you might be pleased about that, Rhea, instead of roaring in here, throwing a childish fit over it."

Chastised, Rhea glanced down at the paint chart, noting her paint choices and notes scrawled across it. "I'm sorry, Mother." There was nothing else to say.

She squirmed in her seat. "It's just that Carter is doing so many new things around the assembly grounds, making so many changes, and I've had little voice in anything."

Her mother steepled her fingers. "Laurel Springs Assembly Grounds belongs to Grampa Layman, Wes and Mary Jane Layman, Nana Dean, and myself—as your father's heir. Carter met with us to explain all the changes he wanted to finance, to get our approval and our input. We would have been foolish to have turned down a gift of the magnitude Carter offered us freely."

Lillian Dean frowned, looking toward the picture of her husband and Rhea's father, Sam Dean, on the wall. Her voice grew quiet. "I wish

Sam could have lived to see the old place come back to life as it has." Her eyes moved to Rhea's. "It never dawned on me that you wouldn't be thrilled to see these renovations and changes happen."

She tapped the pencil into her palm again. "Many of the ongoing repairs and restorations are ones you always dreamed of and wished we could make since you were a girl."

"I know." Rhea picked at her fingernails, not wanting to meet her mother's eyes.

"Rhea, I realize it has been difficult for you having Carter—and his young son—back here again. I know you loved him deeply and your father and I both knew you wanted to marry. Carter spoke to your father before he died, did you know that? He asked his permission to marry you." She put the paint chart back in her desk drawer. "He did that before he ever went away to college."

She chuckled softly in remembrance. "Your father asked Carter if he planned to wait to marry until the two of you finished college and Carter said he'd like that to happen but he wasn't sure he could hold out that long. It gave Sam a good laugh at a very difficult time for him."

"I didn't know that." Rhea felt a sweep of regret wash over her.

Her mother tucked the pencil behind her ear

distractedly. "I've long wished I'd insisted on you going out to California with Carter that fall. Sam told me he asked you to stay and help me, but he shouldn't have done that. You had your own life to live, and we'd have managed."

Rhea felt tears push at the back of her eyes. She sniffed and pulled her chin up. "It isn't your fault or Daddy's that Carter married someone else, Mother. That was his choice."

Her mother shook her head. "There's something we don't know about all that, Rhea. I sense it. You know I'm a no-nonsense person, and not particularly intuitive, but there's a way Carter looks when that woman's name comes up that isn't quite right. I've buried a spouse and I know some about loss and grief. I don't know what it is—but there's something."

She studied Rhea. "Have you ever talked to him about it?"

Rhea crossed her arms and frowned. "I don't *want* to talk to him about it."

"I see." Her mother cleared her throat. "And I'd wager that stubborn attitude and old resentment I'm hearing lay behind your earlier outburst."

Rhea, annoyed, stood up, preparing to leave.

Her mother's eyes caught hers. "You may think, as your mother, that I don't know much about what goes on with you or about what you're feeling, but anyone who knows you and Carter well would have to be blind and bone dense not to feel the heat in the air when the two of you are together."

Rhea gasped.

"You'd better figure out some sensible way to handle that heat, before some un-sensible moment occurs and you find yourself in way over your head. I'd like a grandchild someday, but I'd like one in the old-fashioned way, after attending your wedding."

Rhea tried to find words to reply to her mother but struggled over any that came to mind. Finally she said, "Carter and I are just friends, Mother."

"And pigs fly," she replied, reaching for the phone as it started to ring and waving Rhea out of the room.

Restless now and knowing she couldn't work in her office, Rhea decided to walk over and help Jeannie finish cleaning out the two cabins on East Cabin Road. She probably hadn't finished with both yet.

Rhea cut across the meeting grounds and through the woods trail to the East Cabin Road. She found Jeannie at a cute cottage called Bluebird Stop, sweeping the front porch.

"It figures you'd show up too late to help out." Jeannie tossed her a saucy look.

"You know I had the tour." Rhea frowned at her.

"I know. I'm just teasing. Lighten up." She looked toward a bundle of laundry on the porch swing. "You could throw that laundry into the truck if you wouldn't mind, though."

Rhea walked up on the porch, gathered the laundry into her arms, waddled down the sidewalk, and tossed the linens into the truck. She stopped with surprise as she looked across the street at a little bungalow called the Crescent Moon.

"Doesn't the cottage look great?" Jeannie called, seeing her pause. "The roof's been replaced and it's totally refinished inside and out."

"I see that." Rhea stalked back up on the porch. "Who said the color could be changed and shutters put up? Was it Carter's idea?"

Jeannie looked at her quizzically, picking up on Rhea's cross voice. "What's eating you today?" She sat down on the porch swing and patted the seat beside her.

Rhea sat down reluctantly, hoping she wasn't in for a session with Jeannie after already dealing with Nana Dean and her mother earlier.

Jeannie smoothed a few flyaway wisps of hair behind her ear. "Listen, Rhea. I told Carter and Billy Wade about that old picture you found of the Crescent Moon when it was first built. Remember? You found the picture in some historical book, made a copy of it, and put it in the library scrapbook at the ad-min building. You told me once it would be nice if the Crescent

Moon could have shutters like in the picture again."

She lifted her hands expressively. "I told them I thought it would be neat to restore it to how it once looked—painted soft yellow and trimmed in black with moon wisps cut out on each shutter. Carter paid one of the carpenters extra to make the shutters. We thought you'd love it."

Rhea felt a flush of embarrassment rise in her cheeks.

Jeannie gave her a questioning look. "Don't you like it? It was your idea, after all." She blew out a breath. "I hope you're not mad at me for telling Billy and Carter about it."

"No." Rhea pushed the swing into motion for something distracting to do. "I just forgot—that's all." She tried to smile. "It looks nice, Jeannie."

Smiling back, Jeannie changed the subject in her usual way. "Guess what?"

"What?" Rhea answered, glad to move to a new topic.

Jeannie patted her stomach. "Billy Wade and I are going to have another baby."

Rhea's eyes flew to Jeannie's in surprise. "Really?"

"Really. I found out yesterday." She rubbed her tummy affectionately. "I hope it's going to be a little girl this time."

Rhea looked toward the truck in alarm, thinking of the big load of laundry she'd just thrown into the back. "I don't want you doing heavy lifting or too much work around here for a while."

"I won't be—and neither will you. Carter found two women to clean the cabins now instead of us. Whoopee!" She punched a fist in the air. "Won't that be sweet?"

Rhea bit back the reply that tried to rise up.

Not noticing Rhea's change of mood, Jeannie babbled on. "Those two Barker sisters that live near Caton's Grove were tickled to get the job. They've been cleaning houses here and there, trying to make ends meet, so this steady job is a godsend to them. Estelle says they're hard workers, real good Christian women, and that we're lucky to get them. Isn't that great?"

Jeannie glanced at her watch suddenly and stopped the swing's motion with her foot. "Oops. Sorry to rush off, Rhea, but I've got to go to cheerleader practice with the girls."

Rhea looked at her in alarm. "Is it still safe for you to do that?"

Jeannie laughed as she stood up, grabbing the broom to carry to the truck. "Don't worry so much. You're as bad as Billy Wade." She wrinkled her nose. "I'm not going to do any handstands or splits or anything—just supervise."

"Okay." Rhea stood to hug Jeannie good-bye and felt an odd discontent slice through her. Everything was changing. Even Jeannie. Something hurt deep inside Rhea to think of the sweet new life growing inside her friend.

Watching Jeannie drive away, Rhea tried to decide what to do with the rest of the day. Nothing she considered held any appeal—and she felt no desire for more company after the morning's events.

Her mind still rolled with the words of her mother, her grandmother—and the words Carter said to her last night in such an anguished tone. *What do you want of me, Rhea Dean?*

The question turning in her mind, Rhea decided to go to the old Costner ruins to think. She knew she could sit there against the old stone fireplace, quiet and alone for an hour or so, and collect her thoughts.

The long walk around the lake, through the old Gilliland property, and across the woods trail on Low Ridge, did Rhea good, but she stopped in shock as she rounded the corner at the Costner cabin site.

The ruins were gone! Trees had been cleared, and the beginnings of a new house sat on the old cabin site, a winding paved drive leading up to it.

Rhea walked closer to study the place. The two-storied home was completely framed, the roof on, the windows and doors in place. Her heart ached as she took in the details. She knew immediately it was Carter's new house. Hadn't he mentioned he might be building here? Rhea sighed. Now that she thought about it, she knew she'd heard Billy Wade talking about the house and she'd occasionally seen construction trucks heading in this direction when she was on the west end of the assembly grounds. This was Layman property, after all. It had always been Carter's dream to build here. And hers. Which was probably why she'd tried not to think about a house going up on this spot.

She sat down on the front steps and started to cry. Between the events of last night and today, this was simply the last straw.

Engulfed with confusion and regrets, Rhea dropped her head into her hands and sobbed.

Chapter 16

Carter heard Rhea before he saw her. He'd been behind the old Gilliland place, checking repairs at the vandalized springhouse, and he'd shamelessly trailed Rhea across the ridge, keeping at a distance behind her, unseen. He thought she might be going to Rocky Knob. He planned to follow her there—so they could talk more about what happened last night. With surprise, he saw her head across the ridge toward his new house.

Rhea never wept easily, and Carter knew something was wrong for her to be sobbing audibly like this. He crept up and sat quietly beside her on the rough porch steps before she sensed his presence.

She glanced at him in annoyance and sniffed. "Great. Just what I needed after everything else today."

"Thanks for the compliment." He tried to get her to grin.

She shook her head and looked away. "I'd really like some time by myself right now, Carter."

"Five good reasons why first." It was an old game they used to play. "Then I'll leave."

A cloud crossed her face. "Oh, all right. You asked for it." She gave him a stubborn and irritated frown. "One, Nana Dean says it's obvious something is going on between us. Two, my mother practically agreed with her—which humiliated me, coming from her."

She swept a hand toward the assembly grounds below. "Three, everywhere I look you're changing things at Laurel Springs, and even though that's good, it's hard to deal with—since I'm having so little say in it and that hurts somehow." Rhea sucked in a shaky breath.

"Four, Jeannie is having another baby, and I entertained a pitiable fit of personal jealousy when I heard the news today. I'm not getting any younger, you know." She raised her chin. "And, five, when I come up to the old ruins to enjoy some time alone, I find a new house springing up here, as well." She shook her head and gave him a defiant look. "So, it's just been one of those days, Carter."

She scooted farther away from him. "So, now would you leave?"

Carter shook his head in amazement. Rhea, normally a secretive person who kept her feelings close to her heart, had just dumped a major load of revelations on him. "Wow." He ran a hand through his hair, trying to digest it all. "I don't think I can leave after that."

She glared at him. "I played by the rules. Just like in Truth or Dare."

"You did," he acknowledged, still not budging from his spot on the porch steps.

He sat quietly beside her, thinking over her words while looking across the panoramic view of Laurel Springs spread below him. He'd missed the place so much and never tired of sitting, just like this, to look out over the land, green with summer. His eyes wandered across the lake, sparkling in the sun, and down the quiet road-ways, winding in pretty curves through the property—all so loved, familiar, and dear.

Rhea, growing impatient with his silence, cleared her throat. "I thought you were leaving," she said pointedly.

Carter turned to look at her. "I'll give you five good reasons why I can't leave." He held up a hand to count off the points. "One, Nana Dean and your mother are right; I do think people are starting to suspect something is going on between us. People aren't blind, you know. Two, I haven't talked with you as much as I should about all the changes. I wanted to, but you've been so prickly with me I wasn't sure how to handle it." He swallowed. "Three, I kept hoping when you saw me making the changes you and I always dreamed of doing at Laurel Springs, that you'd soften toward me a little."

Rhea's eyes trapped his. "You thought you could buy my affection?"

He scratched his arm in discomfort. "That sounds like an awful way to put it."

"If the shoe fits . . ." Her voice trailed off.

Ignoring her eye roll, he moved on, a faint smile playing on his lips. "Four, you and I can easily take care of that baby-jealousy issue and create some little Dean-Layman kids to run around this place the same way you and I did."

He heard her gasp but ignored it. "And five, I'm building this house, exactly the way you and I always dreamed, to please you, not to upset you. I even used the stones from the old Costner chimney in the rock fireplace in the den." He held up a key and dangled it. "I'd like you to see it—and show you through the house in its rough state. What do you say?"

She studied the key. "This day couldn't get any worse." She sighed and stood up. "Besides, I might as well go along since you're *not* going to leave me in peace."

Grinning in pleasure at this turn of events, Carter went to the front door to unlock the house. "You always said you thought we should build a house that looked somewhat like the old Costner place that burned down. Remember? The only picture we found showed a gabled two-storied house with a broad porch across the entire front. . . ."

"To catch the fine view across the valley." She sighed. "I remember."

Carter smoothed a hand over the panels of the front door. "You wanted the house painted white with shiny black doors and shutters in the Layman tradition. I plan to do that when it's finished."

"And with a swing on the front porch." She looked around.

"I've ordered it. And rockers."

He watched her try to hide a quick smile as he opened the door into the foyer. "I still have my old notebook where we sketched out the plans we thought would be great for the house."

She looked at him in surprise. "You kept that old thing?"

His voice dropped. "I've kept a lot of things you'd be surprised about, Rhea Dean."

She turned her attention back to the house, avoiding his eyes.

He walked her through the downstairs rooms, framed and ready for the interior work to begin—

finishing the baths and kitchen, hanging drywall, painting the interior walls, and laying the hard-wood floors.

"The architect's plans are very similar to the old drawing—living room, family room, dining room, kitchen, and master bedroom on the first level, four bedrooms and baths upstairs." He led her through the spacious rooms. "I added an office downstairs because I need a place to work at home, but I made sure the architect designed broad porches front and back, to enjoy the outdoors whenever possible."

She stopped in the framed-in kitchen area, looking to the left. Her voice came softly. "You remembered to put in a little breakfast area so it would look out into the woods and across the rock patio."

He made no comment, pleased she'd noticed.

"What about furniture?"

"There's plenty of time for that." He took a chance adding, "I hoped you might help me pick it out."

She didn't answer—just stood looking out the kitchen window.

When the silence lengthened, Carter asked, "Do you want to see upstairs?"

She trailed him up to the second floor, watching her step on the partly finished stairs, walked through the bedrooms, and stopped to peek out the upper windows to catch the views.

Rhea made few comments during the tour, but Carter noticed her mouth quirk in a hidden smile now and then, saw her eyes grow misty with memories, watched her trace a hand gently over the big rock fireplace just finished in the family room, recalling the crumbling chimney they'd leaned against so many times. She liked the house —even though she wasn't saying so.

Rhea stood quietly now, examining one of the small bedrooms. He could almost follow her thoughts. "We'd make better babies than you and Marshall Sutton." Carter couldn't resist the remark.

She scowled at him. "You were doing pretty good at being nice before that snide observation, Carter."

"Sorry," he said, but he knew he didn't really mean it. "How's that going with him, anyway? Marshall practically shoved me into the wall the other day when we met coming out of the Walmart at Newport."

Rhea blew out a breath. "He's not happy with me because I won't commit and say I'll marry him." She moved over to look out a window. "Sometimes I wonder why he wants to. It's not very good between us when we . . ." She hedged. "Well, you know."

He wisely made no comment—this time of candor with Rhea was too precious to risk damaging.

When her silence lengthened, Carter walked

across the room and stood behind her, slipping his arms around her, looking out the window with her at the panorama below.

"It's nice here," she offered in a small voice.

She leaned against him with a soft sigh of resignation, and Carter's heart ached with pleasure.

Interrupting the moment, Taylor's high and frightened voice called from downstairs. "Dad, Dad . . . where are you?"

Even Rhea turned toward the door in alarm, hearing the upset and anguish in Taylor's voice.

"Here, Son. Upstairs." Carter sprinted toward the door, but Taylor plowed into him before he got there, throwing his arms around him.

Tears streamed down his face as he wrapped himself tightly against Carter's legs. Carter squatted to pull him closer into his arms.

He sobbed, literally shaking.

Finally beginning to calm down, he leaned away with a sniff and saw Rhea. "Hi, Rhea." He smiled, remembering to be polite even when upset.

"Hey, Taylor. What happened to upset you?" Rhea put a kind hand on the child's back, patting him gently.

"Yes, what's wrong, Son?" Carter sat down on the floor, pulling Taylor down to sit beside him. Rhea dropped down to join them, so that they formed a little circle, Taylor still leaning against Carter for support.

More tears slid down Taylor's cheeks. "I came

looking for Dad. Mamaw said he'd gone over to the Gilliland place to check on the springhouse that got vandaled." Taylor took a shaky breath. "When I didn't see him, I went up the road to the old Sutton cabin, thinking Dad might have gone there."

His eyes widened. "I heard someone inside the cabin. I thought it was Dad, so I called and went in, but someone threw a quilt over my head and grabbed me. A man, I think. It felt like a man. I couldn't see much."

Carter's heart began to beat an angry staccato. "Did the man hurt you?"

Taylor shook his head. "No, but he scared me *real bad.* He threw me over on that old bed in the cabin, all wrapped up in the quilt, and then he ran out before I could get the quilt off. He shut me in the cabin, too, Dad." Tears threatened again. "He put something against the door so I was trapped and couldn't get out."

Rhea patted his leg reassuringly. "But you did get out, Taylor."

He sniffed. "Don't get mad but I broke the window at the back so I could climb out." His words poured out in a torrent now. "I heard the man run down the walk out front so I tried the door to get away but it wouldn't open. I started to get scared he might come back so I decided to sneak out the back window. It's low and near the ground, but the window wouldn't open easy. I couldn't make the latch move, so I hit it with the miner's shovel to try to make it open. Some of the window broke but then the latch thing moved, and I pulled up the window and climbed out."

He took a deep breath. "As soon as I got out, I ran back through the woods and started across the ridge away from the cabin. I didn't know if the man was still around and if he might try to get me again."

Carter hugged the frightened boy tighter against him.

Comforted, Taylor continued his story. "I felt scared in the woods at first until I found the trail along the ridge, then I knew where I was." His eyes found Carter's. "I was going to go to Rhea's house to call you, but when I saw the door open at our new house, I thought you might be here."

He threw his arms around Carter again. "I was really scared, Dad. I thought that man might do something awful to me, come back and smother me or hit me with a big stick like what happened to you."

Taylor rubbed his tear-streaked face on his sleeve. "Do you think this was the same mean person that hit you?"

"I don't know, buddy." He rocked the boy lovingly against him, deeply grateful he hadn't been hurt.

Rhea leaned over to pat Taylor's knee again. "You were very brave, Taylor, to keep your head and climb out the window and run. That was smart of you." She flashed Taylor a smile when he looked at her with a touch of pride. "And don't worry for one minute about that old window. Your dad and I can replace it easily. The important thing is that you're okay."

She looked down at a spot on his leg crusted with a little blood. "Did you get that cut on the window?"

Alarmed, Carter began to examine his son, finding a cut or two on his legs and one on his hand. He noticed angry scratches on his arms and legs, too. "What happened here, sport?"

Taylor wrinkled his nose. "There were some blackberry bushes or something behind the cabin, and they got me, I guess."

Carter saw Rhea grin at his words. "Well, we need to get you over to your Mamaw and Papaw's house so we can clean those scratches and cuts—and put some medicine on them." Rhea stood up and offered Taylor a hand. "I'll bet we could rustle up some cookies and milk, too. A guy who's had a close encounter with danger deserves a cookies and milk snack, don't you think?"

Taylor nodded, his eyes brightening. "And maybe even banana pudding. Mamaw was making some before I left the house."

Rhea laughed. "I am absolutely certain Mary Jane Layman will decide your escape from danger is worthy of banana pudding, too."

Carter stood up, taking his son's hand as they started toward the stairs.

The next hour or two passed quickly for Carter, walking back to the Layman house, calming Wes and Mary Jane, tending to Taylor, calling the sheriff and going over all the details again with him. Taylor, worn out from the trauma, finally fell asleep on the living room sofa.

Carter motioned to Rhea, and they slipped through the kitchen and out onto the screened porch. His parents had already gone back outside to finish gardening chores they'd dropped in a flurry when Carter arrived carrying Taylor earlier.

"Whew, what a day," Carter said, leaning back in a wicker chair and propping his feet up on a stool.

Rhea settled in the corner of the porch swing and curled her feet up under her. "I want a sip of your lemonade." She reached across to snag Carter's glass from the side table.

"Help yourself." He sighed and leaned his head back against the chair.

"Carter, do you think the same vandal that scared Taylor today hit you?"

"Even the sheriff thinks it's probably all linked, Rhea, that it's either the same person or a part of the same group or gang." He retrieved the lemonade she'd put back on the table and drained the glass.

Rhea drummed her fingers on the arm of the swing. "I just don't get all of this at all."

"Me neither. But I especially don't like the idea that my son might have been injured."

Rhea shifted her position. "I think the vandal thought Taylor might recognize him, don't you? That would explain why he threw the quilt from the bed over Taylor's head. My guess is that Taylor caught him unexpectedly in the cabin looking for something."

"Like what?"

She shrugged. "I don't know. I wish I did."

They sat and thought about this for a few minutes.

"You know what I think?" Carter asked, leaning forward.

"What?" She looked at him with interest.

"I think whatever the man was doing, he got interrupted." A faint smile played on Carter's lips. "My guess is he'll come back."

Rhea's eyes flashed. "Or he might come back because he's afraid evidence could have been left behind."

"Maybe." Carter considered her point. "Ursell went to the cabin to search and look around. He didn't find anything."

Rhea smiled. "But the vandal might not know that. Besides, only the vandal knows why he was there and if he left evidence behind that Ursell didn't find."

A muscle in his jaw bunched. "When do you think he'll come back?"

She scratched her chin, thinking. "I'd go after dark, wouldn't you? When there was less chance to run into anyone."

"An interesting thought." Carter flexed his fingers. "I think I'll be visiting the old Sutton place tonight."

Rhea sat forward. "That might be dangerous, Carter. Maybe we should suggest Ursell or one of his deputies stake out the place."

"Ursell wouldn't do it. The idea would seem too much of a whim to him." His eyes narrowed. "But not to me. I think there's a good chance the man might come back. I'd like the chance to take a piece out of him if he does." He shrugged, conscious of Rhea's indrawn breath. "Even if the vandal doesn't come back, I'd like an opportunity to look around the place."

Rhea slanted him a warning glance. "You shouldn't go by yourself."

"I'll be careful."

She shifted again on the swing, dropping her feet to the floor. "Then I'm going with you," she announced.

He frowned at her. "I'm not so sure that's such a good idea."

She gave him a saucy look. "I'm not so sure *you* have any choice."

Carter knew how Rhea could be when she set

242

her mind to something. "Oh, all right. We'll both go after I get Taylor down for bed—and when I can sneak out. I'll come to your window to get you."

"Okay." She stood up now, stretching her shoulders. "I think I'll go home to get some rest. I've really had a killer day."

He grinned at her. "Watch your choice of words."

She shivered. "Don't try to scare me, Carter Layman."

"Don't think this is a joke. We'll need to be very careful." He paused to think. "Wear all black or dark clothes tonight. Bring a light jacket and a few essentials packed in the pockets, or in a waist pack, just in case we need to stake out for a while. I'll do the same."

Rhea gave him a thoughtful look. "Should we tell anyone where we're going?"

He shook his head. "They'd try to talk us out of it. You know that." He stood up from his chair to see her out. "Besides, this little trip may all be a wasted venture. The guy will probably lay low and not even come around Laurel Springs for weeks after this incident with Taylor."

She nodded. "You're probably right. Hardly anything happened for several weeks after you got injured that time." She paused, considering this. "You want to call off going up there tonight?"

Carter flashed a teasing grin at her. "No. What's the matter? You afraid old Jonas Sutton's ghost might come floating in and scare you?"

He watched her bristle. "Don't be ridiculous. You know I don't believe in ghosts."

Carter laughed. "You were scared enough that time in the cemetery when I came floating in wearing a white sheet and moaning." He raised his arms and waved them dramatically.

She kicked at him in annoyance. "I was ten years old. And you tricked me into going to that cemetery so you could sneak up and scare me."

He laughed. "Son of a monkey, we had some good times growing up, didn't we? A whole wealth of wonderful moments."

Her eyes shuttered over unexpectedly. "I'll look for you about dark," she told him, starting out the back door of the porch. "You better go check on Taylor."

Carter reached to stop her, not liking her change of mood, but then hesitated. They were both tired. He needed to catch a nap, too, before tonight. They could talk later.

Chapter 17

Rhea heard Carter's footsteps on the roof as darkness fell over the valley.

"You're late," she said, opening the window to him.

He scowled. "I know. Taylor had some trouble getting to sleep."

"That doesn't surprise me." Rhea fastened on the waist pack she'd loaded earlier and tucked her flashlight into one of its side loops.

Eager to move on, Carter didn't climb in the bedroom. "Are you ready to go?"

"Yes." She climbed over the sill, pulled down the window, and followed him carefully across the roof to the tree.

Staying in the shadows, they cut through the trees behind Nana Dean's herb garden and started along the familiar trail snaking upward through the woods to Low Ridge. At the rock wall, they turned to follow the familiar grassy lane below Low Ridge to the Laymans' farm.

When they neared the turn to Rocky Prong Road, the gravel side road leading to Gold Mine Springs and the old Sutton place, Carter turned to put a hand on Rhea's arm. "Let's don't take the road to the cabin. Let's continue across the road and then swing right to cross the creek, climb up to Rocky Hillside through the woods, and come in behind the Sutton cabin."

"Good idea." Rhea nodded, following Carter as he headed up the path along the stream. "Do you think the vandal will really come back?"

"I don't know." Carter held out a hand to help Rhea over a fallen tree by the stream.

The darkness deepened, and Carter flicked on his flashlight.

A short time later, they crept cautiously toward

the back of the old Sutton place, squatting behind a rocky outcrop to survey the dark shape of the cabin. Night had fallen heavily now, but they could see the back of the log house in the moonlight.

"I don't see any light moving around," Rhea said after they watched for several minutes.

Nodding in agreement, Carter led them closer to look in the back window, two of its panes still cracked from Taylor's escape earlier. "There's no one here now." Carter brushed off the last of the glass fragments from the sill and pushed up the window. "Let's climb in here."

"Okay." Rhea followed Carter into the cabin.

They stood quietly, listening for several more minutes before Carter flicked on his flashlight. Rhea followed Carter around the room then, the two of them examining every inch of the cabin carefully, looking for anything the sheriff might have overlooked.

"I don't see anything unusual, do you?" Carter turned gradually around, fanning the light from the flashlight over the room again. "I guess we'll just go set up a little watch camp behind the rocks now. If our man comes back, we'll hear any movement or see any light from there."

Rhea nodded, her eyes moving over to the old bedstead, thinking of how Taylor had been wrapped in a quilt and tossed there earlier.

"Look, Carter." She put a hand on his arm.

"That bed's not exactly where it usually is. It looks like it's been shifted."

Carter followed her eyes. "It probably got pushed around with all the skirmish with Taylor."

"Let's move it and check underneath, just in case. All right?"

He stuck his flashlight into his jeans pocket and moved to one end of the iron bedstead to help Rhea push it away from the wall.

Rhea shone her own flashlight over the area where the bed stood before. "These floorboards look odd here. See?" She walked over to stand in the area where she could see more closely.

Carter, interested now, started over to join her. "You're right. It looks like one of the boards has been shifted." He stepped over to stand beside her to look down where her light shone.

And the floor fell in!

With a scream, Rhea heard the wood splinter and felt herself tumbling down with Carter into some long, dark dirt hole.

Carter hollered, too, and added a few expletives before the two of them quit rolling and tumbling and finally came to a stop, piled on top of each other in a heap, at the bottom of what appeared to be a deep tunnel.

"What the devil!" Carter groaned and pushed himself upright.

Rhea, lying halfway across him, winced and tried to sit up, too.

"Are you all right?" Carter rescued Rhea's flashlight from the dirt floor nearby and shone it on her.

"I think I'm okay." Rhea rubbed at her arm. "But I've scraped my arm, whacked my leg something fierce, and turned my ankle." She tried to move it. "Ouch." It hurt.

He ran the light down her ankle and pulled up her pants leg to check it. "There's no break. It looks okay." He moved her ankle carefully. "I think you just twisted it a little."

"What about you?" Her eyes moved over him anxiously. "Are you all right?"

"My pride's hurt." He chuckled. "And I've got some nice scrapes and bruises and a bump on my head. But I'll live."

He shone the light upward. "Look at that. We must have fallen twenty feet. You can see the remains of the floorboards above us."

Rhea looked upward. "Good heavens! It's a wonder we weren't seriously hurt falling that far." She looked around. "What is this place?"

"Obviously a tunnel." Carter shone the light along the dirt walls. "It drops down about twenty feet under the cabin and then heads eastward into a smaller passage. See?" He pointed ahead.

Snatching the other flashlight from Carter's pocket, she shone a light toward the smaller tunnel curiously. "Where do you think that passage goes?"

Carter shrugged, brushing dirt off his jeans from the tumble. "I don't know, but we'll need to find out." He looked up and frowned. "We can't climb out of this hole easily, so we'd better hope that passage leads to an outside entrance."

A trickle of fear crawled up Rhea's spine as she shone her light up the dark tunnel toward the broken remains of the cabin floor. "No one knows where we are, Carter, and we didn't bring cell phones with the reception so bad up here."

"Don't panic. Even if we're stuck here for a while, someone will come looking for us. That hole above would be hard to miss." He shone the light upward, moving it around the splintered opening. "Look. There's a trapdoor hanging down from the cabin floor." He pointed it out to her. "The two of us standing over the area must have been too much weight. We probably snapped the latch on the old trapdoor and then broke the floorboards through with no support beneath them any longer."

"Nice to know that now," Rhea groused.

Carter leaned over to examine Rhea, turning her arms over looking for cuts, rubbing a thumb over her face to remove a dirt streak. "You know, I realize now why there are remnants of an old ladder beside the house, grown over in ivy and kudzu. Grampa mentioned once it looked like a mighty long ladder for work on a small cabin like this."

Rhea stared at him. "You think old Jonas Sutton dug this tunnel under his cabin?"

"Well, I hate to mention it, but it's pretty creepy down here." Carter shone the light around. "Doesn't look like anyone's been here in a mighty long time."

Rhea shivered, pulling her arms in to hug herself. "You don't see any rats or spiders or anything, do you?"

"Not right off." He chuckled. "But I'd say there's some critters living in the area. We probably scared them off for now, falling down screaming like we did."

As if on cue, Rhea heard a scuffling in the small tunnel ahead of them. She wrinkled her nose. "I don't relish spending much time here."

"Me neither." Carter flashed his light into the tunnel. "We'd better see if this passage leads anywhere."

The small side tunnel led only about twelve feet to a rocky wall. From the light of their flashlights, Rhea and Carter could see quartz veins in the rock face and occasional minute flecks of gold. They also found a battered wooden box, covered with dirt, wrapped in a rusted chain and locked tight at the hasp.

The tunnel had narrowed as it progressed, and Carter and Rhea found it hard to stand upright at the wall. Squatting, Rhea looked up toward the ceiling. "I guess we're under Rocky

Hillside and not far from the mouth of the springs."

"Yeah." Carter followed her eyes around the passage. "And it looks like we've found old Jonas Sutton's gold stash."

"Maybe." Rhea studied the dirty box covered in spiderwebs and grime. "Do you think this is what the vandal has been looking for all this time, digging up first one place and then another around Laurel Springs?"

"Could be." Carter kicked at the box to judge its weight. "This box is heavy, obviously filled with something, but I doubt we can get into it without the proper tools to break the hasp and chain."

He looked around. "The bad news, Rhea, is that this old passage goes nowhere but right to this wall. Old Jonas must have been picking for gold bits in the rock, and came in to work through the cabin floor each time."

Fresh alarm seized Rhea. "Then we're trapped here." She hugged herself with a shiver.

"Might be for a time." Carter shone the flashlight back down the passage. "The ceiling is too low to stay here, Rhea. Let's go back to the bottom of the tunnel below the cabin. We'll be more visible there when help comes, and we'll be able to hear if anyone gets close, so we can call out."

They worked their way back through the low passage to the broader area below the cabin floor.

Carter spent some time examining the tunnel

wall with his flashlight, seeing if he could dig out toe-holds in the dirt to climb out on. Rhea soon saw his efforts weren't profiting.

She began to gather up the boards that had splintered from the cabin floor. "Let's put these together to make something to sit on, instead of having to sit in the dirt."

Giving up on the idea of climbing out, Carter helped Rhea put the boards together against one side of the tunnel. "We can sit and lean back here," he said, taking off his backpack and dropping it beside the boards.

Rhea unfastened her waist pack and settled down beside Carter in resignation. She looked at her watch. It was nearly eleven now.

"Mother and Nana thought I'd gone to bed early with a book. It's unlikely they'll check on me until morning when I don't come down for breakfast." She looked at Carter. "Did you tell your folks you'd gone to bed or out walking for a while?" She hoped the latter was true.

He touched her cheek. "They went to bed early, worn out from working in the yard transplanting bulbs and from all that happened with Taylor. I told them I was doing the same." He paused. "Unless Taylor wakes up with another nightmare, they won't know I'm gone until morning either."

"Oh, goody." She tried to make a joke but knew it fell short.

Carter turned his flashlight off. "We'll need to

conserve the batteries in our flashlights. For now, we'll keep one on."

Rhea saw a nasty scratch on Carter's arm and dug out wipes from her pack to clean it. They took turns then, checking each other for scratches and cuts, cleaning them as best they could and putting first-aid ointment on them from Rhea's tiny first-aid kit.

Finishing applying salve to a scratch on her cheek, Carter leaned over to kiss a spot below it. "I'm sorry this happened, Rhea."

She tucked the first-aid supplies back in her waist pack. "It wasn't your fault. Don't start trying to blame yourself because we're stranded here." She smiled at him. "Who knew old Jonas had a tunnel below his cabin? I can't believe we haven't discovered it in all these years."

Carter leaned back against the dirt wall. "He concealed it well under the floorboards. Probably the passing of time rotted the trapdoor underneath, and the extra weight of the two of us standing over that area on the floor caused everything to break through."

They dug out water for a drink and shared a package of crackers that Carter had tucked in his backpack.

Rhea looked in his bag and grinned. "You have a lot of snacks in here. At least we won't go hungry or thirsty."

"There is that." He leaned over and kissed her

nose. "It's nice to have your company, Rhea Dean—even in a bad situation."

She gave a disgusted snort. "Well, personally, I'd rather be home in bed."

He chuckled softly. "That sounds good, too."

Rhea kicked at him, overlooking the little frisson of awareness that raced through her at his implication.

"Do you think there might really be gold in that strongbox?" she asked, changing the subject.

"I don't know." Carter fished in his shirt pocket to pull out a small metal item. "Look at this." He placed it in her hand. "I found this on the floor when we were looking around the cabin, right before we started to move the bed. I meant to show it to you but then got distracted."

Rhea turned the item over in her hand. "It's a lapel pin of some type." Borrowing the flashlight, she studied it closely and then looked at Carter with a shocked expression.

"I know what this is. It's a Rotary pin." She pointed to the center of it. "See the wheel spokes in the middle? The wheel design symbolizes civilization and movement; it's been the Rotary symbol since the earliest days of its organization. I researched the club once for one of my newspaper articles."

Carter took the pin to study it. "What are these words here?" He held the flashlight closer.

Rhea leaned over to see. "They say *'Past*

254

President,' so probably whoever this belonged to was a . . ."

A chill rolled over her, and she stiffened, unable to finish her sentence.

"What is it, Rhea?" Carter asked quietly.

"I know whose pin this is."

Carter's eyes found hers.

She stared miserably at him. "It's Marshall Sutton's. I'm almost sure. He often wore it, even on casual jackets. He took a lot of pride in having been the last Rotary Club president."

"Sounds like Marshall," Carter muttered.

"Oh, Carter, do you think Marshall might be the vandal?"

His lip curled. "You know I wouldn't have any trouble believing it, although I won't blame any of it on a good organization like the Rotary."

Rhea chewed on her knuckles in thought. "But why?"

"I don't know. But I'd certainly like to get my hands on him if he was the one who scared my son like he did and hit me over the head with that stick." He practically spat the words.

She stared at Carter in the dark, dumfounded.

Carter fell silent for a short time and then began to speak slowly. "Let's think about this. Marshall Sutton is a great-grandson of Jonas Sutton's. If old family documents or letters existed, telling anything about Jonas's treasure, a blood relative would be the one most likely to find them." He paused. "I'd imagine if Marshall had discovered this sort of information, he'd view any treasure as his, no matter whose property the gold sat on now."

Rhea shivered, considering this.

Carter's eyes narrowed in thought. "One thing we know about Marshall for sure is that he likes money. He likes money and things. I can't imagine Marshall Sutton would feel especially generous about telling the Deans or the Laymans about a possible treasure hidden underground near one of their old houses or sheds."

Rhea caught her breath. "If an old document only revealed that money or gold lay buried some-where, but not exactly where, it would explain why Marshall, if he was the vandal, kept digging around cabins and buildings at Laurel Springs."

Her nerve endings came to full alert. "Carter, if any gold *is* in that strongbox, who would it belong to legally?"

"To Laurel Springs, in a broad sense and, in a more technical sense, to our families since they own the assembly grounds." He stretched his neck, stiff from the fall. "Jonas Sutton died too long ago for Marshall to be able to claim any of his property legally as inheritance. The land passed hands in sale long before Marshall was even born."

He turned the pin over in his hand thought-fully. "However, Marshall might have convinced him-self that any Sutton gold or money *ought* to be his by rights. Also, if he found it and didn't tell anyone—who would ever know? Most everyone around here thinks those old stories about Jonas Sutton finding gold are myth and legend. Marshall could claim he suddenly made a killing in the stock market and no one would be the wiser."

Rhea stared miserably at her clenched hands. "This is really hard to take in, Carter."

"I imagine." He snorted softly. "Did Marshall ever ask you questions about the Suttons or about the gold mining around here?"

She searched her memory. "We talked about it often when we first started dating. I'd written a column for the newspaper about the gold-mining days and another piece solely about Jonas Sutton and the old legend." Rhea paused.

"And?" Carter probed.

Rhea managed a wan smile. "And Marshall told me he hadn't heard much about Jonas before. He wanted me to tell him everything I knew, about all my sources, all the old books I researched. He said the whole story fascinated him."

"I'll bet it did," Carter murmured.

Rhea remembered Marshall's ardent interest and blushed in the darkness. She'd believed that interest was mainly in her.

A small silence descended.

"All right, you might as well say it." Rhea poked Carter in the ribs. "I know you're thinking it. This is the main reason Marshall made such a run on me. He wanted to soak me for information. He wanted more access to the grounds without it seeming suspicious he was here a lot. He also probably figured if we married, he'd have clearer access and title to any gold or treasure found. With my father deceased, and me the only child, he probably assumed he'd become a joint owner in Laurel Springs in time, too."

Carter considered this quietly before speaking. "Somehow, I can't see Marshall Sutton getting excited about fixing up Laurel Springs. I think he'd want to see his money go into something more personal and showy."

"You're being rather nice not to laugh about this." Rhea crossed her arms, her bottom lip pushing out in a pout. "If all this is true about Marshall, I've been a real idiot."

Carter leaned over and kissed her. "No. You always knew, as you told me, things weren't sizzling between the two of you. And you never agreed to marry Marshall."

Tears stung her eyes, and she sniffed once. "I might have considered it more seriously if you hadn't come back when you did. Being with Marshall seemed much worse after that."

"Oh, Rhea Dean," Carter said, burying his face in her neck and raining kisses over her shoulders, before finding her lips. "You shouldn't tell me things like that here in the dark."

She giggled and put her arms around his neck. "I see little risk, Carter Layman, in anything I might say down here. Surely you know I would *never* disrobe and fool around with a man—any man—in an icky, nasty dirt tunnel twenty feet below ground. No matter how attractive he was or how he made my blood sizzle. This place is gross."

Carter laughed, nuzzling her hair as if to test her theory. "You're not especially upset about Marshall, are you?"

"I don't like acknowledging that I'm such a bad judge of character, if Marshall is the vandal." She let her hands roam over Carter's arms and back, obviously enjoying his warmth in the gathering chill of the tunnel. "Can he be arrested for the things he's done?"

Carter nodded. "Trespassing. Vandalism. Destruction of private property. Assault. I don't know if he'll get much—if any—jail time, but the publicity won't be good. I doubt he'll stay in the area afterward as a banker if it is him. It would tarnish his reputation around here."

She bit her lip. "I guess I feel sort of sorry for him."

Carter spit out an expletive. "Pardon me if I don't join you in those sentiments. I spent most of the evening, before coming to get you, trying to get a frightened little boy settled down to sleep. He even said he was afraid of the quilt in his room. I had to take it out."

"Poor little guy." She shook her head and then shivered. "It's cold down here."

Carter pulled her around to tuck her between his legs, her back against his chest.

Rhea leaned against Carter's warmth gratefully.

"Let's try to sleep for an hour or two." He sighed. "It might be morning before anyone comes looking for us."

He wrapped his arms around her. "If it won't frighten you too much, I'm going to turn the flashlight off, to conserve the batteries."

Rhea hesitated, battling fear at the thought, but then sensibly agreed. "Let me hold one of the flashlights, Carter, so I can turn it on if I get scared or hear anything creepy—or if I feel something crawl on me. Okay?"

He put a flashlight into her hands.

Rhea doubted she could sleep, but as Carter rubbed her arms softly in the dark, she surprised herself and drifted away.

Chapter 18

Carter felt Rhea wake a few hours later. Her breathing quickened, and he heard a small moan escape as she realized where she was. He grinned. That last scuttering sound in the side passage probably disturbed her sleep.

"It was nothing," he whispered, feeling her shiver.

She sighed and stretched against him. "Did you sleep any?"

"Not much." He couldn't have slept if he'd tried. Rhea never considered the possibility that Marshall might return—but Carter had. He didn't relish what that encounter might bring.

They rearranged themselves to be more comfortable, but Rhea made no effort to pull out of his embrace. Instead, she curled up against his chest more tightly.

She shivered again and pulled her feet up as another scratching sound echoed in the dark. "I'm glad you're here with me. I'd be scared by myself."

He tucked his arms around her, glad of her company, too.

The quiet and dark stretched around them.

Carter lowered his voice. "I want to tell you about Judith."

He felt her tense. "Surely this situation is bad enough, without getting into that."

Carter ignored her. "This needs to happen, Rhea." He had her captive attention for once, and he planned to talk about this issue while he could.

"Do I get any choice in the matter?" Her voice sounded petulant.

His jaw clenched. "No, not really."

"That's democratic of you." She crossed her arms in irritation.

Carter ignored her, considering where to begin.

"I met Judith Morgan Benton when I went to Sunnyvale to interview for my scholarship with Cogswell Polytech. It was the time Quest flew me out as one of their final candidates for the work scholarship through the game design program."

Rhea muffled a small laugh. "You'd never been on a jet before, and I think you were more excited about flying across country than you were about the interview."

Glad she seemed ready to listen, Carter moved on. "Judith was a glamorous, poised, confident woman—and two years older than me. I felt like a real local-yokel boy with her, but she took an odd liking to me and actually helped me get favor with her father."

She interrupted. "You always stirred attraction in women that you didn't fully understand."

He passed over her remark, moving on with his story. "When I flew out to California to start college that first summer, Judith met me at the airport. She took me to the apartment I would share with Alvin Johnson, showed me around, and flirted with me. I couldn't help but notice it." He sighed. "She was the classic spoiled and pampered wealthy man's daughter, used to acquiring and manipulating everything to her advantage and used to getting what she wanted."

"And she wanted you." Rhea's voice floated softly into the darkness.

"Not really. She only toyed with me as a game —testing me, seeing if she could attract me, playing with me as entertainment. I knew she had no real interest in me." He took a deep breath. "I intrigued her for a while, probably because I wasn't interested in her."

Carter shifted his position, moving his legs, which felt numb from sitting on the floor so long. "I started school at Polytech and Judith went back to design school over in LA. She came home frequently. Because I worked in the Quest offices and spent many evenings at the Benton home going over development projects with her father, I saw Judith often."

He paused, trying to decide what to say. "Judith and I developed a friendship over time. I never acted enamored with her and I didn't fawn over her like most boys and men. She told me that once. I was totally in love with someone else and in time Judith accepted that. I often told her about you and about Laurel Springs."

Rhea sucked in a surprised breath.

"It's true, Rhea. Judith knew all about you. Homesick for you and for Laurel Springs, I talked about all I loved and missed. I spilled my heart about my dreams to fix up Laurel Springs and restore it to its old glory. In time, Judith let down her hair with me, too. She played roles so often in her life, acting some prescribed part appropriate for the situation, that she enjoyed having someone she could behave more naturally with. She said she could be more herself with me." He laughed. "I wasn't one of her fancy friends, just a plain ole country boy."

A small quiet settled between them.

Rhea relaxed slightly. "What was she like?"

Carter shrugged. "You saw her picture—a tall beauty with olive skin, dark auburn hair, brown eyes. Men chased after her and she dominated them, and most women of her acquaintance. Like her father, Judith exuded power, had a strong personality and that natural poise, confidence, and sophistication so often found in the ultrawealthy. Judith knew how to move and act with grace but possessed a savvy, smart head for business, too. She always stayed cool under pressure and she had manipulation down to an art form."

He paused. "She wasn't a Christian woman, in the sense we think of it, and she didn't have a humble bone in her body."

Carter sighed. "I didn't always like Judith. In fact, I often felt sorry for her, which seemed to annoy her. She thought she had everything but she lacked so many of the inner traits that make a person truly beautiful."

He pictured Judith in his mind as he tried to explain. "Judith used people, Rhea, and thought nothing of it. She discarded suitors and friends, like out-of-season clothing she tired of. She spent lavishly and frivolously. Although extremely gifted and talented, all her actions and goals were self-centered. I can never recall a time, in those early years, that she put another person ahead of herself. She took from people, Rhea, but gave little in return except in a broad philanthropic sense to enhance her image and give her recognition."

He felt Rhea shift in his arms, moving to get more comfortable.

"It doesn't sound like you admired Judith much," she said. "Why did you marry her?"

Carter tried to think how to explain. "At the end of that first summer after freshman year, I suffered with a bad case of disillusion and disappointment. You'd promised all year to come to California and kept postponing."

He heard Rhea blow out an exasperated breath. "That time wasn't easy for me either, Carter. Dad kept taking turns for the worse in his recovery, developing other health issues, and then he died in the summer."

The words pricked his temper. "We see that time differently, Rhea. We talked about this once before. Remember? I felt you didn't truly love me enough to come, that you put other things ahead of me."

He put a hand over her mouth when she started to interrupt again. "Let me tell this."

"Fine." She practically spit out the answer.

"Judith moved back home that winter of my

sophomore year, dropped out of school because of her health. She and her father thought she had mono at first. She tired easily, exhibited weakness, sometimes tripped and fell. Judith exhibited an odd set of symptoms." He stopped to collect his thoughts.

"At loose ends, missing her friends, and often bored, Judith worked in the Quest office during this time. Helped out with the business. My best friend Alvin, and most of my school friends, went home for spring break and I found myself lonely and sometimes bored, too. Judith and I talked more. We started hanging out together. Shared lunch, went to the beach."

Rhea snorted. "Sounds cozy."

"It wasn't. I whined about you and felt sorry for myself. Judith and I commiserated with each other about our frustrations."

"Are you ever going to get to the point, Carter? This story is dragging out more than it needs to."

His irritation kindled. "Fine. Here's the long and short of it. Judith had gone in for a doctor visit after yet another test, trying to see why she wasn't bouncing back to health. She learned she had ALS, Lou Gehrig's disease. I didn't know that then, but she told me later before we married that it put her life in fast-forward—changed all her goals. People who get ALS usually die in three to six years. Suddenly, Judith wanted a child, a chance to experience marriage. She knew she didn't have time to wait for the perfect mate to come along. Her window to bear a child was short, and risky, before the disease progressed."

He stopped, reluctant to tell the next part.

"Go on. It's obvious to me that Judith saw you as handy and available for her fast-forward plans."

Carter gave a disgusted snort. "She showed up and brought me dinner and got me drunk."

"What do you mean she got you drunk?" She swiveled to look up at him in the darkness.

"She brought all these fancy mixers, tonics, and liquor. Whipped up drinks all evening for us to try." He looked away from her even in the darkness. "They must have been stronger than I realized. I woke up the next day not even remembering what happened but finding Judith in my bed. She just laughed and patted my cheek and acted like it was funny."

He ran his hand through his hair. "She didn't own up to me about what she'd done until much later. Then she admitted she'd mixed my drinks heavy to get me drunk, knowing I didn't have much experience with alcohol. She'd timed our interlude perfectly, too, to her most fertile window, and found some herbs and meds to increase her chances for conceiving. She admitted she'd have done it again if she needed to. But it didn't prove necessary."

"Wow." Rhea whistled. "That was rotten of her but it was pretty stupid of you, too."

Carter shifted in annoyance. "Don't think I didn't tell myself that more times than I want to recall. I was naïve and stupid about a lot of things, coming from our little rural neck of the woods."

A small rustling noise close by caused Rhea to jump to her feet and flick on her flashlight. "I hate this creepy place." She shone the light around carefully, moving and stretching while she scanned the dirt passage with her light.

Carter stood, too, while he had the chance, his legs stiff from the long time against the wall holding Rhea. The light, dispelling the heavy darkness around them, embarrassed Carter, and he turned his face away from Rhea when her curious glance sought his. He hated the pitying look he saw in her eyes.

She flicked off her flashlight finally, satisfied the area checked out safe, and pulled him down to the boards to sit again.

Rhea tucked herself up against his side. "Tell me the rest, Carter."

"I don't want you feeling sorry for me." He stiffened beside her.

She kicked at him. "If you'd prefer insults and nasty digs, I can come up with a few."

He laughed despite himself. "That you can."

"So?" She urged him on.

Carter let his thoughts drift back in time again.

"I felt shocked, and scared, when Judith told me she was pregnant. It didn't seem real."

He ran his hands through his hair. "Judith acted thrilled, which didn't make sense to me. I knew her future plans. She wanted to finish school, further establish and grow the fledgling design business she'd started, make her mark as a businesswoman in her own right. She often flippantly told me marriage could wait until later. I'd heard her brag that she'd marry a business magnate one day to increase the family fortunes."

Carter sighed deeply. "It took a while for all the truth to come out. All my future was on the line here—my scholarship with the school through Judith's father's company, my work with Quest, my relationship with you, my entire future if I married Judith to be a father to my child." He managed a rough laugh. "Dad and Grampa taught me a man rated worse than a scoundrel who got a girl pregnant and then wouldn't do right by her, marry her, and be a good father to his child."

"When did you learn she'd tricked you—gotten you drunk on purpose?"

He gave a disgusted snort. "Later, just before school ended and before I'd planned to come home to Laurel Springs for the summer. She and her father had a conference with me in Morgan Benton's paneled study. Judith told me about her ALS diagnosis and why she'd gotten me drunk to get pregnant. She laid it out as though she'd been thinking of both of us in initiating this plan. As she explained it, we could marry, she could birth a child and heir to the Benton fortune, and I could become a full partner in Quest and Benton Electronics. The child's future would be assured . . . and, even though we didn't love each other, we were friends, she insisted. She flippantly said you didn't deserve me, after not caring enough to come join me in California. As Judith put it, you deserved to lose me."

Rhea gasped. "The nerve!"

"Judith was never short on nerve, Rhea." He paused. "I remember her draping herself over the arm of her father's chair, crying and telling me that if I still wanted to marry you later, I could. She told me specifically how long the doctors said she would live."

Carter clenched his fists, remembering his frustration at the time. "Judith's father's coldly laid out my financial gain options in participating in Judith's plans. He also clearly told me that refusing to marry Judith would end my scholarship, my career at Quest, and assure me of never getting to see or know my child."

"Would he have done that?"

His anger surged remembering that time. "Absolutely and without a moment's regret. All he wanted was Judith's happiness, for her to have everything she wanted before he lost her. To my favor, Morgan liked me; he said he didn't mind having me for a son-in-law. He told Judith he thought I could be groomed and trained to be a credit to Quest and the Benton name. The two of them sat there and talked about me like I was a commodity. As though I should be grateful they decided to select me."

"Gracious heaven." He heard her swallow in the dark.

"That's pretty much it, Rhea. I could have said no. But I'd have never seen or known my son. You don't fight someone like Morgan Benton. In shock, I told them both I'd think about it." He picked up a stick on the floor to twist it in his hands. "When I went back to agree to their terms, I had demands of my own. I insisted on having everything drawn up by an attorney and signed. When you play ball with people like the Bentons, you make sure you protect yourself very well."

Rhea fell quiet for a space. "What does Mr. Benton think of you being back here now?"

"It was in my agreement that I could come back here after Judith died, bring my child, and that Morgan wouldn't fight me or oppose me." Carter reached over to touch Rhea's face. "I never stopped loving you. I never gave up on our dream. Perhaps you'll still hate me for giving in to Judith and Morgan—feel I should have walked away from them and from my son. It was for my child I stayed. As soon as I held him, I never regretted that decision."

In the shadowy darkness, he saw Rhea pull her knees up and wrap her arms around them, thinking. "I probably misjudged you somewhat in the past, maybe a lot, but this still isn't easy for me. Even knowing everything now." She punched him with a fist. "I'm mad, too, that you didn't call—or write—and tell me this when it happened."

He winced. "I didn't think you'd believe me. It sounds like a soap opera drama. We weren't on the best of terms at that time, and I just didn't think you'd believe me." Carter hesitated. "In all honesty, I was angry at you, too."

"Why?" She turned to him in surprise.

Gathering his courage, he said, "Because I blamed you in part for what happened."

"Me?" She was incredulous.

"Yes." He spoke softly. "I felt that if you'd come to California before Judith came home that she'd never have gone after me. She'd have found someone else to help her fast-forward her dreams, to be the father of the child she so desperately wanted. I felt victimized on both sides."

"Ouch—that's too candid and tends to forget your accommodating role in all this drama, too." She leaned back and wrapped her arms around herself, as if chilled.

Carter sagged against the tunnel wall in relief, glad to finally have all this off his chest. To finally see it laid out in the open.

Rhea spoke at last. "Do your parents know this? And your Grampa?"

He shook his head. "No. Although I think all of them added up the months to Taylor's birth and had some suspicions as to why I married suddenly, to Judith and not to you. I believe it shamed them, and so they never really asked me any questions. As Grampa said once, 'What was done was done.' "

"I see." She considered this. "Will you tell them now?"

"I don't know. Maybe someday." He turned to look toward her, glad the darkness hid the moment. "I guess I wanted to see how you reacted first. Wanted to see if you'd even believe me."

Her mouth quirked in a small smile. He could see it even in the dark. "I believe you, Carter Layman. Even you, with your incredible, highly versatile imagination could *never* think up a whopper like this. Besides, Judith dying lends credibility to the story. As does Taylor."

Carter leaned over to kiss her. "Thanks for believing, Rhea."

"Hmmm. I guess this explains why there were so few society pictures of you and Judith, why she still went so many places on her own, even after you married."

Carter sighed. "Judith tried to do a lot of living in a very short time, even after we married. I made an effort to be a good husband, even under the circumstances, but I stopped sleeping with Judith when she began to run around on me. She enjoyed a number of lovers before her pregnancy showed, and after Taylor came and she recovered her figure, she sowed more wild oats until her disease progressed. She frantically tried to hold on to life for as long as she could. To do and experience as much as possible. I don't say I condoned her actions during that time, but knowing Judith as I did, I understood them."

He spread his hands. "In some ways, I think Judith's actions made it easier. She didn't expect me to pretend things were different than they were. We returned to being friends and grew closer later on, especially after Judith became more tied to home. She had to become resigned to diminishing health at that point and to diminishing abilities in all areas."

"Was Judith a good mother?"

"As good as she could be, I suppose. Mothering was always more about Judith than Taylor, but she loved Taylor in her own way. Probably too fiercely sometimes, knowing she wouldn't see him grow up. She worried he wouldn't remember her. She hated it when she started being really sick, when she couldn't pick Taylor up or play with him anymore. And Judith despised anyone seeing her sick. Her deteriorating emotional and physical condition was difficult for her and for Taylor. She had good days and bad, and Taylor saw more sorrow and suffering than a small child ever needs to see—especially during the last years of Judith's life."

"Why did you all live at the Benton estate?" Rhea's tone sounded curious.

"Why not?" Carter shrugged. "Ours wasn't a normal marriage and her father wanted every minute possible with his daughter. He tried every doctor and every treatment, struggling to save Judith, but even wealth can't stop death sometimes."

He pulled his knees up to change his position. "The Benton estate was big enough for four families. Judith and I had our own wing, like our own house, with privacy enough when we wanted it. Judith didn't cook or clean. She threw her clothes on the floor after wearing them like a child might, knowing they'd be picked up and put away. The Bentons' servants had cared for Judith since she was a small girl. They understood her and ministered to her with a love she hardly deserved when her illness wasted her physically and emotionally. They truly loved Taylor, too, and he needed people like that in his life. I'm grateful to Martha and Pickett for all they did for Taylor and Judith through a long, difficult time."

"Taylor showed me a picture of the new home you bought after Judith died." Carter could feel the wheels in Rhea's mind turning. "I wondered about that."

"It was time for a change. I wanted Taylor and I to build a new life, get out of the Benton mansion, out from under Morgan's heavy grief and away from his control. We needed a place to heal on our own."

He put a hand over to find Rhea's. "I bought a pleasant, livable house I thought you would like, Rhea. As Alvin once said, you could go there knowing Judith never crossed the threshold. Knowing I never lived in that house with her."

Carter heard Rhea catch her breath. "You think I would go to California with you? Leave Laurel Springs?"

"No." He squeezed her hand. "Go there with me sometimes. During the slow seasons at Laurel Springs. When we wanted to fly out for pleasure or a break or when I had business in California."

She didn't say anything.

"You'd like it there. It's beautiful. The ocean and a big park are near the house." He couldn't read her thoughts, so he kept talking. "You've never traveled, Rhea. We can travel together, see new places together, have adventures. I'm a very wealthy man. You won't want for anything."

"That's Morgan Benton's money." She spit out the words venomously.

"Wrong." Carter snapped the word out and turned to grab her by the shoulders. "I earned my own money through all this, Rhea Dean. I did receive some inheritance through Judith and I may inherit through Morgan one day, in trust for Taylor, but I did fine work at Quest. I raised the company to a new level, designed games for Quest that put it on the map in a way it never was before. I made Quest a big player in the game industry, won awards for the company through my game designs, moved it into the big leagues with my *Traveler* games—in sales volume and with the comics and animated movies being created about its characters."

He pulled away from her, anger simmering in his veins. "I may have been bought in one way—but I made the best of a bad situation. I came into my own. I grew through difficulties. I worked hard. I didn't allow myself to grow bitter or to give up my own dreams."

Carter stood up, flicking on his flashlight so he could pace in the small space. "Don't diminish me to only a bought man. I have known my own hardships in these years—but I have not let them destroy me."

"I suppose you could have." Her voice drifted softly through the darkness to reach him. "It would have been easy to have given up or to have become bitter or hard."

She pushed herself to her feet, wincing over her sore ankle and stiff joints from the long time on the dirt floor.

Her temper flared. "Sheesh, I hate it in here. I

have a new respect for all Thumbelina endured trapped in that mole's tunnel for so long."

Carter laughed despite himself, remembering the childhood fairy tale. "Well, at least Marshall hasn't shown up tonight." He glanced at his watch. "We can thank our blessings for that."

Rhea froze in place. "Oh my gosh, Carter. With all that's happened, I never considered that he might come back while we were trapped down here."

She looked toward the hole high above them apprehensively.

Carter walked over to put an arm around her. "It's nearly four in the morning. I think there's little chance any vandal will make an appearance at this hour. I had concerns earlier but not now."

She leaned into him. "I hate to bring this up, but I have to go to the bathroom. Will you hold the light for me in the side passage and close your eyes and not look?"

"Sure." He chuckled. "If you'll do the same for me."

They attended to their needs and then settled back down on the boards to dig through Carter's backpack for more snacks.

Chapter 19

Rhea studied Carter in the dim light from the flashlight they'd propped between them. "I feel like I know you better now, Carter. And before this I thought I knew you better than anyone in the world did."

"Oh, yeah?" He popped a handful of cheese curls into his mouth.

"Yeah." She punched him with a fist playfully, wanting to lighten up the intensity of this time.

Rhea rubbed her neck as she finished off a box of raisins. "I'm sore all over." She looked up at the sloping tunnel above them. "If that tunnel dropped straight down, versus having a little slant to it that caught our falls, we'd probably both have broken something."

"Probably." Carter rustled in his backpack for something else to eat.

Both settled back against the wall after finishing off their raisins and cheese curls. Rhea gratefully let Carter wrap his arm around her again. The chill underground seemed to have stolen into her bones.

Exhausted, they nodded in sleep for a short time.

Eventually, Carter's voice broke the quiet. "Rhea, why didn't you come to California that summer? I know your father died—but I always felt there was something else. . . ." His voice trailed off.

The night hours and the darkness seemed to encourage a candor not possible in the day.

Rhea searched her heart. Carter had shared honestly with her, and he deserved the same back. "Maybe I felt a little jealous."

He jerked in surprise. "Of Judith?"

"No." She felt reluctant to admit the next words. "Of your success. You went to California, got that wonderful scholarship and then, in your first year, the company put your game design straight into production. You stayed that summer to oversee it. I understood why you couldn't come home. You told me that. But you were already on your way, Carter, and I hadn't even started."

He hugged her closer. "But you won your own scholarship at San José University in the Hospitality, Tourism and Event Management program. Remember? You said you wanted to learn how to bring Laurel Springs into the big time. . . ."

She sighed. "I really just wanted to go where you were going. You had to leave Cosby to achieve your dreams in game development. I knew that. My dreams to go to California were 'hitch on' dreams."

She felt him tense, but she continued before she lost her nerve. "In a deep part of me, I didn't want to go. San José is a big city—near

Sunnyvale, of course, which is smaller—but we wouldn't have been right next door anymore, like here at Laurel Springs. I would have been on my own. No major fields of study suited to me existed at Cogswell Polytech. You know that, so I couldn't go to the same school with you. Live in the same town."

"But you said the major at San José was perfect for you. . . ."

Rhea interrupted. "No, Carter, *you* said that. You found the school near yours and researched the academic majors. You researched the available scholarships. You planned everything. I just went along."

"That's not true. . . ."

Rhea put a hand over Carter's mouth now. "Let me try to say this. Please?"

She swallowed the lump in her throat. "You were always such a strong person. I sometimes felt I floated along in your wake."

He snorted.

"It's true. Jeannie was strong, too—popular, outgoing, well liked, and involved in everything in high school. I floated along after her, too, into her circle of friends, into cheerleading, which I never liked. I drifted along on your arm, absorbing your popularity, admired for being linked to you, in the same way I was favored for being Jeannie's friend. And then there was Billy Wade, the star receiver on the football team, also popular. All three of you knew exactly who you were and where you were going." She hesitated. "Sometimes I felt invisible."

Carter shook his head. "Rhea Kaden Dean, you are one of the strongest people I know. You are now and you were then. How could you not have seen that about yourself?"

"I don't know." She shrugged. "When my father got sick, I had to step up and take his place. I felt scared at first, but then I liked those new roles . . . taking on Daddy's administrative and planning tasks, leading the tours, running many aspects of Laurel Springs. I liked the power and responsibility."

He blew out a deep breath.

"To keep from falling behind in college, I went to Walters State Community College with Jeannie and Billy Wade. I found aspects of myself at the college there that I liked, too. I loved the business program and courses." She paused. "Then in a journalism elective, I discovered a whole new aspect of myself. I wrote a newspaper column for a course assignment and the paper asked me to continue to write more."

"You never even told me about that."

"I know." Her voice dropped. "I was afraid you'd pick up on how much I loved doing it and realize how much I didn't want to let it go." She clenched a fist. "It may not seem like a lot compared to your nationally known video games . . . but it was mine, Carter. My personal thing, my own accomplishment, and it mattered to me. I loved the column. I knew moving to California would mean giving up everything I'd begun to value that year, the column, my new roles at Laurel Springs, my sense of individuality, and my feeling of being my own person at last. I would have gone back to being a follower."

He took his arm from around her shoulder and stood up, trying to find space to pace out his frustration. "I always sensed there was something," he said at last. "Why didn't you tell me?"

She crossed her arms against her waist, searching for an answer. "I didn't think you'd understand. You wanted me to come, and I knew you were angry because I hadn't come already. But the more time slipped by, the more I didn't want to go, even though I loved you. California seemed more and more like your world, and this little corner of the Smoky Mountains, and Laurel Springs, seemed more and more like my world. Where I belonged."

He pushed a hand through his hair in irritation. "Dash it, Rhea, you should have told me. I would have understood."

"Would you have understood?" She stood up to move closer to him, picking up the flashlight to guide her way. "Can you look at me—right here, right now—and tell me you would have truly understood?"

His dark eyes met hers and then slipped away. "All right." He kicked at a scrap of board on the dirt floor. "I admit it. I would have tried to talk you into coming anyway. It's what I wanted. I would have tried to plan and figure a way for you to write a column in California, work at a resort around the San José area. I wanted you with me. And I would have reminded you that we would have come back here eventually."

"I know." She leaned her head against his shoulder.

He brushed a clump of dirt off his jeans. "So you only *told* me you didn't come because of your father dying. You thought I'd understand that you needed to stay for that reason."

"It wasn't a lie. Daddy asked me to stay, and Mother and Nana really did need me. Even Laurel Springs needed me, Carter, especially with you gone. Someone needed to stay here to fight for the dream."

She felt a touch of her old anger rise. "You worked hard in California, but I worked hard here. Many times I despaired that we could keep this place afloat. The need for repairs grew and grew. Often unexpected bills arose, frightening all of us until we found ways to earn extra money to pay them off. Staff had to be let go, and all of us picked up extra work tasks to add to our own. It wasn't a lie that I needed to stay here, to fight to see Laurel Springs survive. But I wanted to be honest tonight and say that other things influenced my staying, too."

A muscle in his jaw bunched, but he pulled her into his arms, holding her against him. "We thought we knew everything about each other, but we didn't, did we?" He put his hands on her face. "I wish we'd opened our hearts to each other more in the past."

She shrugged. "We were kids. We didn't always know or understand ourselves in those years. How could we explain what we were still figuring out?"

He smiled at her. "Perhaps you're right. But one thing I've always known is that I love you, Rhea. I always have and I always will. No matter what else has happened. No matter what else happens in the future."

Carter traced his fingers over her lips, and his smile twitched with a wicked touch of pleasure as a kick of awareness sparked between them. He lowered his mouth to cover hers, and Rhea plummeted head over heels into the moment, forgetting the dirt, the filth, and the spiders around her. Aware only of the beating of her heart and the feel of Carter tight against her.

She heard herself utter a small crooning sound as Carter deepened their kiss and wrapped her body tighter against him. His hands roamed over her, sending sparks through her nerve endings in every place he touched.

Carter barely suppressed a groan as he rained soft kisses near her ear. "Marry me, Rhea Dean," he whispered. "No matter what has happened between us, we belong together. Surely you feel it—and know it in your heart?" His mouth covered hers again.

Dizzy with desire, Rhea wondered why she couldn't say yes immediately. She knew her body cried yes within her. Why did she hesitate?

Suddenly, sharp voices from above interrupted the moment.

"Carter?" Rhea heard Grampa Layman's strong preacher's voice. "Are you here, boy?"

Carter pulled back with reluctance. "Yes, Grampa. Down here."

Rhea heard Jinx barking with excitement from overhead.

"Is Rhea there with you?" Carter's father's voice filtered down from the cabin floor above now.

"She's here. We're both safe and well, just tired and worn out." He walked over to stand below the opening above them. The lights of his father and grandfather's flashlights flicked over him—and then over Rhea.

Grampa Layman's voice sounded again. "Good Lord, what's happened here?"

Carter sighed. "We'll explain everything when you get us out! Go get some strong rope, or better, an extension ladder. Load it up in the truck. We're both pretty sore and worn out from the fall. Rhea, especially, would find it easier to climb out of this hole on a ladder rather than to have to pull up on a rope."

"I'll head that way right now," Wes Layman confirmed.

Rhea heard his footsteps pace swiftly across the cabin floor.

The dog barked eagerly once more, scratching around the edge of the opening above.

"It's all right, Jinx," Carter called to him.

"You've got a good dog here," Grampa said. Rhea saw him pet the big dog's head with fondness. "He's got a real sense when someone's in trouble. Woke us up about four in the morning, scratching and whining. Our guess is he went in your room and found you missing about that time."

The next hours until morning went by in a flurry. Wes came back with the ladder. Carter and Rhea climbed out, and all of them rode back to the Laymans' place. Then the sheriff was called again.

Rhea felt worn out from the long, tense night and from the extensive explanations that ensued after their rescue. Even more discussion occurred after the rescue of the strongbox from the underground tunnel.

Rock chunks threaded with veins of gold filled the box, but the value of the stash didn't appear to be great. The best finds in the strongbox were a few gemstones, probably mined out of Jonas Sutton's time working in North Carolina.

"Marshall will be disappointed he risked so much for so little," Carter said to Rhea as he drove her home later.

Both of them were stiff and filthy from their night in the tunnel. Wes offered to drive Rhea home, but Carter had insisted he would take her.

Rhea, quiet on their ride, dreaded the battery of questions awaiting her from her mother and Nana Dean. Neither knew she'd been gone until Rhea called them at 5:00 a.m.

Carter stopped the car along the circle driveway before they neared the Deans' farmhouse. He turned off the motor and let his eyes wander over Rhea, a slow smile spreading across his face.

A nervous flick of apprehension moved through her. "I look a sight, don't I?" She'd caught a glimpse of herself earlier in the Laymans' bathroom mirror. "I don't think I ever looked forward more to a hot bath."

He put a hand to her cheek, not willing to let her avoid the subject she feared he wanted to discuss again. "You didn't answer my question I asked you before our rescue team arrived." He traced a finger down her cheek. "Will you say yes? Will you let me love you forever—be in my life and my heart for always? I promise I will cherish you."

She hesitated, dropping her eyes, but not before she saw disappointment flash across Carter's face.

"You're still hesitating, Rhea? Even after tonight and all our confessions?"

She crossed her arms defensively. "It's a lot to take in. And we're both tired. Can't we talk about this more some other time?"

His eyes grew hard. "I don't think so. I need to know what's in your heart."

Feeling pressured, Rhea felt her anger start to rise. "I don't know what's in my heart." She knew her voice sounded testy. "A lot of mixed feelings. I could say I love you, and I would mean it. I've always loved you, Carter. Surely you know that?" Her words rushed on. "I could say I forgive you—for everything that's happened, for all the years, for all the time lost. But I'd be lying to say I can simply put everything behind me, even after learning Judith Benton used trickery to induce you to marry her."

She gave him a stubborn look. "Despite her getting you drunk, you *were* spending time with her. Going to the beach with her, sharing meals together. Knowing she desired you and found you attractive. Risking fate."

Rhea pushed at him with her hand in annoyance. "You did that, Carter Layman. You risked fate by spending intimate time with a woman like Judith. You said yourself you knew what she was like."

She hugged her arms around herself. "I wasn't cheating on you here. I *never* dated anyone else while you were gone, *never* spent time with another man alone. Even if I wasn't sure I wanted to come to California, I was sure I loved you. I believed you would come back to me."

When he tried to interrupt her, she rushed her words on. "I believed our dream would bring you back."

"It did, Rhea." He studied her calmly now, trying to understand. "People can't go back and erase the past, but they can go on. Move past hurts and disappointments. Find new happiness, a new future."

She spit out her next words before thinking. "Well, I'm not sure I can just forgive and forget. I think Judith Benton will *always* be there between us. I don't think I can ever forget that."

Carter's eyes grew hard and filled with pain now. "You're saying you won't marry me because of Judith, because of Taylor, and because you refuse to forgive me for what happened in the past. Even when you know everything now?"

Rhea hated the wounded look she saw in his eyes.

"I want to move on, but I don't know if I can right now." She twisted her hands in her lap. "Maybe I just need more time to digest all of this."

"No." His voice sounded cold. "I think you know exactly what you want, just like you did when you wouldn't come to California with me. To love aright, you have to be willing to give, often more than you receive, and to forgive time and time again. I learned that well with Judith. In the end, I loved her in my own way. I'm not ashamed to admit that. She was my wife; she was my son's mother. We lived together six years. I watched her live; I watched her die."

He turned to look out the car window. "I had another life these last nine years after I went to California. I can't change that. But I wanted the rest of my life to be with you, Rhea." He blew out a deep breath. "I'm sorry you don't want that, too."

"Carter . . ." she began.

He turned his eyes to her, but then Rhea didn't know what to say.

Carter shook his head in resignation. "I've lived with disappointment before. I can live with it again." He reached over to open the car door for her. "I won't die because you said no to me. And I hope you find whatever it is you're looking for."

She got out of the car, wishing she had some words to say to make the moment better. It didn't surprise her that Carter didn't call out his usual warm good-bye as he drove away.

Chapter 20

The weeks after the night spent in Jonas Sutton's secret tunnel dragged by laboriously for Carter. Every day he hoped Rhea would come to him, saying she'd changed her mind about the stand she'd made refusing his marriage proposal.

While angry that night, she'd told him, *Maybe I just need more time.* Carter stayed hopeful for weeks, remembering those words. Now summer, and the heavy tourist season at Laurel Springs, neared its end, and reality reared its ugly head.

"I've lost her," he said out loud as he walked through the covered bridge heading to Billy Wade's house. They met regularly on Billy's porch every Monday morning to discuss the progress on Laurel Springs and the new house.

Carter reached down to pet Jinx, whose ears had pricked at the sound of his voice. "I've done everything I can, Jinx, but I've lost her."

Carter thought about dropping a penny through the cracks in the old bridge to make a wish that things could be different. But how could it help? He was beyond wishing and hoping.

Crossing the Camp Roads intersection, Carter saw Billy propped back in a cane chair on the front porch of the caretaker's house—his and Jeannie's home—waiting for him. A colorful fish-shaped windsock fluttered around its pole in the morning breeze.

"Nice flag," Carter said, walking up on the porch.

Billy looked up from the pile of paperwork on his lap to grin. "Jeannie bought it on the weekend. Puts up a new one every month it seems."

Carter nodded, taking a seat and pouring out a cup of coffee from the battered carafe on a metal table. "I like this one better than the butterflies."

Billy snickered. "There's some of Estelle's fried pies in that box there, Carter. And some napkins underneath."

"You're a good man, Billy Wade Ledford." Carter grinned as he opened the pastry box. "I'll miss these Monday morning treats in the future."

Billy glanced up in surprise. "Going back to California for a week or two again?"

Carter sat back in his chair, finishing a large bite of peach pie before he answered. "I'm going back to stay. It's time for school and a good time for Taylor to make the move."

Rattled, Billy dropped the papers in a heap on the glider beside him. He leaned toward Carter, his eyes full of questions. "Having second thoughts about the country life? I thought you and Taylor both liked it here."

Billy watched him closely when Carter didn't quickly respond. "What does Taylor think about this?"

Carter hunched his shoulders. "I haven't told him yet." He forced the unsettling thought from his mind. "But he's only a kid; he'll adjust."

"I see." Carter felt Billy's gaze bore into him. "What's all this about, Carter?"

He took a few more bites of Estelle's fried pie, washing it down with coffee afterward. "It's hard keeping on top of all the work with Quest from here. I need to be in California more.

Benton's having a hard time; I'm a key player in the company and a partner."

Carter licked the last bites of pie off his fingers. "The renovations are nearly finished now. I can come back and forth to Laurel Springs to check on what few improvements need to be completed."

Billy sat quietly watching him.

Trying a smile, Carter added, "You've done a great job with everything, Billy. I'm grateful."

"This is about Rhea, isn't it?" Billy Wade frowned.

Uncomfortable now, Carter got up to stand, looking out over the front lawn. A late patch of black-eyed Susans waved sunny petals in the light breeze, and a hummingbird flitted in and out among the clusters of orange trumpet vine spilling over the split-rail fence.

"I'll miss it here." Carter reached out a hand to trace it down the windsock.

"Dadgumit." Billy Wade kicked over a small stool in annoyance. "Anyone can see that you and Rhea still have a thing for each other. Can't you get her to see it, too?"

Carter slumped into the chair beside Billy's. "I've tried all summer. Even asked her to marry me, and she turned me down. Said she can't forget I got involved with and married someone else." He dropped his hands between his knees dejectedly. "I can't stand to live around her, loving her and wanting her the way I do. It will be better for both of us if I'm in California most of the time."

"What about Taylor? He's crazy about Rhea, and he loves it here."

"I know." Carter ran a hand through his hair. "But lately, Rhea has started avoiding Taylor, too. He's starting to pick up on the vibes that all isn't well. We both know Taylor's known too much unhappiness in the last few years to endure more, Billy."

"Dang stubborn woman." Billy crossed his arms in annoyance. "Did you tell her all that happened out in California? Why you married Judith?"

"She was the first I told, down in the tunnel the night we got trapped at the Sutton cabin, before I told you and Jeannie and my folks." Carter blew out a breath. "Learning what happened didn't resolve things with Rhea. She claimed I courted trouble spending time with Judith at all."

"Well, we ain't none of us saints." Billy drank down the last of his coffee. "She was right stupid herself running around with Marshall Sutton all those months she did, not discerning what he was like."

"Perhaps." A faint smile flickered over Carter's face. "I guess that rival is out of commission."

Billy snorted. "It still makes me mad his slick lawyer got him off. Even when the sheriff found more evidence in Marshall's townhouse to finger him, he didn't even get an indictment. His lawyer claimed no proof existed he attacked you or Taylor. Of course, the sly dog wouldn't admit it either." Billy flexed his fingers in annoyance. "All Marshall got were a few fines and monetary damage payments for trespassing and vandalism. The man isn't even leaving the area, just transferred himself to the other bank his family runs over in Newport. He even got some folks convinced he had a right to look for what his kin left behind."

Carter shook his head. "There are no guarantees that life will be fair, Billy. You take what comes, and move on and do the best you can."

He turned to pick up the papers Billy Wade dumped on the porch glider. "Let's look these over and do our business so you can get to work."

They spent the rest of their time together talking about the final renovations planned for Laurel Springs.

In his own office later, Carter called Alvin and told him to schedule the jet to pick them up the following Monday.

"You know I'm thrilled you're going to be back here," Alvin said. "But I'm worried whether it's the right thing for you and Taylor." He paused. "Have you told Morgan you're coming back?"

"No." Carter flexed a fist. "But he'll be glad because of Taylor and because he knows all I'll do to continue to grow Quest. You know, he tempted me before to stay in California, offering to give me Quest. I don't want to lose my edge of negotiations with him by letting him learn I might stay for more than a visit this time. Keep this under your hat, Alvin."

"Sure thing." Carter could almost picture the white flash of Alvin's grin. "I'd love to have you for a boss instead of Morgan Benton. He's smart as the devil but he's rather short on diplomacy and humility."

"Tell me about it." Carter shook his head.

A short silence ensued before Alvin spoke again. "Last time you were here, Morgan really upset Taylor—made him cry. Remember? I'd hate to see more of that for the boy after all he's been through."

"I'm going to talk to Morgan about Taylor. Don't worry." Carter considered this. "It's been over a year since Judith died. Morgan should be working through his grief and less likely to put pressure on Taylor like he did before."

"Hmmm. I hope so."

Carter checked his watch. "Alvin, call to see if Martha Oslo will go over and clean the house before next Monday." Carter flipped his day-book open and read Alvin a cell phone number. "She does that when I come in for one of my short stays. Start shopping around for a regular housekeeper for me, too, if you would—someone to be there when Taylor gets home from school and to do the cooking and cleaning. I don't want him staying over at the Benton place. Call an agency if you need to. Tell them I want someone happy and warm-hearted."

"I'll start to work on it," Alvin said before they hung up.

Carter looked around the office he'd created for himself inside the ad-min building. Sandalwood walls, George Masa photography prints on the walls, dark cherry furniture, brown leather chairs, state-of-the-art technology, and—best of all—a big picture window looking out over the old assembly field and across to the church, the cemetery, and the woods beyond.

As Carter got up to walk to the window, Jinx lifted his head from the corner where he snoozed. "These mountains sure do get in your blood, Jinx. I'll miss it here."

Drawn by the church across the field, Carter closed down his computer, pushed the office door shut, and headed out the side door toward the crisply repainted Greek Revival church. The breeze, still blustering and making its presence known, jangled the bell in the belfry, sending a deep gong out softly over the air.

As he let himself in the church door, Carter put a hand out toward Jinx. "Stay," he said, and the dog dropped down in a shady spot on the porch.

Inside the church, Carter stopped to look down

the aisle. The August sunlight streamed in ribbons through the stained-glass windows, playing across the wooden pews and the newly refinished floor.

"The old place looks good," Carter remarked as he walked to the Layman pew, third from the front. He sat down, closing his eyes and hoping some of the peace of the aged building would seep into his soul.

"Need a prayer partner?" said a familiar voice.

Carter looked up to see his Grampa Layman scooting into the pew beside him.

"What are you doing here?" Carter leaned his head back, trying to relax the tension in his neck.

His grandfather chuckled. "It might be more appropriate if I asked you that question. I am the preacher here, after all."

"True." Carter blurted out the next words before losing his courage. "Taylor and I are going back to California, Grampa."

"I gather you don't mean for a business trip, from your tone."

"No." He put his elbows on the pew in front of him and dropped his head into his hands. "I can't stay here loving Rhea the way I do and knowing she won't have me. I hope you, and Mom and Dad, can understand that." He let out a deep sigh. "Taylor's growing fond of Rhea, and she's even been pulling away from him lately. I don't want him to know more hurt. He's been through enough."

"It's hard to hide from hurt and trouble. It has a way of following you no matter where you go."

Carter shook his head. "I've got to do this. It's killing me to be around Rhea every day when she won't forgive me, won't love me. I've done everything I know to do. Tried everything I can to win her. I know, deep in my heart, she cares for me, but she won't yield to it. She doesn't want to give up her anger and resentment toward me."

"Have you tried prayer, Son?"

Carter turned his eyes to meet his grandfather's. "Yes. But I don't think even God can get through to Rhea Dean."

Grampa frowned. "Faith believes and speaks aright, boy. How about you and I aligning our faith here together and believing for a change in Rhea's heart?"

Carter blew out a breath. "It will take a miracle."

Grampa Dean grinned roguishly. "Our God is good at those."

"All right." Carter smiled at his grandfather. "What's our Scripture we're going to stand on?"

His grandfather's eyes twinkled. "How about Mark 9:23—'all things are possible to him that believeth.' "

"Yeah, that'll do." Carter bumped his elbow against his grandfather affectionately. "Let's do it."

The two of them settled in to pray.

Standing up to leave the church later, Carter said, "I still plan on talking to Taylor to start preparing him to leave."

Grampa's eyebrows lifted. "That's kind of a non-faith action after praying like we did."

Carter put a hand on his Grampa's shoulder. "It may take a while for even a faith prayer to get through to Rhea Dean. And, in all fairness, Taylor needs some time to settle himself about going back next Monday. To say his good-byes to people and places he's come to love."

Carter left his grandfather thinking on this while he made his way out of the church and along the familiar Assembly Road toward home. Jinx trotted along beside him happily, and Carter knew the dog would miss the freedom of being off the leash once they returned to California city life.

Coming down the drive toward the big Layman farmhouse, Carter found Taylor swinging idly in the old tire swing that hung from a giant maple beside the house.

"Hi, Dad," he called. "Hi, Jinx."

The dog ran over to nuzzle the boy with warm canine affection.

Carter sat down on the whitewashed bench under the tree nearby, patting the seat beside him for Taylor to join him.

"Something's wrong, isn't it, Dad?" Taylor studied him with solemn eyes as he sat down.

"No, nothing's wrong, Son. But I need to tell you that we're going back to California for a while. Longer than usual this time." Carter dropped his eyes from the probing gaze of his son's. "I've finished most all I needed to do to fix up Laurel Springs, and now I need to fix aspects of Quest that have gone lagging while I've been gone so long."

He offered Taylor a smile. "You'll be able to go to school down the street from our house on Vista; we can go to the park and to the beach again whenever we want. Go to Disneyland. Connect with all our old friends. Be home again."

Taylor scowled at him. "But you said Laurel Springs was our home. We came back to Laurel Springs to live here forever. You said so. We're even building our own house here."

Carter scratched his neck with discomfort. "You know I kept our California house, too. I always expected we'd go back and forth. Live a little in both places."

Taylor looked down at his feet. "I guess it doesn't matter if I want to go or not, does it?" He searched Carter's face with eyes wet with tears. "It never matters what kids want when adults make up their minds about things."

He jumped off the bench and ran toward the house, leaving Carter feeling like a complete heel.

"That went well," he said to Jinx.

The dog licked his hand and then headed off to follow Taylor, offering no opinion.

Carter heaved a sigh. He'd have his mother and father to face next. The evening promised to be a long and emotional one.

Chapter 21

Rhea had felt more and more uncomfortable around Carter as the summer weeks slipped by. They'd bared their hearts to each other in the tunnel below the old Sutton cabin, and yet, Rhea still found herself unable to let go of the past. Carter's searching eyes whenever they got together now made Rhea feel guilty. She knew he kept hoping she would change her mind about his proposal, and she could see from his actions that he felt hurt over her refusal.

Over the last two weeks, Rhea even found herself avoiding Taylor. There seemed to be a winsome yearning in the child's eyes lately—wanting more from her than she felt ready to give.

Around the assembly grounds, the ongoing renovations daily transformed Laurel Springs. Every building sparkled with fresh paint, and newly paved roads and neat landscaping met the eye at every corner. Reporters and journalists visited to take pictures and do write-ups on the continual changes occurring. Tourism increased rapidly with the media coverage, and more groups called daily to schedule fall retreats and weekend workshops at Laurel Springs.

Rhea sat in her office in the ad-min building thinking about it. She knew she should be grateful and should be able to deal with her feelings for Carter Layman in a more mature way. Hiding out from him and his son was hardly the way for a grown woman to act.

Rhea laid down her pen, realizing she was getting nowhere with her writing today. She looked wistfully at her notes about the history of covered bridges for her newspaper column next week.

"Each covered bridge is unique," she read, trying to focus her thoughts. "More than ten thousand covered bridges once dotted the American landscape but now only seven hundred fifty remain. They remind us of a time when the world moved at a slower and less hectic pace and each covered bridge evokes memories of past times. In some rural communities, it was traditional for a man to be granted a kiss from his sweetheart when they passed through a covered bridge."

Rhea's mind drifted. Carter kissed her for the first time in the covered bridge here at Laurel Springs in October when the maples and oaks around the old bridge were a glory of red and orange. She could never walk or ride through the bridge without remembering.

She pushed her notes aside with irritation. "I

should never have started an article on this subject right now."

Annoyed at her inability to concentrate, Rhea headed through the back door of the ad-min building and across the back paths to the Laurel Springs store. She needed some lunch and hoped a visit with Jeannie and Estelle would lift her spirits.

Entering the store, she saw Jeannie's tow-headed son Beau waiting to get an ice cream cone.

"Hi, Beau." Rhea leaned over to ruffle his hair.

The child jerked away and pumped out his bottom lip at her. "I don't like you anymore, Rhea Dean."

His mother shook a scolding finger at him from behind the counter. "Beau Ledford, you watch your manners, and you tell Rhea you're sorry for saying that right now."

He stuck his chin up defiantly. "I'm not sorry. It's because of Rhea Dean that Taylor's having to move back to California, and he's my bestest friend."

The room fell deadly quiet, and Jeannie's eyes widened.

Beau crossed his arms and gave her a sulky look. "You know it's true, Mama. Daddy said so at breakfast this morning. I heard him."

Estelle snickered behind her hand while Jeannie dashed out from behind the counter to take Beau's arm and head for the door. "Your behavior is not allowing you to have ice cream today, Beau Ledford. You walk right on back to the house and tell your daddy how you've acted. He's mowing the grass and I'll bet he decides you need to help him with some of his yard chores."

"He will 'cause you'll call and tattle on me," Beau challenged, allowing himself to be shuffled out the door after a few more verbal exchanges.

"I'm real sorry about that, Rhea." Jeannie came back into the store and slipped behind the counter again.

Estelle held out the ice cream cone she still held. "What do you want me to do with Beau's chocolate ice cream cone?"

"Just put it back." Jeannie snatched the cone in irritation, dumped the chocolate scoops back into the ice cream bin, and flipped the cone into the trash.

Rhea watched Jeannie and Estelle exchange pointed looks.

"What's going on?" Rhea leaned against a table near the counter, watching her two friends.

Estelle looked at her in surprise. "You haven't heard that Carter and Taylor are going back to California?"

"For another business trip?" Rhea straightened the napkin holder and salt and pepper shakers on the table.

Jeannie shook her head. "No, for good. Hasn't Carter told you?"

Rhea's open mouth of shock told the answer.

"There. You see? It's that kind of communication between the two of you that's caused this." Jeannie shook a finger at her. "You're going to regret not being willing to forgive and forget with Carter Layman one day. You mark my words. And Carter and Taylor leaving Laurel Springs is about to break all our hearts."

She pressed a hand to her mouth, tears starting in her eyes.

Estelle looked at Rhea apologetically. "She's right upset today."

"No kidding," Rhea said, beginning to feel annoyed.

Rhea walked closer to Jeannie. "I did not ask Carter to move away, Jeannie Ledford. How can you blame me because he's decided he wants to return to California?"

"You are so dense." Jeannie slammed her hands down on the counter. "The man is in love with you, always has been. He came back to win your love and now you've rejected him. He told Billy Wade he can't stand to keep seeing you every day when you won't forgive him, won't love him back, and won't marry him. So he's going back to California."

Jeannie blew a strand of short hair out of her face. "Poor Taylor is so upset, Mary Jane says he cries himself to sleep every night. I hope you're proud of yourself for making a little boy and a grown man so miserable."

Rhea felt her face flaming. "You can't make yourself love someone when you don't, Jeannie."

"That's a lie and you know it." Jeannie snatched up a dishtowel and shook it at Rhea. "You have never stopped loving Carter Layman. You're just too stubborn to admit it."

Rhea saw Estelle's eyes sharpen with interest.

Crossing her arms in irritation, Rhea tried to make Jeannie understand how she felt. "Carter hurt me. You know how I suffered for a long, long time. I can't put that behind me simply because Carter is back now and wants things to be the way they were."

Jeannie leaned over the counter toward Rhea. Her voice grew soft. "I love you, Rhea Dean. But I believe you are making a *big* mistake not to ut the past behind you and be willing to move on."

Estelle chimed in. "My granny always said, 'Forgiveness is an attribute of the strong.' "

Rhea gave her a withering look. "Thank you very much, Estelle."

Jeannie hid a laugh behind her hand.

Remembering she'd come for lunch, Rhea slipped behind the counter to make herself a quick roast beef and Swiss sandwich. She wrapped it in paper and stuffed it in a paper sack with a canned cola.

"I need to get back to the office to finish my column for the newspaper," she said, ringing up her own sale. She doubted she could enjoy lunch in the store with the looks Jeannie and Estelle continued passing between them.

Sunday service at church the next day proved even worse. Mary Jane broke down and cried during the service and several people directed pointed looks in Rhea's direction. Carter wisely avoided attending. Nana Dean said her friend Maureen whispered that the boy broke down weeping over breakfast and had to be kept home.

Needless to say, lunch at the Dean house after church was strained. Her mother and grandmother hardly offered two words as they ate.

Annoyed at the unending silent treatment from her mother and grandmother, Rhea finally banged her glass on the table, startling them both. "Enough of this. If you have something to say, say it."

Her mother leveled her with a narrow-eyed glance. "It's your life, Rhea. Your father and I interfered in your decisions relating to Carter Layman nine years ago and I've often regretted it. I don't want to interfere this time. I'm keeping quiet."

"Well, I'm not." Nana Dean studied her with soft eyes. "Why won't you marry the boy, Rhea? I know you love him. Can't you forgive him?"

Rhea toyed with her silverware. "Forgiving

and forgetting are two entirely different things, Nana."

"No, I don't think so." Nana reached across the table to lay a hand on Rhea's. "To say you can forgive but can't forget is only another way of saying you won't forgive. God brings the forgetfulness you need to move on once you set your heart to truly forgive. It's like standing in faith. Your feelings change when you make the right stand in faith."

Rhea's mother interrupted. "She's too stubborn to let those feelings go, Nana. You're wasting your time trying to reason with her."

Nettled, Rhea got up and started taking the dirty dishes to the kitchen. She moved through her chores quickly, changed out of her Sunday skirt, into her shorts, and headed to the barn to find Jewel.

"I need a ride to clear my head, girl," she said to the horse as she slipped a bridle over her head.

Shortly after, she rode through the back field, up Rocky Prong Road past Gold Mine Springs and onto a well-worn path leading through the woods and into the Great Smoky Mountains National Park. After a final climb through a stand of hemlock, she emerged onto a high mountain trail.

The ride along the mountain ridge cleared her head but didn't resolve the mix of feelings in her soul. Returning to the barn, Rhea found Taylor

Layman waiting for her, sitting on a bale of hay.

He stood up politely, his face brightening. "Your Nana said I could wait for you here."

"How long have you been here?" Rhea asked as she dismounted and started to unsaddle Jewel.

"Just a little while." Taylor handed her a cloth to wipe Jewel down with after the long ride. Then he strolled along while Rhea walked the horse briefly around the corral.

"I'm leaving tomorrow," he told her finally.

"I heard."

"I don't really want to go back to California." He hung his head. "But my dad says he has to go back to work."

"Perhaps he does."

Taylor shook his head. "No. He's just saying that to me."

Rhea wisely kept silent.

"I'm sorry you don't like me because of my mother."

Shocked, Rhea turned to look down at the child. "That's not true, Taylor. I like you very much."

He sighed deeply. "But not enough to want to be my mother."

Rhea led Jewel into her stall and shut the door.

"Let's sit and talk." She patted the place beside her on a wooden bench in the barn.

Taylor sat down, fidgeting as Rhea considered what to say.

"It's a very big decision to get married," she offered at last.

His eyes searched her face. "But you were going to marry my dad before." He shuffled his feet. "So I figured it was because of me you said no this time."

Rhea felt her annoyance rise. "Your father shouldn't have told you I said no to his proposal."

"Dad didn't tell me." Taylor's brown eyes grew huge. "I heard Mamaw and Papaw talking. Dad would be real mad if he knew I eavesdropped—and super madder if he knew I told you what I heard."

"I see." A smile twitched at the corner of Rhea's mouth. "Does your dad even know you're here, Taylor?"

He shook his head solemnly. "No, but I wanted to say good-bye and I needed to talk to you."

"What did you need to talk about?" Rhea waited.

Taylor shuffled his feet in the dirt on the barn floor again. "I know some things I'm not supposed to know," he said at last.

Rhea lifted an eyebrow. "Is that right?"

He picked at a scab on his arm. "I know my dad was supposed to marry you but he married my mom instead because she was going to have me."

Rhea suppressed a gasp.

"I didn't just learn that from Mamaw and Papaw," he added quickly. "I heard my Grandfather Benton and my mother talk about it, too."

"Eavesdropping isn't a very nice habit, Taylor."

He sighed. "I know, but sometimes you're just in the wrong place at the wrong time and you hear stuff. If you come out, you know you'll get in more trouble because you heard something you shouldn't have." Big chocolate eyes looked up at her for understanding.

"I see," she acknowledged, remembering being trapped in that situation all too well herself a few times.

Taylor picked up a piece of straw from the floor to fiddle with it. "When my mother and I were having some of our special times before she died, she talked about you."

Rhea barely disguised her shock.

"She showed me your picture and she told me how my dad loved you before he married her." He chewed his lip, thinking. "I asked her if she tricked him to marry her. She didn't get mad. She laughed and said she did. She told me she had to try to grab hold of life fast before she lost it. That she wanted to have me and be a mother, and a wife, before she died."

Taylor smiled. "She said my dad was the nicest man she'd ever known. She picked him to be my dad because he was so good."

Rhea felt appalled to learn Judith discussed a

matter of this magnitude with a small child. She wondered if Carter knew.

"Mother told me that when she died, Dad would take me back to Laurel Springs where he'd come from. She said she thought I'd like it and she told me she thought I'd like you. She asked me not to be mad if Dad wanted to marry you."

Rhea looked at the child curiously. "And are you mad?"

"No." His face lit up. "I like you. I really do."

"Thank you." Rhea couldn't think what else to say.

"I have something for you." Taylor searched in his shorts pocket and pulled out a crumpled, folded envelope. He made an effort to straighten it and then offered it to Rhea.

"What is this?" Rhea asked.

"It's a letter from my mom. She wrote it to you the day we were talking."

Rhea sucked in a breath. "I don't know if you should give me this, Taylor."

He offered her an innocent look. "Why not? She wrote it to you and she told me to give it to you someday. I just forgot it for a long time. When we flew back home a few weeks ago, I remembered it. I found it with all the other things she gave me in my treasure box."

Rhea looked at the envelope in her hand, not sure if she should open it. "Did you read this, Taylor?"

He grinned. "I tried a little, but I can't read much. I'm only six and starting first grade. Maybe you could read it to me." He frowned. "Unless you don't want to."

Rhea unfolded the letter, hands trembling as she saw the neat script flowing across the sheet of paper, and started to read.

Dear Rhea Dean,

I have heard about you since the first week Carter came to California. I saw the pictures you sent him, I shared in the news from Tennessee you detailed. I laughed at your stories and wept over your sorrows. I began to feel as though you were a sister. I looked forward to you coming to California—even though I envied you Carter's love. When you didn't come, I grew angry at you. When I learned I had ALS and would die, I decided Carter and I would make a nice team. I wanted a husband and a child. You didn't seem very interested in Carter.

I know I acted selfishly. Dying is not a happy time. Carter shared joy with me, despite all, and he gave me Taylor, a beautiful child. I can't regret anything here as time slips away. However, I can hope you'll forgive me for borrowing your kind man. He never stopped loving you—although I believe he came to love me toward the end. I know I grew to love him.

I envy you the years and lifetime ahead with him. And with my son. I know Carter will go back to you and try to win you. Please love them both well and try not to think too harshly of me. I came to know Carter's God near the end, so I hope I will see you all on the other side someday.

Be kind to Taylor. He is a very wise and kind little boy and I know he will be a good man like his father.

Embrace life, love, and joy while you can.

They slip by all too quickly.

Sincerely,

Judith Morgan Benton Layman

Hands still shaking, Rhea folded the letter back up.

"That was a nice letter," said Taylor.

She touched a hand to Taylor's hair, brushing it back from his forehead. "I think your dad should see this."

He frowned. "Dad might get mad at me about it."

"No. I don't think he will." She leaned over to kiss Taylor on the forehead. "Do you think it would be all right if I give this to your dad?"

Taylor considered this. "Okay, but he went to see Billy Wade and then he said he was going to his special mountain place. That's why I could come see you. He won't be back until later."

Rhea leaned her head back against the stall behind their bench for a moment and closed her eyes. So much emotion.

"Are you okay, Rhea?" Taylor's voice sounded anxious.

She found the child's hand. "I'm fine, and I don't want you to ever worry again about whether I like you or not. Do you hear? I like you very, very much."

He sighed. "I guess I'd better go back. I asked Mamaw if I could walk over to tell all of you good-bye, but she said not to stay long."

Rhea managed another smile. "How about if I ride you back home on Jewel? She won't mind another chance to get out today."

His face brightened. "That would be fun. I won't get to ride again for a long time. Until we fly back and visit at Thanksgiving. Dad promised we could come then."

Getting up, Rhea walked across the barn to talk to Jewel in her stall. She saddled and bridled the mare quickly and soon had Taylor tucked in front of her in the saddle. After dropping Taylor off at the Laymans' front porch, Rhea headed back out the Laymans' driveway and then kicked Jewel into a trot, heading up the trail to Low Ridge and toward Rocky Knob. She had some business to attend to with Carter Layman—and hoped he would still be at the mountain knob when she arrived.

Chapter 22

Sunday had dragged slowly for Carter. He'd skipped church earlier in the day to stay home with Taylor. The child started weeping over breakfast, the tears prompted by those of his grandmother. Carter's mother wasn't taking his decision to return to California well.

At Billy Wade's later, he faced more anger from Beau, who didn't want to lose his new friend. It pained Carter to share good-byes with these longtime friends. They had quickly grown close again.

Now he sat on the rocky outcrop at Rocky Knob, high above Laurel Springs. He drank in the scenes before him with his eyes, hoping he could hold the memories close in his heart to think of later.

A footfall behind him caused him to turn his head.

"Up here feeling sorry for yourself, Carter?" Rhea walked carefully out on the shale ledge to sit down beside him.

For once, Carter didn't welcome her company.

"What are you doing here?"

"For one thing, I'm ticked off at you." She pulled her knees up and wrapped her arms around them. Carter's eyes slid over her sun-browned legs with longing.

"You didn't even have the decency to come and tell me you're moving back to California yourself. Typical." She snorted. "I learned about it while getting emotionally chewed out by Jeannie yesterday and then I enjoyed the pleasure of being snubbed by half the congregation at church this morning because of it."

"It was my decision."

"Yes, but I get to live with the fallout of it since you fingered me as the reason you're heading back out West."

Carter closed his eyes wearily. "Rhea, I don't need this conversation today."

"Well, too bad." She gave him a stubborn look. "We have some things we need to discuss."

He looked longingly back to where his horse, Traveler, was tied up in a grassy patch near the trail.

Rhea's eyes caught his. "Don't even think about it."

Resigned, Carter stretched out his legs on the sun-warmed rock. "I guess you want to talk about the continuing renovations at Laurel Springs. I fully intend to finish everything planned. Billy Wade and I met today to talk about it. I also met with your mother, my folks, and Grampa. You don't need to worry that my return to California will change any ongoing or future renovations planned."

A red flush stole up her neck. "I don't give a rat's ass about the plans for Laurel Springs right now." She turned angry eyes to look at him. "I came up here to talk about you and me."

He blew out a breath. "I think you've made it clear there is no 'you and me,' Rhea."

She stretched her legs out beside his. "And to think you've always said I act like a drama queen."

Carter watched her dig into her shorts pocket to pull out an envelope.

"Is this a good-bye note?" He couldn't avoid a sarcastic tone.

"You'd better watch your tone. It's a long drop off this rock," she warned. She handed him the note. "Actually, this is a letter your son brought me a short time ago."

He scowled at her. "Taylor can't write a whole letter. He's only six."

"Taylor didn't write this."

Carter ran a hand through his hair. "Listen, I'm sorry if my mother or dad wrote something to you that upset you and had Taylor deliver it. I'll talk to them. And I'll talk to Taylor."

"You sure jump to quick conclusions." Rhea stretched backward to lie down on the rock, an old familiar pose that stirred Carter's blood.

"Read the note, Carter," she said, closing her eyes to the bright sun.

He opened the envelope and felt his pulse

quicken to see Judith's curving script across her familiar signature blue stationery. He read the note slowly and then folded it back into the envelope.

As he finished, he saw Rhea sit back up, watching him now.

"Where did Taylor get this? Did he say?"

She nodded. "He explained that his mother wrote it at one of their special talks."

"That's what she called their visits together toward the last year," he clarified. "Judith spent time with Taylor on days when she thought she could handle it productively, when her symptoms were less severe."

Rhea sent him an angry look. "You realize she sat and explained to a five-year-old child why you married her. She laughed about it. She told him she picked you out especially to be his father. And she had the nerve to confide in him **that she stole you from me. To tell that child you'd** undoubtedly come back here to try to win me back when she died. Taylor wasn't even six years old at that time, Carter."

She picked up a rock and threw it over the cliff with irritation. "What kind of mother would do that to a young child? Dump that kind of emotional garbage on a little boy?" She crossed her arms and scowled. "That child has been carrying that weight around all this time. Knowing more than any little kid ought to know about grown-up matters. No wonder he's so serious and intense. He's been treated like a small adult, expected to understand things beyond his ability to fully comprehend."

Rhea kicked another loose rock over the edge of the cliff. "It makes me mad enough to spit."

Carter sighed and shook his head. "Judith was always direct. She said what she thought. She seldom acted with diplomacy and rarely considered how her words and actions would affect others."

"Tell me about it." She pulled her knees up to wrap her arms around them again. "It was not an easy situation to find myself in. Taylor believed himself the reason I didn't want to commit to marry you. He thought I didn't like him."

Carter shrugged. "You do keep him at a distance. Children are keen to pick up on things like that."

She pushed at him. "I didn't want him to get more attached to me than he was until I felt sure about my feelings for you. People had already told him we once were sweethearts. He entertained enough ideas already without me fueling them further."

"Yeah, well, a lot of people entertain ideas that don't pan out." Drat it, she annoyed him. "He'll get over it."

Rhea gave him a smug smile he didn't understand.

She leaned down to retie her shoelace. "What's the weather like in California right now?" she asked casually.

"Hot and dry this time of year, eighties most days on average, sixties at night. It's the least comfortable time of year in Sunnyvale."

"Seems like I remember hearing that."

Irritation crawled up his spine. "What's your point in this polite chatter?"

She gave him a sweet smile. "I wanted to know what to pack."

"What?" He turned his eyes to study her, trying to decide what kind of game she was playing now.

"Well, you don't think I'm going to let you go out there again to have some other unscrupulous woman finagle you into marriage."

His heartbeat picked up despite his best intentions. "What are you talking about, Rhea Dean?" The woman always drove him crazy with her subtleties.

"You are *not* leaving me again." She turned her intense blue eyes toward him. He could see the gold flecks in them in the sunlight. See the sprinkling of freckles across her nose.

He counted to ten to keep his patience in check. "Rhea, what are you saying to me?"

She shrugged. "You said I made it clear there is no 'you and me,' but that's not totally true. I never said that. There will always be a you and me,

Carter Layman." She leaned over to touch her lips briefly to his, sending a shock of feeling through him.

He eyed her cautiously. "Don't play games with me."

She stretched her arms casually, like a cat. "I've heard California's weather is a lot nicer in the fall. If we flew out later, planned a wedding first, we might enjoy it more. And to be quite frank, I think Taylor would be happier going to school here at Smoky Mountain Elementary in Cosby with Beau. For a small, rural school it has a surprisingly good reputation. You can check it out on the Internet."

He grabbed her arms and turned her to face him. "Are you saying you will marry me now?"

She patted him on the cheek. "I never thought you were slow, Carter. Wasn't I just discussing a wedding? We can get married in California if you'd like, but I think it would hurt Grampa Layman's feelings if he didn't get to do the ceremony."

Carter tried to process Rhea's words.

She bit her lip and put her face closer to his. He could smell the lemony, citrus smell of her now, and her breath whispered across his senses as she spoke. "You can kiss the bride before the ceremony, Carter Layman."

Trying to wrap his mind around this new reality,

Carter held back. "What made you change your mind?"

She dropped her eyes for a moment. "Judith Benton. I knew what you shared with me about what happened, but when I read Judith's words something changed in me. Some old hurt place broke away, and I knew what she said rang true. Time does slip by all too quickly. We need to embrace life, embrace love, and savor joys while we can."

Rhea put her hands on his chest. "Besides, I knew after I rode the ridge trail today that I couldn't let you go again." Tears welled in her eyes. "Don't leave me, Carter. Stay with me or take me with you. I just want to be with you. Don't leave me again."

Her tears were his undoing. He wrapped her against his chest, feeling his own tears too near the surface. "I won't and I'll never let you go again, Rhea Dean. Never."

She sniffed. "We're going to see that Taylor is a happier little boy in the future. He's much too serious for six, carries too much adult burden. I want us to plan a lot of fun times for him—where we'll laugh and cut up, be silly and play together. He needs that."

Carter's heart swelled.

Rhea turned wet eyes to look deeply into his. Her voice dropped to a sultry whisper. "If we marry soon, we might have a child not long after

Billy Wade and Jeannie. They could play together at Laurel Springs, like Beau and Taylor do, like you and I did."

"You're killing me, Rhea." Carter couldn't find words to express his joy. He'd dreamed of this moment for so long.

She gave him a saucy look. "I explored the house again at the Costner ruins one day when you weren't there. I slipped in through a window left unlatched. It's shaping up nicely. I heard Billy Wade say it ought to be finished by Thanksgiving. It will need furniture then to be a home, you know. I have a lot of ideas for that."

"I'll bet you do." He grinned at her.

She put a hand out to push a strand of hair out of his face. "We could live most of the year at Laurel Springs like you said, Carter, and other times at the California house. What street did you say it was on?"

"Vista. Vista Avenue."

She smiled. "That's a nice name." Rhea chewed her lip thoughtfully. "I've never traveled. I've never been far from Tennessee. Will I like it in California?"

"You'll like it." Watching her chew on her lip, Carter lost his last remnant of control, pulled her into his arms, and found her lips with his.

"Oh, I thought you'd never kiss me again like this," she murmured against his mouth.

He deepened the kiss while pulling them back from the precipice of Rocky Knob to sit against a rocky face in the shadows. As his hands found their way over his favorite places on Rhea's body, the sizzle hit with hot familiarity.

She crooned his name, wrapping her arms around him, reveling in the passion and intensity stirring between them. Lost quickly in loving Rhea Dean, it took Rhea's soft voice, a short time later, to bring Carter back to reality as his hands began to try to separate her from her clothes.

"I don't want people counting back the months when our child is born like they did with Taylor." She pulled away, her eyes dilated and aroused, to give him a melting smile. "We'll have a whole lifetime to explore loving together. I hope you learned a little expertise as a previously married man."

He let his hands trace their way down her arms lightly. "The best lessons in loving I ever learned—or have to learn—will be from you, Rhea Dean. I love you with all my heart. I always have and I always will."

She sighed deeply. "I love you, too, Carter Layman. It took me a while for the cold places in my heart to thaw, but they're melting quickly now." She giggled.

With reluctance, he kept himself from wrapping her into his arms again, afraid he couldn't stop his emotions a second time. "Do you think we could go tell everyone our good news, Rhea?"

She nodded, still running her fingers along his leg, tantalizing him with her touch. "We should tell Taylor first. I want to be sure he's happy about this decision."

Carter laughed. "Are you kidding? This is the kid that encouraged me to go after you in California because he thought you were hot."

Rhea frowned. "That's hardly a nice way for a boy to talk about his future mother."

"I think Taylor will whoop and holler with joy. Don't worry."

She bit her lip. "About that letter. I don't want you scolding Taylor for bringing that to me. For not telling you about it."

"I won't." He stood and reached down to offer her a hand. "But I want Taylor to talk to me—and to you—more freely about things Judith might have told him. Things he may not understand and have questions about. A kid his age shouldn't feel he needs to keep secrets locked up or to fear sharing with those he loves."

Rising to her feet, Rhea leaned into him, wrapping her arms around his waist. "I feel like I've come home in my heart, Carter."

"You have." Carter hugged her to him, overwhelmed with the rush of emotions. "You truly have. I promise."

Later that night, after all the excitement of

sharing their news with family and friends, Carter gave Rhea a final reluctant good-night kiss on her front porch.

He looked up toward her window as he started down the porch steps toward his car.

"Don't even think about it," Rhea said. "The two of us can't handle any more temptation right now." Her mouth quirked into a smile. "Besides, we only have a few weeks to wait."

They'd set a wedding date for not far in the future, and no one had tried to talk them into waiting any longer.

"The sooner, the better," Rhea's mother had said. "I'll sleep better not worrying about that boy climbing in my windows at night."

Rhea had gasped at her words.

Carter chuckled to himself, remembering this now as he walked to the car, climbed in, and shut the door. He looked back to see Rhea still framed in the light of the doorway. So beautiful.

Her voice floated out over the night as she let herself into the door. "See ya later—and love you forever, Carter Layman."

Carter closed his eyes in joy. Life didn't get much better than this.

Discussion Questions

1. Why is Rhea Dean not glad to learn from her friend Jeannie that Carter Layman is coming back to Laurel Springs for a visit? What happened in the past to end their relationship?

2. What brings Carter Layman from California back to Laurel Springs? Who does he bring with him? How does Carter's first meeting with Rhea go? What did you learn about Carter's feelings for Rhea as they meet again?

3. The main setting for this book is the Laurel Springs Camp Assembly Grounds—a vacation retreat center since the early 1900s in the Cosby, Tennessee, area at the base of the Smoky Mountains National Park. Who established Laurel Springs in its earliest days? How has it changed over the years? What old dream did Rhea and Carter once share about Laurel Springs? Many resorts similar to Laurel Springs were established around the United States in the late nineteenth and early twentieth centuries. Have you ever visited one?

4. The Deans and the Layman family share ownership of Laurel Springs and both have

homes on the property. Share your impressions of these families—of Wes and Mary Jane Layman and Grampa Layman—and of Lillian and Nana Dean. What different roles has each family played at Laurel Springs? How has the breach in the relationship between Rhea and Carter affected these families? How is Carter received when he first visits the Deans?

5. Carter tells Rhea, "We don't always get what we want." What did Carter want that he didn't get? What took him to California, and what caused him to stay? At the end of Chapter 3, Carter tells Rhea two reasons why he came back to Laurel Springs. What were those reasons?

6. Both Rhea and Carter bear resentments toward each other about their break-up. Carter is angry Rhea didn't come out to California with him as planned. Rhea is angry that Carter doesn't understand why she didn't come. What reasons does she give for not going to California? Later, as the book unfolds, what other admissions does Rhea confess about not wanting to go to California?

7. There are always special memories between longtime close friends who have grown up

together. What memories begin to surface in the scene at the covered bridge, at Rocky Knob on the mountain, and as both remember past times swimming to the raft, dancing at the gazebo, and climbing into each other's windows? How do these and other recurring memories make it harder for Rhea to keep Carter at a safe distance?

8. Old words of good-bye that Carter and Rhea always shared—"See ya later and love you forever"—surface early in the book and play their way throughout the story. How does Rhea respond to these words when she first hears them? When is the only time in the book that you hear Rhea say these words?

9. Judith Morgan Benton was already ill when she began to pursue Carter Layman in California. What disease did Judith have? How did it affect her before she died? As the book progresses, you learn more about Judith and Carter's marriage. Why did they marry? What did you think about Judith and her father, Morgan Benton? How did they use their wealth and position to influence Carter's life? What concessions for himself did Carter insist on in their agreement?

10. Past friends play a strong role in this book, like Billy Wade and Jeannie Ledford, long-

time friends of Carter's and Rhea's. What did you like about these characters? How were they good friends to Carter and Rhea? Do you have longtime friends in your life like these? How have they been a help to you in difficult times?

11. Rhea is seeing Marshall Sutton as the story begins, and Marshall has already expressed a desire to marry Rhea. What is Rhea and Marshall's relationship like? What do Jeannie and Billy Wade think about Marshall? How does Carter respond when he meets Marshall again?

12. As Carter begins to use his wealth to revitalize Laurel Springs, Rhea has very mixed feelings about the changes. Why isn't she thrilled to see these changes she's longed for? Why does seeing Carter's new house on the old Costner cabin site cause her to cry?

13. Why does Rhea have a difficult time at first accepting Carter's son, Taylor? How does their relationship change with time? How does the hike to Hen Wallow Falls and the cookout help change Rhea's feelings toward Taylor? What does Taylor give to Rhea at a later time in the book that changes her feelings toward Carter?

14. Laurel Springs is having trouble with vandalism in the book. As the book progresses, what do you discover is behind the vandalism? Who is perpetrating it? How does Carter get hurt by the vandal at the Costner ruins and what happens to threaten Taylor at the old Sutton cabin? How do Carter and Rhea both find themselves in a dangerous predicament because of the vandal?

15. When he is hurt, Carter admits to his grandfather that he has let his faith slide. What counsel and help does Grampa Layman give him? How does he counsel Rhea in a similar way later in the book? Have you had situations in your life when you've found it hard to forgive someone for a wrong, or to forgive yourself for mistakes you've made? How did you move on and who helped you as you did?

16. Carter creates games for Quest, an interest started as a boy, and he has become very successful with his career. What does Carter learn—with surprise—that Rhea is doing as a side career besides working at Laurel Springs?

17. Rhea fights and fights not to allow herself to love Carter again. As she tells her grand-

mother, "I don't want to be a second chance or a second choice." How does their enforced night together in the tunnel beneath the Sutton cabin help her to understand Carter's actions better? Yet, Rhea still refuses to marry Carter after this night or to let go of her old hurts. When Carter plans to return to California in disappointment, what events turn Rhea around? What happens when Rhea goes to find Carter at Rocky Knob before he plans to leave? How did you like the closing scene?

18. Of the main and side characters in this book, which ones did you like best? What did you enjoy most about this book? Do you wish you could stay at a place like Laurel Springs?

Center Point Large Print
600 Brooks Road / PO Box 1
Thorndike, ME 04986-0001 USA

(207) 568-3717

US & Canada:
1 800 929-9108
www.centerpointlargeprint.com